Contents

Author's Note

One day, having not written a single word in many years, my wonderful wife asked me to tell her a story. At the time nothing came to mind, no plots or ideas, though after a few days I returned with not just a story, but an entirely new world. It seems all that dormant creativity had been building; storing that sleepless and unrelenting urge to look past what we can see and touch. My world became consumed by another, by people and conversations, their thoughts and their dreams, all pouring out of me at the same time. As many fantasy writers before me, I knew it was all over when I started drawing a map, setting the scene for the story that would come. This is that story, I hope you enjoy reading it as much as I enjoyed writing it.

The story is based around a young man named Ewan; he is from our world but is cast into a medieval fantasy land, known as the Kingdom of Farreach. In a realm of knights, kings and unparalleled betrayal, he sets in motion events that will alter the very history of this new world. Civil war is brewing and murderous plots start to unravel, yet at the heart of it all runs a love story that will change a kingdom forever.

-D.S. Aitken

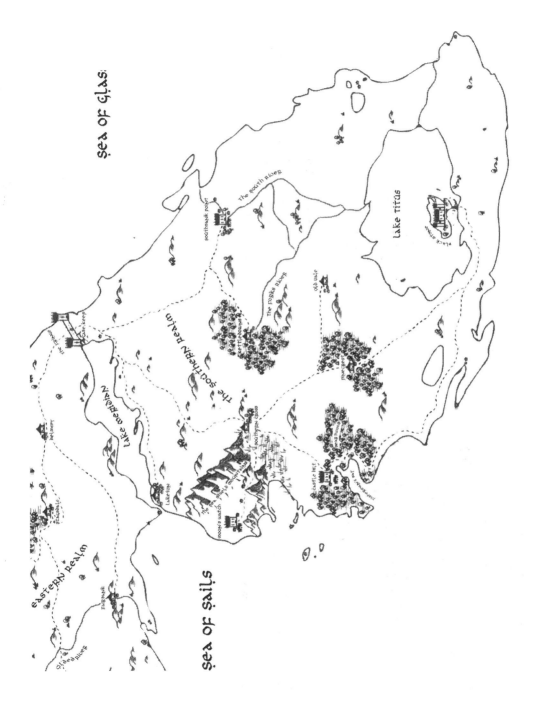

sea of glas

sea of sails

eastern realm

Lake merian

The southern realm

Lake titus

House Greyfell

Adwen Greyfell (Deceased) ——— Elora (Mason) Greyfell

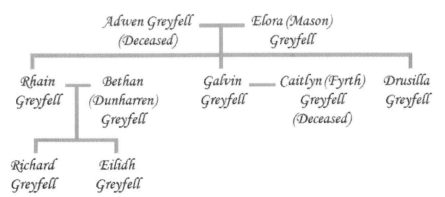

Rhain Greyfell ——— Bethan (Dunharren) Greyfell

Galvin Greyfell ——— Caitlyn (Fyrth) Greyfell (Deceased)

Drusilla Greyfell

Richard Greyfell

Eilidh Greyfell

House Associates

| Ewan Anderson | Nesta Mason | Sir Darrion Tarn | Lord Dale Tarn | Sister Margret |

House Dunharren

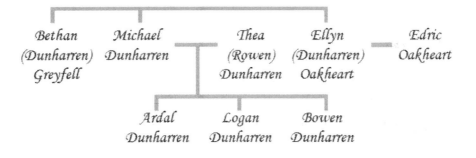

Bethan
(Dunharren)
Greyfell

Michael
Dunharren

Thea
(Rowen)
Dunharren

Ellyn
(Dunharren)
Oakheart

Edric
Oakheart

Ardal
Dunharren

Logan
Dunharren

Bowen
Dunharren

House
Associates

Lord Peter
Rowen

House Anvil

Walter	Torin	Gwyn
Anvil	Anvil	Anvil
(Deceased)		

Tristan
Anvil

House
Associates

Lord Farris	Sir Thomas	Lucille
Gillain	Gillain	Gillain

House Fyrth

Wolfrick
Fyrth
(Deceased)

William
Fyrth

Alva
Fyrth
(Deceased)

Caitlyn (Fyrth)
Greyfell
(Deceased)

Stewart
Fyrth

House
Associates

Sir Stefan
Barron

The Fabled Trilogy

Fabled: The War of Antlers

followed by

Fabled: The Bears of the North

and

Fabled: The Fallen Sword

Prologue

The morning was quiet and dark with the grass still weeping dew from its blades. The mist rolled down the hillside like a stampede of wild horses, tumbling over and over each other in a desperate race to reach the vast expanse of the valley below. Astride either side, there stood a dense forest reaching as far as the eye could see. This made the fields below the only stretch of grass not encroached by a wall of trees, as if it were a fight to remain open and free beneath the dying stars. This field was no stranger to conflict. The ground was heavy with the burden of war and the mist, which now settled in the morning air, retained the smell of death between its thick grey folds.

The dawn's first light broke over the trees and began to fill the valley with its soft morning glow. It chased down the shadows and forced them to rapidly retreat back up the side of the valley, into the shelter of the forest above. In that moment the sound of a horn cut through the stillness of the morning, a long low blast that rattled the trees so the leaves were made to cling to their branches. Then came the sound of marching, heavy feet pounding the ground with a very determined tone, a resolve that could only mean one thing, war was drawing near once again.

The world swayed and moved with the forceful yet rhythmic beat until all of a sudden it stopped, the air was still again. Through the trees on one side of the valley stepped out an enormous white stag, yet it had no fur to speak of, from antler to hoof it was made entirely of glass. There was not a single imperfection, it was flawlessly white and managed to look both fragile and strong at the same time. The creature moved forward out of the shadow of the tree line, looking out beyond the mist. It walked with a powerful and majestic stride; its antlers an elaborate array of intertwining pieces that caught the morning light.

The white stag looked towards the far side of the valley, where out of the trees emerged an almost identical beast, save for it being made of black glass. This darker being also walked with immense grandeur; great in size and beauty. It stood there, a polished silhouette set against the back drop of the trees, its antlers rising high and sharp. These inconceivable and dreamlike creatures simply locked eyes and stood their ground; their gaze conveyed anger as well as their terms. Despite the emotional and literal divide between these two commanding beasts, there appeared to be some form of familiarity that surpassed the mutual respect between enemies.

After the brief introduction was concluded, the two stags bowed to each other, both knowing that settlement was not an option that morning. They came with the intent of war and neither one wished for anything else. Without signal or sign, those responsible for the sound of heavy marching appeared out of the trees on either side of the valley, two glass armies, one black and one white. The men in the front ranks of each side were armed with tall spears, their heads tipped with finely etched glass blades, poised ready to be thrust into the enemy, shattering them to shards. Behind this wall of spears stood those with shield and sword, their rounded shields were flawless panes of hardened glass, their swords unsheathed standing long and sharp. The morning took one last breath of the stillness before both horns were blown and the armies flowed into the valley below.

White glass crashed into black as the ranks bled into each other on the battlefield. Their spears were forced through the opposition, causing their brittle frames to crack as shields were splintered when they took the brunt of falling swords. The valley became a dazzling spectacle as the sun danced around the broken shards, littering the ground with pieces of the fallen. The two great stags met in the centre of the valley with their war raging on around them, their antlers collided with one another, sending beautiful glass sparks into the air. Locked together these two beasts battled for power, rearing and kicking as they fought.

They crashed into each other time and time again in a desperate fight for control. This duel between the two creatures seemed to surpass the infinitely larger battle raging on in the background. Despite the cries of death and the cheers of victory, the stags were the focal point; a collision of black and white within a sea of glass.

The battle lasted hours and the ranks began to diminish until there were none left save their majestic captains; antlers splintered and broken. None were to survive that day, none were meant to breathe in one more mouthful of fresh morning air. The stags fell on each other once more but their bodies were now cracked and brittle. These two colossal creatures broke upon each other and shattered themselves, joining all the other shards with no distinguished or grand grave. They were consumed by the piles of coloured glass that littered the ground.

It was at that very moment, alone in his bed, King Adwen suddenly awoke. He was drenched in sweat, not from the dream, but from the fever that ailed him. All men who have seen war have troubling dreams; King Adwen was well accustomed to both. He was an elderly man late in his years and had lived a long and prosperous life as King and protector of the Kingdom of Farreach. The fever that he suffered from had come as quick and swift as a rushing tide; it washed over his body with a burning heat from which he could not escape.

His old grey eyes searched about his chamber, hoping that no one had seen him in his vulnerable state. The room was empty; his only company was the fire that roared in the corner. Two stag statues made of white marble stood on either side of the fire place, their antlers entwined which reminded him of his dream.

The door opened and his wife, Queen Elora, and her sister Nesta Mason entered his chamber.

"How are you feeling my love?" asked the Queen.

"Nothing hurts other than my pride," he replied, lying to everyone including himself.

"You seem in good spirits my King," said Nesta.

The King was good friends with his wife's sister, back in their youth the sisters both had crimson hair as bright as forging flames. Age had turned them a dull reddish grey colour. The King had broken tradition when he chose to marry Elora, for she and Nesta were not of a noble House. Their parents were farmers but when they died they were forced out of their home. One morning when the King was out riding, he noticed Elora with her hair of fire and fell in love. Elora became Queen and her sister Nesta joined her side in the Citadel of Kings, becoming the royal family's healer for her medicinal skills.

"Like I said it's only my pride that needs healing Nesta, no King should be forced to his bed no matter what his age," he said with a smile.

"You're not as young as you feel husband," replied the Queen.

"Nay I am as young as the woman I feel, and she remains beautiful despite her constant nagging," said the King with a laugh that muffled the severity of the fever.

"How is he sister, truthfully?" asked the Queen.

Nesta looked at the King before she indulged her sister's worrying. The King gave her a hard stare that she seemed to understand without question. She placed her hand against the brow of her King and he saw her heart sink.

"I believe he'll be fine," said Nesta after a moment.

"See my love, I remain unbeaten," said the King, "now leave me in peace so I may battle this sickness alone. I will see you in the morning strong and well."

"So be it my King," said the Queen as she and her sister stood up to leave.

The King watched as they left the room without another word. When the door closed behind them and he was alone again, he gave in to the storm of shivers he had been holding at bay. The King clutched the furs of his bed around him, pulling them close over his shaking and frail body. After years of defeating his enemies in the field, he simply refused to be beaten by sickness. He hoped, as he shut his eyes, that his pride would not be the end of him. But it was, for once his eyes closed, they never again opened.

As the mighty and noble King died in bed an old man; someone much younger, worlds away, was just about to wake.

Chapter One

The Green Mirror

Ewan Anderson's eyes opened slowly to a soft breeze from the window of his large bedroom, the curtains fluttered ever so slightly as the chill crept in, making its way under the warm sanctuary of his duvet. He curled his legs closer to his chest in order to retain some of the heat his sleepy self sorely missed. Ewan eventually gave up this folly and sat up in bed, his room was old and dusty with the dark wooden floor full of cardboard boxes. Each of which was scribbled with a roughly drawn 'Ewan's Bedroom' in a thick black ink that made an acrid tinge hang in the air.

That morning was the first time Ewan had woken up in his new room, still uncertain of the unfamiliar walls. His feet fell from the softness of his bed onto the hard wood below, an all too cold and strange feeling for that time of the morning. Hopefully his mother would allow him to put some carpet down or at the very least a rug, for he longed for the warm cushioned floor of his old room, the material so thick and plush he was able to curl his toes and grip the warmth.

Finally used to the wood beneath his feet he stood up, taking a deep breath he rubbed the last remnants of sleep from his tired eyes. Ewan made his way over to the solitary yet grand window on the far side of the room, rain lashed against the glass but no weather could ever interrupt the beauty of the scene that lay before him. Ewan looked out upon green rolling hills as far as the eye could see, dotted with small clusters of trees. He reached out with his hand and pressed it against the window, hoping to touch the beautiful world outside but only feeling the chill of the glass. The window framed this image in such a way it appeared to be a picture of a magical land not of our own. Ewan's mind would forever wander, always wishing he was on some far off adventure, away from the world he knew.

With his hand still pressed against the glass, Ewan saw his faint reflection. He was a young man in his last years as a teen with blonde hair that would often fall over his face. His eyes were of a deep green and lay above high cheek bones that were dotted with a few freckles. His new home was in the country, far from the city life he was used to, where he had never seen so much green. He drew in one last look of the world outside before turning back to his room. Dropping to his knees he looked through each of the boxes before him, he could not understand how all his possessions filled the small cluster of cardboard. Whilst sliding a box across the still very cold floorboards, a flash of green caught his eye somewhere between the cracks in the wood.

Pressing his face against the floor he saw there in the crack lay a piece of bright green glass about the length of his hand. Now this ordinarily would not provoke further inspection but the colour of the glass was unlike anything Ewan had ever seen before. Even in the darkness under the floor it shone like a shard of emerald green ice; giving off a soft glow in the dark. He looked about for something to pry up the floorboard to retrieve the shard but found that it was already loose; the thick plank of wood came away easily and he set it aside.

Gently Ewan reached in and pulled the shard out of its wooden crypt. He blew away the dust and admired it as it shone brighter still, never before had he thought a simple piece of glass could be beautiful. His green eyes were reflected back at him as they danced about on the gleaming surface; he turned it over and over in his hands. It did not feel like a piece of ordinary glass, it felt light yet stronger than metal. His transfixed state was suddenly broken by a shout from downstairs.

"Ewan your breakfast is ready!" his mother called.

He took one last long look at the green shard before placing it on top of his bed without even thinking.

"Be right down!" he replied.

Ewan got dressed, opened the door and made his way out into the hall. The new house was in no way new, the long halls and many rooms as dusty and uncared for as his bedroom. Down a grand staircase where paintings hung behind moth eaten sheets, Ewan made his way towards the sound of his mother's voice. He entered the kitchen where she was cooking bacon and his sister was eating cereal at the table. He went over to his sister and kissed her on the head.

"Good morning tiny," he said to her, "how are you?"

"Not too bad," she uttered through a mouthful of half eaten cereal.

"Did you sleep okay in your new bed?" he asked.

"Well I couldn't tell you because half way through the night I somehow managed to find my way into mum's."

"Which I didn't mind at all due to the heating not kicking in yet," said their mother.

"We have heating?" Ewan joked.

They all laughed as his mother finished the bacon sandwiches she was making and joined her two children at the table.

"And you Ewan, did you sleep well in your new bed?" she asked.

"I had a very strange dream that hasn't come back to me yet, other than that though I slept really well."

"Well your sister and I have to run into town so that we actually have some proper food in the house, would you like to come or would you prefer to have a wander around?"

"It will take more than just an afternoon to explore this house," he replied.

"Well it's an entirely different world to the city so don't go getting yourself lost on our first day," his mother said.

Ewan finished his sandwich and headed for the door.

"I make no promises," he said with a smile just as he was leaving.

He thought he'd start outside and although the rain had now stopped, the air still retained that fresh wet smell that filled Ewan's lungs as the heavy wooden door shut behind him. His house rested in the middle of nowhere, surrounded by vast grounds that did not seem to end. It had been left to his mother in the will of a great aunt Ewan had barely heard of let alone knew. They had lived their entire lives in the city and a move to the country seemed just what they all needed.

The house rose up behind him, a huge hulk of Georgian stonework with grand tall windows. Both ivy and time had made their mark on the building, yet it stood defiantly against their efforts. It took Ewan a long time to circle the large house, trying to take in every inch of his new home, though it proved impossible as there was simply too much of it. Once his circle was complete, he took one last look at the impressive structure before heading out into the large grounds.

The morning passed quickly as Ewan found himself lost amongst the vast gardens that encompassed his new home, most of it spent trying to find his way through a large hedge maze, grown more difficult over time as nature sought to take back the once well kept paths. When he finally made it back to the large house the morning was well and truly behind him, the sun now high in the sky.

The front door opened as heavily as it did when he had left. Ewan closed it behind him and removed his now muddy boots, setting them to one side. The house seemed very empty and he guessed his mother and sister were still in town.

"Hello!" he shouted, "either of you two home?" his voice echoing up into the high ceiling.

He received no reply and his original deduction was proven true. With the outside mostly explored, Ewan thought he would take the time to investigate the many rooms of his new home. On his way down to breakfast that morning he had noticed a second staircase at the end of a large hall and presumed an attic lay beyond; he thought that was a perfect place to start.

He ventured upstairs and sure enough at the end of the hall, lay a dark and dusty entrance to the upper realms of the house. The stairs gave off an unnerving creak as it moaned through his entire ascent. Ewan's head breached the level of the ceiling and entered the attic space above. Light shone into the attic from rows of small windows, dust danced in front of the beams of light, unsettled by the intruder who now disturbed the room's long and uninterrupted peace. Ewan climbed up the rest of the stairs and into the attic, his eyes took some time to adjust to the darkness that the rays of light failed to illuminate.

The attic was just as large as the house below, littered with old furniture, paintings, and other remnants of the past hidden beneath dust covered sheets. Ewan wanted to uncover all the forgotten treasures locked away from the face of the world, with only time and darkness for company. Though one dusty sheet caught his eye more than others, mainly due to its sheer size; covering something underneath, concealing it behind its moth eaten folds. Ewan inquisitively approached the sheet; whatever was hidden underneath was clearly taller than him and easily twice as wide.

His hands gripped the dust covered rag and he poised himself to remove it with one swift stroke. Ewan closed his eyes and wrenched the sheet into the air, he felt the dust fall around his face as he kept his eyes tightly shut. After the dust had again settled, Ewan slowly opened his eyes and they were filled with a flash of green. What stood before him was an enormous mirror made from the same glass as the shard he found under his floorboards; an unmistakable emerald green surface that was without a single scratch or imperfection.

The mirror was edged with an ornate golden frame made of thick rich metal; it curved round the glass in an elaborate design of floral swirls. Ewan could not believe what stood before him; he did not even trust his own reflection that mirrored his look of pure wonder. In the bottom right hand corner of the mirror Ewan noticed that a small section of the glass was missing, leaving a golden sliver set amongst a sea of green. The shape of the empty space was the same size and cut as the piece of glass still lying atop Ewan's bed downstairs.

He fled down the wooden steps nearly killing himself in the process. Ewan raced through the large house and burst into his bedroom, snatching up the piece of glass. Before he knew it he was standing once again before the green mirror, this time with the shard in hand.

For some reason he was very hesitant about placing it in the mirror. Eventually he knelt down on the dusty wooden planks that made up the attic floor, holding it inches away from its rightful place in the mirror. It slid effortlessly into place and the broken lines that separated it from the rest of the mirror fused shut with the whisper of cracking ice.

Ewan jumped back as the surface of the mirror suddenly frosted over and it became a dazzling sheet of green crystals. The glass appeared to move and shift as if it were a glacier trapped within a golden frame. Ewan approached the mirror once more with his hand outstretched, as his finger met the glass the frosted green crystals parted and his finger slipped right through the mirror. At first Ewan did not believe what was happening but then found the courage to immerse his entire hand in the glass.

The air on the other side was warm against his skin and he could feel a distinctly real breeze brush through his finger tips. Ewan shut his eyes and with his hand in the mirror he could hear waves lapping against a distant shore. None of it made any sense, he was miles inland, far from any sea yet the sound came from the mirror where the rest of the house lay silent.

Ewan had no notion as to what world lay beyond the shiny green glass, nor did he have any idea as to whether he would be able to return even if he could pass through. Before he could make the decision for himself, his hand was pulled further into the mirror. Panic took him as some invisible force began to draw him through the glass. Ewan tried to call out for help but before his words escaped him, he was pulled from the world he knew and disappeared entirely through the mirror. Moments later, the sound of his mother and sister returning echoed through the empty house.

Chapter Two

Daughter of a King

The waters of the Sea of Glass rested as still and calm as always. Standing at the edge of her balcony, Eilidh Greyfell looked down at soft waves gently lapping at the base of the Falling Cliffs. Her long crimson curls flowed in the sea air; her red hair was a gift from her grandmother Elora, for the rest of the Greyfells were all dark in comparison. From her balcony she could see to the southeast the forest of Beachwood, where its dense trees went right up to the sandy shores. She enjoyed riding through the shallow water of the beach whenever she was given leave from her studies, which was not very often.

Eilidh turned back to her chamber, falling down onto the large double bed and curling herself up in a heap of furs. It was quite warm for the start of spring but she loved the softness of the fur against her cheek. Eilidh was young with fair pale skin and freckles to match. She was a Princess of the Kingdom of Farreach and lived within the Citadel of Kings, a large palace at the very edge of the capital city of Gleamport.

"Princess Eilidh," she said to herself softly.

She still found the words strange to hear, for despite always being a member of the royal family, she had not been considered a Princess for very long. Only those directly beneath the King and Queen were also granted royal titles. The complications that came with such her own title troubled her greatly. Her grandfather, Adwen Greyfell, was considered by all to be King but her father, Rhain Greyfell, did not have the luxury of such a simple claim when the King died some weeks before. However, Eilidh was in the eyes of many a Princess and therefore the responsibilities of such a status came regardless of whether she felt like one or not.

There was a knock at the door and in swept her teacher and carer Sister Margret, a large older woman full of cheer who held her reputation as high as the welfare of those she had charge of. Eilidh knew the woman meant well but she could not help but be irritated by her overly friendly persona.

"Good morning Princess," Sister Margret said as she immediately started to tidy up around her, another thing Eilidh sorely disliked.

"Good morning Sister Margret," she replied with practised enthusiasm.

"And how are we feeling this morning?"

"A lot better if I knew I was going for a ride later rather than being stuck indoors with you," she said with a smile.

Sister Margret was well accustomed to Eilidh's lack of interest and was well used to taking her comments on one of her chins.

"Well that could be arranged if you manage to finish your studies with time to spare, but first I believe your father wishes to have a word with you," replied Sister Margret.

"Did he say what he wanted?"

"The King did not say and I did not presume to ask, only that he needed to speak with you, however, you will not even pretend you are going to leave this chamber in the state you are in, first we must wash the night off of you."

Once Sister Margret had fetched the young Princess a bowl of steaming hot water, she went about the room doing this and that whilst Eilidh undressed and washed. The hot water trickled from the sponge over her naked body washing off the night as Sister Margret had said. Eilidh brought her hands to her chest and smiled in the mirror, for she had only recently been given a woman's body.

"Stop feeling so proud of yourself," interrupted Sister Margret with a very noticeably smirk between her lips.

"Should I not be?"

"Not when one is still smaller than the other."

Eilidh fired a look of daggers back at her but she knew that the comment was in jest. Sister Margret had known young Eilidh since she first opened her eyes. She knew every inch of the young Princess and could read her like an open book.

Once Eilidh was washed Sister Margret dressed her in a crimson silk gown that was adorned with gold stitching. Eilidh looked at herself in the mirror, it was her favourite dress.

"I always love how it brings out the colour of your hair," said Sister Margret with the faintest tear in the corner of her eye, "you truly are a young woman these days."

Eilidh sat down in front of the mirror and Sister Margret began to tame her wild curly hair to little end.

"I suppose that will have to do my child," she said as she put the brush down in obvious defeat, "now off to see your father, we shall convene in the library for your studies once you are done."

Eilidh left her chamber with a small push of encouragement from Sister Margret. The halls of the Citadel of Kings were made of pale white marble cracked with streaks of blue, on the walls hung banners with the heraldry of her House coloured the same as their marbled setting; a white stag prancing across a field of azure. The stag had been the heraldry of House Greyfell since they first began their royal dynasty hundreds of years ago.

Down the hall she could see the entrance to her father's chamber, a large wooden door made of solid dark oak and studded with brass nails. It was and always had been the King's chamber; it was still very odd to go looking for her father there. Her grandfather King Adwen often told her stories within those walls and she was sad to have him leave her life so suddenly. Young Eilidh also felt for her now widowed grandmother; stripped of both husband and the title of Queen in the same hour.

Outside the large door Sir Darrion Tarn stood watch. He was the Captain of the King's Royal Guard, the youngest in the history of the Kingdom her father would always tell her. Sir Darrion had squired for her father when he was but a boy. He was a young man in his prime, slight yet strong and not overly tall, light brown hair tied neatly behind his head. The men of the Royal Guard wore armour made of polished steel that bore a nest of antlers forming a crown engraved on their breastplates. This was accompanied by a long blue cloak trimmed with white fur. Sir Darrion's attire was of this fashion with a brightly coloured fox running down the scabbard of his longsword, the heraldry of House Tarn.

"Good morning my Princess," he said in a friendly manner as she approached the door.

"Good morning Sir Darrion," she replied with a smile.

He was always very kind to her and other than her father, she trusted the noble Captain more than any other man, even over her older brother Prince Richard.

Eilidh raised her hand to knock on the door but it opened just as her fist was about to fall on the wood. Her father, King Rhain, stood there looking at her. The King had very stern features that he seldom put aside, with dark brown hair, the streaks of grey the sign of his age.

"Good morning little one," he said gently.

"Good morning father."

With the formalities out the way, and already forgotten, her father embraced her with sincere affection. She hated the fake portrayal of propriety but they both knew that it was necessary. Eilidh loved her father dearly and moments when they disagreed were few and far between.

With his arms still around her, Eilidh realised that she loved the smell of leather and toil that hung to his clothes. Despite his status her father was a simple man at heart; a soldier. Eilidh saw a lot of herself in her father, the reluctance to attend studies and the desire to be out riding in the fresh air certainly did not come from her mother.

"So what did you want to see me about?"

"Come in and I shall tell you."

"Good luck," Sir Darrion whispered to her just before the door of the closed.

Inside the room it was warm and the floor was heavily laden with soft furs which she liked. A grand fireplace was ablaze in the corner with two stag statues on either side, their antlers locking in front of the flames. Her father turned and their eyes met from across the room.

"I wanted to talk to you about Tristan," her father explained, "now that you are both engaged to be married and he has been staying here in Gleamport these last few days, I thought it best that you get to know each other a little more. I will not have my only daughter married off to a man she barely knows."

"I would like that very much," said Eilidh with a grin.

"Accompanied of course," replied her father without a grin.

"Of course father," Eilidh said mimicking the seriousness of her father's tone.

The man her father had chosen for her was the son of Lord Torin Anvil, Keeper of the Hammer Hills and Thane of the Western Realm; Tristan was his only child and heir. He had moved to Gleamport recently and Eilidh was very pleased with her father's choice. Tristan was a good man and Eilidh held the few moments they had spent together close to her heart.

"Tristan seems to be a good and honourable lad and although no man is good enough for you, I believe he comes quite close. His charms are second only to the support his father has given me from the Western Realm, right now I need all that I can muster."

"Father, why is most of the Kingdom supporting you and not uncle Galvin?"

He obviously did not expect such a question so early in the morning and seemed to be in no mood to try and answer it.

"Another time perhaps child, now away to your studies before Sister Margret makes me join you."

Again Eilidh was given a light push out of the door and enjoyed it as little as the first one. She quickly found her way down to the library where without a doubt Sister Margret was waiting eagerly for her arrival.

The library was a large circular room with books lining the walls around them. Thousands of dusty tombs full of knowledge and past events that Eilidh could not be the least bit interested in. She did, however, always love to stare at the pictures depicted on the domed ceiling above, horrific and brutal battles portrayed in such beautiful and elegant strokes. Her father had told her about the truth of the battles he had fought in and she was not fooled by the artistic grandeur.

"So what did your father want with you?"

"He wished to talk about me spending more time with Tristan," said Eilidh.

"Did your father say what he thought of the young Anvil lad?"

"He said he thought Tristan seemed good and honourable."

"That seems true enough, but if he should ever prove otherwise, it will not be your father he has to worry about. I have not grown soft in my old age, especially when it comes to matters concerning you," said Sister Margret with a playful nudge.

The comment should have pleased young Eilidh but she sat there very pensive.

"What troubles you child?" asked Sister Margret seeing the distant look in the Princess' eyes.

"I want to know why everyone thinks my father should be King and not his brother. He has never wanted the crown."

"I believe that is a question for your father."

"I have tried but he won't answer," replied Eilidh with frustration in her voice.

"Very well," said Sister Margret, "as you well know your grandfather, King Adwen, had three children, a daughter and two sons. Your aunt Drusilla being a woman has no claim to the Kingdom, but since your father and uncle are twins neither one has a more rightful claim than the other."

"Yes I know but uncle Galvin not only wanted to be King where my father did not, he also seemed so sure he would be," interrupted Eilidh.

"So was the entire Kingdom, I will have you know," said Sister Margret, "it was well known that Galvin was always your grandfather's favourite; I cared for them both as children the way I care for you now. Galvin was good at everything he touched; he succeeded over your father in all aspects despite them being twins. Everyone always expected him to one day be proclaimed the King's heir and they all supported it."

"But grandfather Adwen never named his successor."

"That is exactly right my child, when your grandfather died a few weeks ago he had never formally announced his heir."

"But then what changed the hearts of the people from supporting Galvin as they once had?"

"Now that is a question you do know the answer to my Princess."

Eilidh fell silent. She did indeed know the answer to the question.

"The death of his wife," she said quietly.

"Yes," said Sister Margret with a sigh, "when Lady Caitlyn died last year Galvin's spirit died along with her. He became secluded and shut himself away from the Kingdom along with the people in it."

"He was never really the same after she died," said Eilidh sadly.

"No he was not. Your father saw his own brother turn cold and fall from the King's good graces. It never upset your father to forever live in the shadows; he always loved your grandfather and did not want to see his Kingdom fall to ruin in the hands of a broken man. It appears that most of the Kingdom agreed and that is why your father is now King."

"Most but not all," said Eilidh.

"No I am afraid that is right, despite the fact three of the Realms acknowledge your father as King, the south has yet to do so," replied Sister Margret.

"So why does the Southern Realm support uncle Galvin?"

"As you know House Fyrth are the Thanes of the Southern Realm but they above all else desire power. Lord William Fyrth only married his daughter to your uncle Galvin in the hopes that she would one day become Queen."

"But Lady Caitlyn died," said Eilidh.

"Exactly," replied Sister Margret, "and now Lord William is supporting his once son by law in another attempt to gain some kind of grip over the Kingdom, however, for the life of me, I can't understand why your aunt Drusilla thought it wise to follow Galvin south."

Drusilla was the younger sister of the two twins but like her father and most of the Kingdom, she preferred her brother Galvin.

"They were always very close," said Eilidh.

"Indeed they were," replied Sister Margret in a disapproving tone, "now with your permission can we please begin your studies or do you have any other lengthy questions?"

Before them on the table was a large map of the Kingdom. It was made of old parchment that Eilidh disliked the smell of, the corners were torn and the creases along its folds were beginning to crack. The map clearly showed all four Realms and all that lay within them.

"Now I know your knowledge of the noble Houses doesn't require any attention but due to the up and coming coronation banquet, your father has asked me to go over them with you," said Sister Margret.

"If we must," replied Eilidh.

"Yes we must," said Sister Margret as she tapped at the map.

Her finger pointed towards the western icy region where the Kingdom met the Sea of Sails, where the water crept in to the land creating a large bay.

"The Rift," explained Eilidh.

"Lords and Keepers?" asked her teacher.

"House Gillain."

"Very good," said Sister Margret, "their stronghold and heraldry?"

"They are Lords of Fort Morton and their heraldry is a snow owl due to their wintery land."

"Well what a good start to the morning," she said cheerfully.

Next she pointed to a mountain range north of the Rift but still frozen and covered with snow.

"And here?" she asked.

"The Hammer Hills," said Eilidh with a smile, "where Tristan is from."

"That is right, perhaps you should be smitten with all the Lords' sons, then you might answer my questions with more enthusiasm," said Sister Margret with a hint of sarcasm, "what are his father's titles?"

"Torin of House Anvil, Lord of Mount Steel, Keeper of the Hammer Hills and Thane of the Western Realm, as well as my future father by law," added Eilidh with a smirk.

"Very clever young lady," replied Sister Margret, "what about their House heraldry?"

"A golden anvil."

"It is indeed," said Sister Margret.

Her finger then landed at the northernmost part of the map where an island off the mainland was covered in trees.

"What about here?" she asked.

"That's an easy one."

"Pray tell."

"My mother's homeland of Forest Isle, Lord and Keeper is her brother and my uncle Michael of House Dunharren."

"Don't forget Thane of the Northern Realm and your father's best friend," added Sister Margret.

House Dunharren had long been Keepers of the woods that made up Forest Isle. It was cut off from the mainland of the Kingdom by a long thin birth of the sea known as the Northern Straits. Eilidh's mother, Queen Bethan, grew up in the great city of Oakenhold on the island with her older brother Michael and younger sister Ellyn. Eilidh's father and her uncle Michael had been friends since they were boys, meeting every chance they could; spending their time together hunting, training and when old enough, fighting. As brothers in arms and defenders of noble Houses they had been to war together which only served to strengthen their bond.

Eilidh loved to see the two of them together. When out of the prying eyes of those they rule that think them men, her stern faced father and burly uncle become boys again. She had not seen her uncle's family in quite some time but they would be attending the coronation banquet to swear fealty to her father. She knew Richard would be pleased, her older brother and her eldest cousin, Ardal, were both of the same age and went hunting together.

Once her studies were complete and she was thoroughly sick of all the noble Houses of the Kingdom, Sister Margret gave her leave to go riding as promised. Eilidh took off out of the library at a run, scared of being called back to recite more well known and trivial details. She escaped into the hall at such a pace she nearly tackled her brother to the ground as he was unknowingly walking past.

"Sorry," she gasped.

"Trying to get yourself killed?" asked her brother angrily.

"Sorry," she said again, this time more earnestly.

Eilidh had never been truly close to Richard, not through lack of trying on her part; they were simply very different. He looked a lot younger than he was, with childlike eyes and boyish dimples. That day he wore a dark blue tunic made of soft silk with a silver brooch that clasped a short cloak hung over one shoulder. Her brother always acted like a Prince even before he was one, he took everything so seriously and Eilidh seemed to irritate him no matter how hard she tried.

"Off for a ride are we?" asked Richard.

"I am," she replied, not knowing whether he actually cared or not, "are you looking forward to seeing Ardal when uncle Michael arrives?"

"I'm hoping father will arrange a hunt, I haven't killed anything in weeks. I was under the impression Princes could do as they please."

Eilidh, like her father, did not wish to fall on such grace, yet Richard seemed to live for it. He looked down on those beneath him not with a desire to share their simplicity but an ill placed sense of superiority. Despite her brother's flaws she pitied his narrow perspective and tried to see the good in him, unfortunately she did not often find it.

"Well go see to your little horse," he said.

"I shall," she replied with spite, "and it wouldn't hurt to be a little kinder."

"I have no need for kindness sister, not anymore."

Those last words hung in her thoughts as she made her way down to the stable. She believed a man like her brother had no business becoming King; it was when this thought entered her head that she understood why her father sought to be King even though he did not desire it. Young Princess Eilidh promised herself then that she, like her father, would not let his Kingdom fall to ruin.

The stable was set in the courtyard just outside the Citadel of Kings. When she reached the fresh air of outside she could see the city of Gleamport spread out before her. The Citadel stood alone from the rest of the city on a thin outcrop of the Falling Cliffs. It stretched out over Royal Bay like a sword, the Citadel a shining jewel set into the tip of the blade. The Falling Cliffs were aptly named after either side of the outcrop had fallen into the Sea of Glass hundreds of years ago, leaving only the slender stretch of rock untouched. The unique stretch of rock was known as Greyfell's Sword, the Citadel long being held by Eilidh's ancestors.

In the stable stood her horse waiting saddled and ready, reins held by capable stable hands. Eilidh looked on with a smile at the elegant creature that she could call her own. Her name was Willow; she was a flawless creature that none in all of the four Realms could rival. Set against her perfect white coat was an equally perfect golden mane. The light caught it in such a way it would shimmer and float like water; a cascading river of gold.

Eilidh's hand ran through the golden hair of her old friend, the horse responded to her familiar gentle touch.

"Hello you," said Eilidh, almost expecting a polite answer in reply.

She mounted Willow with a practised fluid motion, falling deep into the leather of her saddle. Her feet found the stirrups hanging by the horse's side and within an instant of finding their place, off they both shot along the length of the Sword, beyond the walls of the Citadel and onto the mainland of the cliffs.

"You be careful young lady!" shouted Sister Margret as she came rushing out to say goodbye.

But both girl and horse were far away and the concerned shouts were appropriately ignored.

With the Citadel far behind, Eilidh raced through and out of the city. Beachwood lay beneath Gleamport further down the cliffs, where it levelled out to meet the water. The trees came into sight as they curved down the last slopes of the cliffs. Eilidh loved how close the wood was to the waves, mere strides separated the shallows of the beach from the tree line with the soft white sand acting as a barrier.

Willow headed straight for the water, kicking up sand and salty spray with her hooves. Eilidh's crimson hair flowed far behind her as she felt the sea splash against her face. Those moments when time seemed to slow down meant the most to her, she did not have to be a Princess or a Lady but just a girl on her horse. She was truly happy. Right up to the point where Willow stumbled and she was sent flying from her saddle into the cold water of the sea.

Chapter Three

A Chance Meeting

Ewan awoke with the feel of soft grass on his face and the sound of gentle waves in his ears. His cheek lay flat against the ground, the air that he breathed bounced back at him in a suffocating recycled cloud. The sound of the sea washed over him; due to the closeness of the water he was expecting sand instead of grass. Ewan slowly cracked open his eyes to the world around him.

Thoughts of the mirror came flooding back to him in a flash of green. Ewan lifted his head from the soft grass and forced his eyes to believe what they saw. He was surrounded by trees, their branches looming overhead thick with leaves. Through them, not far from where he was, Ewan could see waves lapping against a white sandy shore. He had no explanation as to where he was or how he had got there. His first thoughts were that he was dreaming but his stiff body sprawled out on the hard ground betrayed them. Wherever he was it was no dream.

Ewan climbed to his feet and it took him a long time to regain his balance. When he finally settled he looked around for the green mirror, though it was nowhere to be seen. The door, through which he had been cast, appeared to have closed firmly behind him. Despite the very real breeze he felt brush against his face; logic told him he was still very much asleep. Raising his hand, he pinched his arm and winced, for the pain was just as real as the wind.

Fear crept over him; his dream did not pass from a truth to an uncertain memory as they usually did. He expected to blink and simply wake up in his new bed, ready to begin the day all over again. His thoughts then drifted to his family that he had left behind, wondering what became of him without so much as a note or a simple goodbye.

Fear stopped stealing its way into his heart as he suddenly became aware of the moisture from the grass being soaked up by his socks. His eyes drifted down.

"You've got to be kidding me?" he said aloud to himself.

He had managed to get pulled into an entirely different world, all without a pair of shoes. So there he stood, alone, stranded and in socks. Before he let himself be overwhelmed by uncertainty, he decided the simplest of thoughts, to place one wet sock in front of the other.

It seemed a good idea to head towards the sea, getting out of the trees would give him a better look at the landscape. The wood was alive around him as he pushed through, the sound of birds and insects filled the air, interrupted only by his soft feet against the grass. Through the trees was a beautiful beach, the likes of which Ewan had never seen. As he emerged from the darkness of the wood he was blinded by the brightness of the light. Before young Ewan lay the crystal clear water of a sea that gently rose and fell against the sand.

The beach seemed to be part of a large bay for Ewan could see shores on the opposite side, which were separated by the sea, forcing its way into the land. The beach curved round and high to his left, he could see cliffs rising from the water, rock walls sharp and steep as if they had once been sheered clean off. Jutting out of these cliffs he saw a large palace glinting in the sunlight, he could not tell if it was real or not. As he stood admiring the ambiguous building, out the corner of his eye, he saw something red floating in the shallows of the waves.

He strained his eyes on the object and quickly realised that it was a person face down in the water. Without thinking he ran into sea, the cold spray washing over him. Wading through the shallow waves, he took a deep breath and plunged under the glassy surface. As he got closer he saw that it was a girl, her fiery red hair floating out in front of her. He turned her over in the water and pulled her back to shore.

He had no notion of what to do, so again without thinking, he breathed a deep long breath through her soft lips. The girl lay deathly still with no sign of life behind her closed eyes. Nothing happened so again Ewan breathed a deep breath into her mouth. Suddenly she spluttered and coughed her way back into life as relief washed over young Ewan.

Despite being pressed against her face just moments before, this was the first time he actually took in what she looked like. She lay there still not fully awake with crimson hair wet and clinging to the sand about her. She had beautiful pale skin, void of any imperfection save the freckles dotted about her cheeks. Her lips were as red as her hair, forming small soft curves within her gentle face. Her attire looked very medieval to young Ewan. The wet dress clung to her, revealing her slender frame. So when she began to stir Ewan made sure it was her eyes he was looking at and not that which lay below them.

"Don't be afraid," he said gently, "I found you in the water."

The young girl's eyes opened to the sound of his voice, they were an icy light blue and searched Ewan's face for answers. He could not help but notice how remarkably beautiful she was.

"Who are you?" she asked nervously.

Ewan did not know what to say; until he knew more about her and the world he was in, he thought it best to leave out certain details.

"My name is Ewan Anderson," he said with slight hesitation.

"I was in the water?" she asked with confusion.

He nodded in reply.

"Well thank you Ewan, my name is Eilidh of House Greyfell."

"What were you doing out here?" he asked.

"I was riding, first time I've fallen in years," her eyes looked over him curiously, "you must forgive me after just saving my life, but where did you get such odd clothes?"

He suddenly became aware that his clothes must seem very strange indeed and the fact he was not wearing any shoes certainly did not help.

"Well in my defence they did look a lot better dry," said Ewan with a smile, trying to avoid the question.

"If your clothes had stayed dry I might not have stayed alive, thank you again," said Eilidh returning the smile.

"You're very welcome."

"I don't know the name Anderson," she went on, "do you live in the city?"

Ewan did not know which city she meant or what he should tell her. His life before the green mirror was still clear in his mind, though he had no idea how to even begin explaining the truth of it.

"I don't remember," he lied.

"You don't remember where you live?"

"No nothing, I know my name but that's it. The first thing I can remember is waking up lying in the wood," he lied again.

"So you know nothing about the Kingdom or where you come from?"

"Kingdom?" Ewan replied.

He did not want to lie to her but he could not see any other option. Ignorance is bliss when the truth might get you killed, he paraphrased to himself.

"The Kingdom of Farreach of course," said Eilidh with a confused tone.

Ewan knew he would sound just as patronising trying to explain to someone back home what country they found themselves in.

"My father King Rhain Greyfell is Keeper of Royal Bay and Thane of the Eastern Realm in which we now sit."

It all sounded very important but the only title that he knew the meaning of was King, though that was enough for him to realise the importance of the young girl he had just saved.

"So if your father is King that would make you a Princess?"

"That's usually how it works," she replied with a teasing smile.

"So not only did I save the life of a beautiful young girl but also the daughter of a King?" said Ewan surprised at his own boldness.

He watched as Eilidh's cheeks blushed as bright as her hair yet she did not shy away from the compliment.

"It would appear that way," she said, "a feat worthy enough to be considered a guest in the Citadel of Kings at least."

Ewan was pleased yet could not help but give off a look of uncertainty, as he had no idea where the Citadel of Kings was despite of how important it sounded.

"Forgive me," Eilidh continued after realising her mistake, "the royal family of Farreach live in the capital city of Gleamport, in a palace known as the Citadel of Kings; you would honour me by staying as our guest. I know my parents would welcome my saviour."

Ewan was happy to accept; he had no idea what he would have done with himself if Eilidh had not offered such a kindness.

"Thank you Princess," he said at last, "I really appreciate your help."

Eilidh smiled at his acceptance as Ewan stood up and helped her to her feet.

"The only problem is that we must walk, for I seem to have misplaced my horse."

"That's quite all right Princess," he said as he held out his arm for her to hold.

She welcomed it and pointed them in the right direction. They walked along the beach with the water lapping inches away from their feet. Ewan enjoyed the feel of the soft sand through his socks; he gripped at the grains through the supple material and held them there with each step. The trees began to thin out as they moved further into the bay and beach turned into cliffs, Ewan once again saw the shining palace above them, this time more clearly.

"This is Royal Bay," Eilidh pointed out, "and that building there is the Citadel of Kings."

The Citadel lay at the far end of a thin outcrop of the cliffs, a finger of rock pointing out into the bay. Ewan glimpsed the start of Gleamport beyond the rocky edge.

"The cliffs around the bay are known as the Falling Cliffs. Hundreds of years ago they were swallowed up by the Sea of Glass, all but Greyfell's Sword. My family's ancestors claimed the palace away from the city at the very tip of the Sword, and there it has stood for generations."

"Were they not scared it might someday fall away like the cliffs around it?"

"Legend says that the day the Sword falls is the end of my House, I suppose they hoped that day would never come."

They reached the foothills of the cliffs and Ewan stepped from sand onto the gently sloping grass that topped them. As they made their way towards the city, Ewan noticed the sun was beginning to set out over Royal bay and something about it just did not seem right.

"Eilidh you said we are in the Eastern Realm of the Kingdom right?"

"I did."

"And the sun always sets in the east of Farreach?"

"Of course it does, it's hardly going to set in the west is it?" she replied with a giggle.

He was in an unknown land worlds away from his own and yet he still thought it odd that the sun should set anywhere other than the west. Whether he was dreaming or even dead, the natural certainties that he was used to being completely different, still made him feel very nervous indeed.

The walls of Gleamport lay before them, the very peculiar sun setting behind the high buildings. The city was made entirely of white stone, the towers upon the walls standing tall. Atop these towers blue flags were flying with a graceful white stag embellished in the centre. The walls of the city curved around the cliff in a perfect half circle.

As they neared the gates Ewan saw a host of what appeared to be knights approaching them, their polished armour and blue cloaks glinting in the setting sun. He had been right about the medieval look of Eilidh, before now the city and the knights were creations of history and fantasy; not a reality that loomed over him. At the forefront of the host was a young knight, a brightly coloured fox running down the length of the scabbard that held his longsword; the hilt as polished as his armour.

"My Princess," the man said with earnest concern in his voice, "when your horse returned without you we feared the worst. I was in the process of organising a search party. Who is this boy?"

"His name is Ewan Anderson; he saved me from the sea after I fell from Willow. I'm sorry that I worried you Sir Darrion but I'm unhurt," she said to the knight.

"I'm glad to see you alive and well Princess, what is to be done with him?"

"He is my guest Sir Darrion, in payment for his bravery."

Ewan thought it best to remain silent throughout, the knight clearly cared about the young Princess and he did not want to speak out of turn. Sir Darrion nodded and parted his men to let them pass.

"Very well, I will escort you and master Ewan to your father at once," he said as he led them towards the city, "the King and Queen have been worried sick ever since Willow returned alone."

"I'm just glad that she returned at all," said Eilidh with relief.

"And your guest Princess," asked the knight, "does he have a voice of his own?"

"He does, a fair one, though no memories to accompany it."

The knight stopped in front of them.

"What do you mean?" he asked with a puzzled look.

"I'll explain when I see my parents."

As they walked through the gates of the city Ewan was amazed by everything he saw. Gleamport was busy with merchants and citizens as they prepared the city for nightfall. The sound of blacksmiths hammering the last of their steel and food sellers shouting out final orders filled the dense air of the streets. Ewan had seen medieval festivals where people would act out the roles of the time but nothing compared to the reality of the environment around him. His senses were filled with the smell of cooking meat and smouldering white hot steel.

"Are you okay?" asked Eilidh in a low voice, still close beside him.

"It's just all so busy," he replied, overwhelmed by what was going on around him.

"This is the capital," Eilidh said in earnest, "being near the sea has made it the trading centre of Farreach. A port lies in the bay on the other side of the Sword, sheltered by its blade. Everything from food to clothing comes through here and though our steel might not rival that of the Hammer Hills, we're a lot easier to get to than those snow covered mountains."

The city was large and if Ewan had not seen it from the bay below, he would not have believed it lay on the edge of a cliff. It spread out before them with white stone alleys going off in every direction. Leading from the front gate was a long street that seemed to stretch through the entire city. In the distance Ewan could see the Citadel of Kings standing tall and proud. Eventually they reached the end of the street, where the city hugged the very edge of the cliff.

Greyfell's Sword reached out in front of them from the mainland like a bridge that had no other side. A large gate stood at the entrance with another host of knights guarding it. The Citadel lay beyond, made up of gradually increasing tiers that grew larger and eventually peaked at the Sword's tip. The gates opened before them with just a nod from Sir Darrion as he led them forward.

The Sword was edged with a small white stone wall that ran along both sides. Between the wall and the wide path that they walked on were gardens of green grass, small trees symmetrically lining the entire length of it. More knights were evenly spaced out along the path, unmoving with tall spears held tightly to their side.

A large circular courtyard lay just in front of Citadel, with a stable off to one side. Eilidh stopped and Sir Darrion turned to face them.

"Would it be okay if I saw Willow before explaining to my parents?" she pleaded.

"I thought you might ask," Sir Darrion sighed in defeat without even putting up a fight, "go on then," he said gesturing towards the stable.

"Thank you," she said as she led Ewan across the courtyard.

The inside of the stable was hot and smelt of hay. Ewan follwed the young Princess along to the stall where her horse eagerly awaited her arrival. Ewan had never seen such a grand creature; the horse was as white as snow and had a mane of golden hair. Eilidh placed a hand on her head and Willow instantly became calm.

"You two good friends?" he asked her.

"Before today we were, it might take some time to forgive her for leaving me," she said with a small smile.

Willow seemed to respond to her comment, her large round eyes looking almost guilty.

"I'm teasing," Eilidh said to the horse again with a smile, "it wasn't your fault you fell."

The horse seemed to appreciate the sympathy as well as the strokes from Eilidh's soft hands.

"We better go," said Eilidh at last, "my parents will never let me hear the end of this, let alone Sister Margret."

"Who's Sister Margret?"

"My teacher and carer but she likes to act as a second mother," she replied with a sigh.

As they emerged from the stable the courtyard was now littered with more than just knights. A large woman full of hysteria ran towards them at some speed despite her size.

"Let me look at you child," she exclaimed as she reached them, her voice out of breath from the short sprint.

She was dressed in a light grey dress with her dull grey hair tied neatly up out of the way. She looked the Princess over from head to foot.

"You must be Sister Margret," said Ewan with some courage behind it.

"Indeed I am, and what part did you play in her disappearance?" she demanded.

"The part of saving my life," interjected Eilidh, "I fell from Willow into the sea. Ewan here pulled me from the water, otherwise I would have drowned."

"Well then," coughed Sister Margret realising her abruptness, "I suppose we owe you a debt of gratitude rather than a host of accusations. I apologise for my rudeness, but this girl means more to me than the entire Kingdom."

"I can see why Sister Margret," said Ewan, "she is indeed special."

Sister Margret looked at Eilidh and they both smiled at each other.

"Oh I like this one," said the old woman with a cheeky grin.

"So do I," replied the Princess looking at Ewan.

From behind the roundness of Sister Margret approached a man and woman. Eilidh left Ewan's side and ran into the arms of them both.

"Father! Mother!" she said as she met them in an embrace.

The King and Queen both looked relieved to hold their daughter once more. The King was a simple looking man, not overly adorned with jewellery or elaborate clothing as Ewan thought a King would be. He was dressed in studded leather with a longsword swinging at his hip and a crown of antlers nestled atop his dark brown hair. He had a stern face that broke only with the sight of his daughter.

The Queen was dressed in a light blue gown, the neckline trimmed with gold. Her hair was as black as the night sky and fell from under a small and delicate diadem, holding the same likeness as the King's crown. She was very beautiful for her age but with her black hair and dark skin, she looked quite different from her daughter.

"I'm so happy you're safe," said the King still caught in her embrace.

"When Willow returned alone we couldn't help but worry," added the Queen.

"I'm sorry that I worried you both, it wasn't my intention. But I'm not hurt."

"And who is your young guest Sir Darrion has just told me about?" asked the King turning his attention to Ewan.

"He pulled me from the sea after I fell," said Eilidh.

"Is this true?" the King asked Ewan directly.

"It is my King," Ewan said trying to sound as respectful as possible.

"And Sir Darrion tells me you have no memories before saving my daughter?" the King continued.

"Again true my King," he lied once more.

The King took a moment and without a hint of subtlety, weighed up Ewan with his stern eyes.

"Well I'm only thankful that you remembered how to swim," the King said at last with a smile.

He left his wife and daughter and held out his hand to him. Ewan shook the hand of the King with a firm grasp and was met with one in return.

"A good strong handshake," the King said to him, "you can always tell a lot about a man by the way he shakes your hand."

"I think saving your only daughter's life tested his character enough my dear," said the Queen with a smile, "leave the poor lad alone, he is our guest after all."

"Indeed he is," said the King releasing his hand, "thank you Ewan, our home is yours to treat as your own. Eilidh would you find him one of our finest chambers?"

"Aunt Nesta's chamber is free and quiet fine," pleaded Eilidh.

"True enough, I'm sure my mother won't mind. It's been some time since her sister fled," said the King.

With that sorted and Ewan's nerves at their absolute limit, Eilidh led him through the large wrought iron doors of the Citadel, held open by more knights. Inside the Citadel was as grand as outside. The halls and stairs were made of pale marble and large chandeliers holding copious amounts of candles hung from the high ceilings. The white stag he had seen on the flags over the city was displayed inside the halls as well, embroidered onto tapestries and rugs.

Sir Darrion was the only knight to remain in their company. He walked behind them in silence as Eilidh answered Ewan's many questions.

"So Nesta is your father's aunt?" he asked.

"Yes, Nesta Mason is the sister of my grandmother Elora, the previous Queen," she replied.

"And what did your father mean when he said she had fled?"

"My father has not long been King, nor I a Princess. My father's father, King Adwen, ruled before him but he died a few weeks ago," said Eilidh.

"I'm sorry to hear that," said Ewan with sincerity.

"Thank you. He was a good man and my grandmother, Lady Elora, loved him dearly. Her sister Nesta was the healer here in the Citadel. When King Adwen died my grandmother blamed her sister for his death and she fled the city."

"And so when your grandfather died your father became King," Ewan summarised to himself.

"Yes," said Eilidh with slight hesitation as they reached his chamber, "but I'll explain it all in the morning I promise. I might even get Sister Margret to help; she has a great insight into most matters, trust me. That and I think she's rather fond of you."

"A fondness I hope you share Princess."

"You'll have to wait and see," she said as she placed a soft kiss on his cheek, "thank you again."

She continued on down the hall by herself and Ewan watched her until she turned a corner and disappeared. Only he and Sir Darrion remained.

"I want to thank you myself," he said to Ewan, "the Princess means a great deal to us all here in the Citadel. You will not find one kinder."

He opened the door for Ewan and with a light tap on the back, followed the Princess down the hall. Ewan turned to face the now open door and the room that lay within. He could see a balcony that looked out over the bay, the thin silk curtains on either side swinging lightly in the evening breeze.

He stepped into the room and closed the door. He made his way out onto the balcony and found himself at the very back of the Citadel looking out over Royal Bay. The last rays of the sun were setting in front of him over the eastern horizon, shimmering over the water as they desperately clung to the silky waves. He took one last long breath of the evening air before heading back into the room.

His new bed was far better than his other new bed; it was a four poster marvel of wood covered with an assortment of furs. Ewan let his damp clothes fall to the floor before getting in. He curled up in the many furs and shut his eyes. He half expected to wake up back at home to the sound of his mother calling him from downstairs. The day passed in front of his eyes as a blur of strange people and places. Just before he fell asleep, he had convinced himself that it was all a dream.

Chapter Four

The Crested Concave

That night the moon shone full and bright. The entirety of Royal Bay glinted as the moonlight danced softly over the still water. A cool midnight breeze flowed in from the east, filling the halls of the Citadel. From his bed, King Rhain could see the moon high in the sky out through the balcony of his chamber. The pale marble of the walls glowed soft silver under the clear night sky. His wife's black hair was a deep silhouette against the light. It ran down her naked shoulders like a river of delicate ebony; long, dark and soft as silk.

He had made love to her that night, their shadows mirroring their affection. After, they lay entwined amongst the furs of the bed, her smooth olive skin against his. His lust for her had not dwindled with time, in fact he longed for her more now than he had in their youth.

Rhain loved the closeness that making love to his wife brought them. He loved the moments after almost more than the act itself, the feel of his wife's heavy breath against his chest as he ran his hands through her black hair. The darkness of it and her skin showed she was from the Northern Realm; very few south of the Old Forest had hair as black as hers.

Rhain ran his hand over her back; she shivered as his fingertips traced small circles on her soft skin.

"What are you thinking about my love?" he asked her softly.

"Just about young Ewan," replied Bethan.

"You're thinking about that young lad now? Shall I go and fetch him for you?" he said with a smile.

"It would take more than the youth of a boy to steal away my desires for you," she said, "I was just thinking about how lucky we all are that he was there to save Eilidh."

"He did us a great service," replied Rhain, "very strange that he has no memories."

"Indeed it is, though as long as our daughter is safe it matters not."

"Well said my love. That and he seems to have a good heart."

"Did your handshake tell you that?" asked Bethan teasingly.

"No it did not," said the King thoughtfully, "however, his eyes did."

The next morning the King rose before the sun shone over the capitol. He had an important council meeting at dawn and did not want to be late. He left the Queen sleeping for he did not have the heart to wake her. He got dressed quietly, his usual attire of studded leather. Around his waist he fastened a longsword with a blade of black steel; a rare metal only forged in the fires of the western Hammer Hills. It was named Sable and belonged to his father; Rhain was rarely seen without it. The grip was made of dark red wood, matching the scabbard, and the crossguard of untarnished gold forming a pair of antlers, with the pommel fashioned into the shape of a crown; embellished with the Greyfell's stag.

Rhain looked at himself in the large mirror resting on the floor; taking a deep sigh he reached for the crown that lay atop a cushion on a mantle of its own. The golden antlers curved round forming a perfect jagged circle. He donned the crown and no longer recognised the man staring back at him, for he felt more himself with a sword at his hip than a crown on his head.

He opened the heavy door of his chamber to find Sir Darrion waiting for him. Ever since he was a boy, Sir Darrion was the first to rise. In all the four Realms, there were two men that the King trusted with his life; Sir Darrion was one of them. The knight bowed gracefully as the King shut the door softly behind him.

"Good morning my King," he said.

"Good morning Sir Darrion, early as ever I see."

"There are some things that never change my King."

"Yes but unfortunately there are some things that do," he replied sternly.

Rhain started down the hall and Sir Darrion was quick on his heels. The meeting that had been arranged was regarding his brother Galvin and his recent allegiance with Lord William Fyrth, Thane of the Southern Realm.

"Do you really think that Galvin will go to war alongside Lord William and the south?" asked Sir Darrion.

"I honestly don't know."

"Well we know that House Fyrth are not above starting a rebellion," said the knight in a grave voice.

He knew that Sir Darrion was right. The Southern War had ended fifteen long years ago but the scenes of battle were still fresh in the King's memory and heart. At the time it was not Lord William that was Thane of the Southern Realm but his older brother Lord Wolfrick Fyrth. The south was the largest of all the Realms, rivalling all the others put together. Lord Wolfrick had a hunger for conflict and sought to start a southern rebellion against the rest of the Kingdom. The Houses of the south rallied behind their Thane and so the Southern War began.

Rhain, only a Prince at the time, fought out in the field in his father's name. However, it was his twin brother Galvin that had the honour of leading the Royal Guard. The war lasted a whole year but the Kingdom finally gained the upper hand

and managed to push the rebellion back. The last battle took place at the thin piece of land that joined the Southern Realm to the rest of the Kingdom, known as the Fringe.

The Fringe lay just within the southern border, where Lake Meridian seeped into the land from the west. From the banks of the lake to the shores of the sea, on the small piece of solid ground the Fringe had to offer, lay Gate Keep. It stood thick and long, stretching from west to east, a gated wall with high battlements. Through its core ran a tunnel, wide enough for entire armies to funnel through, gated at both ends. It was the only way in and out of the Southern Realm and it guarded the passage well. House Sayer were the Lords of Gate Keep and Keepers of the Fringe, allied with Lord Wolfrick and his rebellion.

The southern force had retreated behind the safety of Gate Keep and the King's army knew better than to attempt a siege on the castle. So they lay in wait, right on the southern border, out of range of the many archers that lined the walls. The town of Helmsby, where they had made camp the night before, lay far behind them. Rhain's brother Galvin stood at the forefront of the enormous army, shining like a beacon in front of the glistening armour of the Royal Guard. Rhain commanded a small battalion on the eastern flank by the shore. Michael of House Dunharren, the second man he trusted with his life, was on the western flank with the rest of the Northern Realm.

Gate Keep lay in the distance, the flag of House Sayer rippling in the wind from the high towers, a grey gate set against a field of pale green. The front gate of the castle slowly began to creep open; the sound of metal grinding on stone filled the Fringe. As the gate retracted upwards the vast armies of the south could be seen in the long tunnel. Thousands of men funnelled into a thin long line, swelling out into further ranks at the far southern side of Gate Keep.

Horns sounded from the walls of the castle and Lord Wolfrick's armies charged from the safety of the tunnel out into the field. Rhain watched from afar as Galvin raised his sword, the King's army pushed forward at his command. They marched gradually increasing in speed; Rhain noticed that as the gap between the two armies slimmed, the men of the Southern Realm were still coming through the tunnel of Gate Keep. Lord Wolfrick had called on every able bodied man of the south for a last effort in his rebellion. The King's army broke into a sprint to cover the last of the ground between them and their foe; flesh crashed into steel as the two vast armies bled into one another, the battle of the Fringe had begun.

The battle seemed to last a life time. By midday Rhain had lost count of how many southerners he had cut down. Young Sir Darrion fought tirelessly by his side, only a squire at the time, though Rhain could not have hoped for one better. Even at the young age of fifteen, Sir Darrion had been a better swordsman than most men. After that day he had been given the name the Fox of Tarn, suited to his House heraldry and the agility and precision he had displayed in combat. They fought back to back and carved a bloody circle into the southern force, any who dared enter was met with the cold bite of steel.

As yet another rebel fell beneath Rhain's sword Sable, a giant of a man pushed his way through the battle to face the young Prince. Lord Wolfrick stood before him, towering above. Rhain had never been a tall man but Lord Wolfrick, who was almost twice his age, was also almost twice his height. He had no helmet and his hair was the golden blonde of House Fyrth, his face heavily bearded and rugged. He wore steel plate armour enamelled blood red. Over this was a yellow surcoat embellished with a red osprey across the front, the bird of prey being the heraldry of House Fyrth. Both hands wielded a giant greatsword, its broad blade also made of black steel.

The shimmering weapon was pointed at Rhain. Sir Darrion tried to move between them but Rhain pushed him aside. The young Prince and the giant that sought to slay him moved into the centre of the circle, slowly pacing the edges, blades poised and ready.

It was Lord Wolfrick that struck first, a heavy overhead blow that would have severed Prince Rhain in two, if he had not sidestepped the stroke. He countered with Sable, thrusting the sword at his opponent from below. Lord Wolfrick parried the strike and black steel met, sending out a high pitched ring. The blades scraped closer together and the two men stood face to face. Rhain could feel the hot breath of Lord Wolfrick on his cheeks.

Rhain stepped back and regained his ground, he met blow after blow, each one heavier and stronger than the last. Rhain tried again and again to pass the giant's guard but his greatsword was always there to meet him. Lord Wolfrick countered one of his attempts and brought the huge sword down on Rhain's upper leg. It sliced through armour as well as flesh, leaving Rhain wounded and kneeling before his enemy.

Lord Wolfrick raised his sword high above his head and there it hung, savouring the death to come. Rhain closed his eyes. Sable held loosely in his weak grasp. It was then that Rhain found a sudden strength deep within him, gripping his sword as tightly he could he stood up on his wounded leg and thrust the blade through the exposed neck of Lord Wolfrick.

The light left his eyes and Lord Wolfrick's giant body slid the entire length of Sable before falling to one side, taking the Prince's sword with him. Rhain stood over his fallen enemy, not believing his own victory. He grasped the handle of Sable and released it from Lord Wolfrick's neck. He raised the blood slick black blade over his head and his battalion around him roared and cheered.

Despite killing the instigator and champion of the rebellion, his brother Galvin was the one honoured by their father with the victory of the Fringe. Though it upset Rhain for his own victory to be cast aside by his father, the story of Lord Wolfrick's death was told amongst his men with his name, not his brother's.

After the Fringe the southern rebellion was quickly quelled, William Fyrth, as younger brother of Lord Wolfrick, became Thane of the Southern Realm. Rhain's father thought it best to make peace with Lord William, for he did not have the same hunger for conflict as his older brother. King Adwen, in order to bring a swift end to the war, decided to arrange a marriage between Lord William's daughter, Lady Caitlyn, and Rhain's twin brother Galvin. Lord William eagerly accepted under the assumption that his daughter would someday become Queen by Galvin's side.

This of course never happened. Rhain's sister by law died a year ago, baring no children to Galvin's name. Rhain was very fond of her; she was a gentle and kind soul. Her hair was long and golden, her features fair and slender. Lady Caitlyn was aware that her husband was always favoured over Rhain, yet never agreed with or encouraged it. She had been taken by an ill and swift fever not unlike Rhain's father.

Now trouble in the Southern Realm was brewing once more. Rhain knew that Lord William would exploit Galvin's claim to the Kingdom and use his brother as a puppet, pulling the strings in the direction of war. The years had not made Lord William kinder, this war would be worse than the first. Rhain, as King, would not allow his brother or Lord William to ruin the peace his father had worked so hard for.

The meeting that day was being held in the Crested Concave, a grand council room on the highest floor of the Citadel. He and Sir Darrion journeyed up through the vast halls. They emerged high in the Citadel with a thin corridor before them, the morning light refracted through the glass windows that lined both sides of the walls. At the end of the corridor was a narrow passage with a small spiral staircase, that wound up the inside of a thin tower. Two members of the Royal Guard were standing watch, Sir Darrion's best swords as the King had requested the night before. They stood to attention as their King and Captain approached, allowing them passage. The staircase was very narrow and steep, the King had never liked being in such small spaces, the walls appeared to close in the further they ascended. Eventually light loomed over their heads and the stairs came up through the floor of the Crested Concave.

The room was large and square with tall windows that looked out over the fours Realms of Farreach, each one matching the four points of a compass. They were stained with the heraldry of the four greater Houses that were Thanes of each Realm. A large square table sat in the centre of the room, each side with its back to a window. The eastern end, on the far side of the room lay empty, two chairs laid out for the King and his Captain. The window looked out over Royal Bay from the highest point of the Citadel; the glass was a brilliant bright blue with a dashing white stag depicted in the centre. The King and Sir Darrion made their way round to their chairs and took a seat.

There were three other men sat around the table. On the western end nearest the stairs sat two of them, young Tristan of House Anvil, the man betrothed to his daughter, and his protector Sir Thomas of House Gillian, a knight of the Rift. Tristan was older than Eilidh and tall and strong in build. His hair was the auburn colour of House Anvil and fell down in small curls. He was dressed in a black tunic over fine golden chainmail.

Sir Thomas had been sent with him to Gleamport by order of Tristan's father, Lord Torin, Thane of the Western Realm. He was the most decorated knight of the west and his father, Lord Farris Gillain, was Keeper of the Rift. The knight wore steel plate armour with a long white cloak embroidered with a silver owl. Sir Thomas and Sir Darrion were similar in age and the two often trained together when he was not guarding his ward Tristan.

The third man at the table sat to Rhain's right at the northern end. He was Peter of House Rowen, Lord of Wood's Horn and Keeper of the Old Forest. Lord Peter was an elderly man though still known to be fierce in battle; his black hair had turned grey and like most northern men he spoke his mind, no matter his company. He wore a long dark green cloak, an oak leaf brooch of soft gold fastened it in place. The window behind him was stained brown with the fearsome black bear of House Dunharren. He sat in place of his Thane, Rhain's best friend and brother by law, Lord Michael, who had not been able to travel from Forest Isle. The south end of the table lay empty with the red osprey of House Fyrth, silently listening in for their vacant masters within the glass of the window.

"My Lord and Lord Heirs," declared Rhain, "thank you all for coming, especially you Lord Peter. I know it was a long travel south for just one meeting. Know that you are a welcome guest until the banquet."

"It is my honour my King, Lord Michael sends his regrets for not attending but he said I speak as Thane in his stead."

"As do I for my father," said Tristan from across the table.

"Your Thanes are lucky to have such worthy voices," replied Rhain, "I am also glad Sir Darrion and Sir Thomas are here to speak for their Lord fathers."

"As Lord of Castle Grove and Keeper of the Glades, my father pledges House Tarn to you my King," said Sir Darrion.

"You know my father to be a loyal man," said Sir Thomas, "the Southern War was a long time ago, but the west suffered greatly, we depend on the trade from the Southern Realm. My father will not lightly sever ties once more that could cripple our House."

"Sir Thomas speaks the truth," said Tristan, "the south has long been the greatest supporter of the Rift's fishing trade and buyer of our black steel. My father, as Thane, must look to the best interests of his Realm."

"And what of the interests of your King?" questioned Sir Darrion.

War would cripple the entire Kingdom, thought Rhain, not just the Western Realm. He understood that each man must protect his own, but the Kingdom must face a rebellion together or it would surely fall.

"My father never wished for war, yet he was forced to fight one," replied Rhain, "make no mistake; I will not see good men suffer under my rule. I understand the position your fathers are in, but we must remain united. Send word that their voices have been heard and that I will speak with them further at the coronation banquet."

"Has Galvin or Lord William sent word from the south?" asked Lord Peter.

"No word has been heard," replied Rhain.

"Let them stay there," declared Tristan.

"That solves nothing," interjected Lord Peter, "if the south means war we cannot sit idle while they muster an army."

Rhain appreciated Tristan's youthful spirit, there was a time he too thought the Kingdom's problems sorted themselves. He did not want to go to war with the south again, let alone with his own brother. Rhain had never wanted to be King, but he also refused to see Galvin destroy the land that their father had held together for so many years. With the death of his wife, Lady Caitlyn, Rhain watched his brother's love for the Kingdom slip away. Their father had always told them that as a King you must love every rock in the river, caring for every child born under your rule. Galvin once thought like this, with Caitlyn at his side he would have been a good King, but her death had made him cruel.

"I will not allow my brother or Lord William to corrupt my father's Kingdom. They will not disgrace his memory," said Rhain with rising passion in his voice.

"The other Realms are behind you," said Sir Darrion.

"Aye they are at that," added Lord Peter, "the day I bow to the south is the day the Sword falls," he said spitting on the ground.

"So be it," said Rhain, "I do not hope for war, but if Galvin and the south intend to start one, I will lead the rest of the Kingdom to finish it."

Chapter Five

First Lessons

Ewan stood upon the Eastern shores, staring out at the gentle waves. Closing his eyes he remembered the chilling touch of the green mirror and the world he had left behind. It was the morning of his third day in the strange land, on the very beach he had arrived on. Alone upon the sand he searched for answers as he had done the day before, yet they remained hidden. He felt the sea breeze against his skin and heard the waves break upon the sand, telling himself it could not be real and yet when his eyes opened it was.

The day before, whilst the King was busy at council, Ewan had spent it with Sister Margret, who he already very much liked. When he woke up she had refused to let him get dressed in his damp and sand covered clothes. She marched him straight to the bathhouse and when he returned there was a light green tunic made of fine cloth waiting for him. Along with this he wore soft leather riding trousers and high boots. Sister Margret was very pleased with his new attire and said that he looked very handsome.

The rest of the day consisted of lessons about the Realms of Farreach and the vast amount of history contained within them. He was taught heraldry and Houses, lands and titles, and almost everything in between.

"Were you born in the capitol?" he had asked Sister Margret.

"No child, I'm from the Western Realm, a small town called Brittlebank that rests next to the frozen Brittle River," she had replied.

"Is it always cold in the west?"

"Yes dear, I think I originally moved east just to see if grass did indeed lie beneath the snow," she had said chuckling.

Throughout the rest of his lessons, the occasional appearance of Princess Eilidh had been the only thing that had kept him going. She seemed well used to Sister Margret's manner of teaching and was able to help unravel the mass of information before him. That and Ewan found her incredibly beautiful.

When he returned from the beach later that morning, the young Princess sat opposite him, enjoying her breakfast as much as he was. She wore a pale blue silk dress, her fiery red hair falling down her back. Ewan was in his green tunic once more, Eilidh had told him the day before that it brought out the emerald colour of his eyes and he had not taken it off since.

The room where they ate was a large banquet hall, shields decorated the walls and large chandeliers hung from the high ceiling. Long tables with benches filled the floor with one very grand table at the end of the room, raised higher than the rest on a large stone step. It was late morning but the room, apart from the few servants that had brought their food, was all but empty.

"So is this where the coronation banquet will be held?" asked Ewan.

"It is," said Eilidh swallowing the last of her breakfast, "in three days time this room will be full of people, the Lords of each noble House will swear fealty to my father."

"How many noble Houses are there again?" he asked with a smile, realising he should know the answer.

"Not paying attention were we?" she said teasingly, "there are eleven noble Houses in total, though five of those lie within the Southern Realm and therefore will not be attending the banquet."

The trouble brewing in the south had been explained to Ewan the day before. He had learned about the Southern War and the turmoil it had brought to the Kingdom. Eilidh had explained how her uncle Galvin had fled south into the arms of House Fyrth along with his younger sister Drusilla. It seemed Ewan had landed in a world on the brink of another rebellion.

"Do you think the south will start another war?" he asked her.

"I believe they will," she replied, "my uncle will not give up his claim lightly and Lord William will use the dispute to whatever advantage he can."

"And I don't even know how to use a sword."

"Yet," replied Eilidh smiling, "I've heard my father has requested Sir Darrion start your training the day after tomorrow."

"You can't laugh at me."

"I most certainly can," said the Princess, "I don't know much about swordplay, I could, however, teach you a thing or two about wielding a bow."

Ewan had spent just as much time pulling a bow string as he had swinging a sword. Yet he was not going to pass up an opportunity to spend time with Eilidh, even if it meant making a fool of himself.

"I'd appreciate the help Princess," he said.

"I wish my cousin Ardal was here sooner, he'll arrive for the banquet with the rest of House Dunharren."

"His father, Lord Michael, is your mother's brother right?"

"I see you were listening," she said, "Ardal is one of the finest archers in the Kingdom, his arrows never miss."

"Your father said something about me joining them on a hunt after the banquet."

"Yes, there will be a hunt in Beachwood a few days after, let's hope you know how to loose an arrow by then," said Eilidh grinning.

"What will we be hunting?"

"Mainly deer, Beachwood is teeming with them."

"So when do we start our lessons?" he asked her hopefully.

"Now is as good a time as any," she said standing up from the table.

Ewan finished the last of his breakfast and eagerly followed the young Princess out of the banquet hall.

The barracks of the Royal Guard lay at the southern end of the Citadel's courtyard, across from the stable. It was a large building made of white stone, the walls forming archways along its front. The training yard lay behind, with archery targets, made of woven straw, set up at the very edge of the Sword. Nothing but sky lay behind them, as they looked out towards Beachwood. This is where Eilidh had taken him for his first lesson. Within the training yard was the armoury, Eilidh made her way over to a small weapon rack that was lined with all manner of deadly instruments. The young Princess ran her hand over a long slender bow made entirely of white wood.

"This is Kimber," she said as she handed him the bow.

The pale shaft was smooth against his skin, there was not a single imperfection down its length, Ewan had trouble picturing it in its once rough and bark covered state. The taut string that ran from each end was made of tightly wound blue and white thread and held the bow in its tense curve.

"It's a beautiful bow," said Ewan softly.

"A gift from my uncle Michael, he carved it himself," Eilidh replied, "I insisted on being trained to use a weapon and my mother thought it more lady like than swinging around a heavy sword."

"Are all men of the north good archers or just your cousin?"

"They are skilled in all matters concerning wood; living in the forest has made them renowned woodcutters and huntsmen, making them experts with the axe and bow."

Ewan handed Kimber back to the hands of her master. From the weapon rack Eilidh took another bow of a far more simple nature, as well as a small leather quiver filled with arrows, fletched with feathers as blue as her silk dress. Placing both bows aside she fitted Ewan's right hand with a three fingered leather glove and his left with a leather brace that ran up his wrist and forearm.

"What are these for?" he asked her.

"The glove will help you grip the bowstring and the brace will protect your wrist from the feathers of the arrow," she replied as she tied his leather laces.

After putting on her own glove and brace, Eilidh picked up the two bows and handed Ewan his. It felt heavier after handling Eilidh's delicate Kimber. The wood had been treated with a light brown lacquer and a black leather grip was tightly strapped to the centre of the shaft. Ewan held the weapon in his left hand and flexed the bowstring with his right. He was surprised by the strength of it; the wood creaked with power as it curved under the weight of the string that imprisoned it. Eilidh pulled a handful of arrows from her quiver and pierced them into the soft ground in front of them.

"Now lift your bow up with your left hand and grip the string with the first three fingers of your right," she said as she demonstrated with her own bow, "draw the string back to your cheek, hold it and breathe."

Ewan did as she said and pulled the string all the way back until the knuckle of his thumb brushed against the skin of his cheek. He held the bow there, the wood quivering to be let loose. The targets were at the end of the long training yard and he tried to picture the imaginary arrow flying straight and true. He breathed deeply, holding the bow in its tight curve; before slowly releasing it back to its true form.

"Good," Eilidh encouraged.

"Thank you," said Ewan, welcoming the Princess' praise.

"Now let's try it again, this time with an arrow. Watch me first."

Eilidh plucked an arrow out of the ground and with her bow horizontal; she slid the arrow down the shaft and nocked it to the string. The point of the arrow was fashioned like the tip of a spear, leaf shaped with a long curved point. With it in place she raised the bow up and drew back the string.

Ewan watched as Eilidh handled Kimber with an ease and familiarity that made it look simple. The white bow stayed obediently in its taut curve as the young Princess steadied her breathing and took aim. She released the arrow and it found its mark within a blink of the eye, burying itself in the small red circle at the centre of the target.

"Okay, now you're just showing off."

"Well you won't bring down any deer with an attitude like that," she said with a grin.

"Fair enough, you just make it look so easy."

"And you will too, if you work at it," replied Eilidh, "right now you try."

Ewan plucked his own arrow and levelled his bow out as Eilidh had done. He rested the arrow against the wood and nocked it to the string. He lifted the bow up slowly, making sure the arrow stayed flush to the shaft. Tightening his grasp on the leather grip, Ewan pulled back the string and took aim.

"Take your time," Eilidh said from his side, "steady your breathing and just let the arrow go."

The target appeared to be very far away and his arrow seemed very small, but he slowly breathed out, let the arrow loose, and watched it as it sailed high over the target and out over Royal Bay.

Eilidh attempted to stifle her giggling as Ewan let the string slacken and the bow fall to his side.

"I thought you said you weren't going to laugh."

"Don't be so hard on yourself," she replied, "I've seen far worse. You should have been there when my brother Richard fired his first arrow. Sir Darrion almost met his end."

Ewan had been treated by Eilidh and House Greyfell with nothing but gratitude and kindness, apart from her brother Prince Richard. Ewan had only a few dealings with him, but he had made it clear that he regarded Ewan as little more than a peasant that had stumbled into a palace. Eilidh had apologised for her brother's abruptness, Ewan found himself wondering how Richard could be related to the tender hearted and gentle Princess he had quickly grown so fond of. With the death of his grandfather, Richard Greyfell was now known as the Stag Prince, a self appointed title he was led to believe.

"This time I'll help you with Kimber," said Eilidh as she set his simple bow aside and handed him her white one.

The young Princess took an arrow out of the ground and came up behind Ewan. She handed him the arrow and he quickly had it nocked and ready. Her left hand closed over his as he held the shaft of the bow. Ewan spread his fingers ever so slightly so hers could slip gently in between his own. Holding Kimber together, Ewan felt her other hand delicately clasp his right forearm as it held the arrow in place.

"Now, we're going to pull back the string and I'll help you position your arms," said Eilidh.

Her head rested against his shoulder and her words brushed lightly against his ear. With their fingers entwined around Kimber, Ewan could feel her soft pale skin against his. Together they drew back the string, Ewan, Eilidh and Kimber working as one. With the bow fully drawn, Eilidh altered his aim and raised his right elbow slightly.

"Slowly breathe out and then loose the arrow," she said in his ear.

They stood close together, their bodies flush. They emptied their lungs as one and Ewan closed his eyes and loosed the arrow. It seemed a long time before he opened them, but when he did, he saw his arrow, resting in the small red circle at the centre of the far away target, the two arrows as close as they were.

"Well done!" a voice shouted from behind them, breaking them from their trance as they quickly stepped apart.

Standing there Ewan saw Sir Darrion, the Captain of the Royal Guard, and two others he did not recognise. One was clearly a knight, around the same age and build as Sir Darrion, yet he wore plainer armour and a white cloak decorated with a silver owl. The other was much younger yet older than he or Eilidh. A handsome man with curly auburn hair, dressed in a tunic of black and gold, an anvil finely stitched to the front.

"Tristan," said Eilidh addressing the younger man, her face red with embarrassment, "I thought we were meeting at midday."

"It is midday my Princess," he replied pointing to the high sun overhead, "and this fine lad must be the saviour of my forgetful wife to be."

Ewan was shocked by what this Tristan was telling him. Not only had he not realised they had spent the entire morning together, but this man was claiming that he and Eilidh were engaged.

"So you're promised to this man?" Ewan asked Eilidh, trying to mask the sadness in his voice.

"I see the time is not the only thing my Princess forgets," said Tristan for her, "yet she certainly makes up for it with beauty and charm."

Ewan did not need to be told this, he knew it all too well, hence his disappointment at the news.

"I'm sorry Ewan," said Eilidh making her way to Tristan's side, "I presumed Sister Margret would have included our engagement in her lessons," still with a face as red as her hair, "this is Tristan of House Anvil, Lord Heir to the Hammer Hills and the Western Realm."

"I'm afraid she didn't," he replied biting his tongue, "but I believe congratulations are in order," he said as he held out his hand to Tristan.

"Thank you Ewan," Tristan said as he met his outreached hand, "for your courtesy and bravery, I shall look for a way to repay your courage in kind. But now I believe these two knights require the use of the training yard, and I require the company of the beautiful Princess."

"Then I won't keep you," said Ewan with his best fake smile, "thank you Princess for your time."

"I will look for you later," she said as Tristan took her arm and led her out of the training yard.

"I will see them back to the Citadel," said the other knight to Sir Darrion.

Sir Darrion gave the knight a nod and he too vanished out into the courtyard. Sadness filled Ewan's heart, for though he understood that he had no claim over the young Princess; all he desired was a chance. He must have worn such feelings on his face for he finally realised Sir Darrion was staring at him.

"I will not tell you to look away young Ewan," the knight said to him, placing a kind hand on his shoulder, "I understand hidden desire better than most. I would, however, advise a small amount of caution in the future. More hinges on their marriage than you know, you must not interfere."

Ewan made his way back to his room in the Citadel, Sir Darrion's warning ringing in his ears. He had never felt so strongly about a girl before, only to find she was promised to another. Sister Margret had somehow managed to neglect telling him about the engagement. She did, however, explain that very few highborn married for love, consolidation of power tended to lie within the bounds of matrimony. As unfair as it seemed, Ewan understood the custom was not unfamiliar in the history of his own world.

He walked the halls of the Citadel of Kings with a sorrow hanging over him. He was, however, thankful to see that Tristan seemed to be a good man. He could not bear the thought of a man mistreating her, she had been so kind to him and he would not allow her to be hurt. Ewan approached the door to his room and as he opened it his melancholy was replaced by surprise. An elderly woman sat on the bench at the foot of his large bed. Her hair was a dull reddish grey.

"Good afternoon Ewan," she said politely, "my name is..."

"Lady Elora," Ewan interjected, "previous Queen and husband to the late King Adwen."

"I see Sister Margret has already gotten her hands on you," she said with a smile.

"All of yesterday."

Lady Elora was dressed in purple satin, her reddish grey hair falling free. Though being elderly she seemed to have retained her beauty, her skin was pale but clear and her face unwrinkled, her eyes the same icy blue and likeness as Princess Eilidh. She stood up and walked towards Ewan with grace in every step. She embraced him and gently placed a kiss on each cheek.

"I wished to thank you myself for saving my granddaughter," she said, "I'm sorry I didn't come sooner."

It had been two days since he had pulled the young Princess from the Sea of Glass and despite appreciating the gratitude he had received; Ewan did not know how much more he could take.

"I welcome your thanks Lady Elora."

"May I ask how you recognised me?"

"You have the look of your granddaughter," Ewan told her.

"I'm glad to hear my beauty wasn't wasted," she said with a smile.

Ewan saw more of Eilidh in her grandmother than just her eyes; the old woman had her spirit as well.

"I'm sorry for the loss of your husband," he remembered, "I've heard he was a good and noble King."

"He was," she replied with a sad voice, "and an even better man."

"May I ask you a question my Lady?" he enquired nervously.

"For saving my grandchild you may ask me two," she said in return.

"Staying in your sister's chamber I couldn't help but wonder about the reasons why she's no longer here."

"That my dear boy is not a question."

Ewan realised his mistake and considered his question once more.

"Why did you blame your sister for your husband's death?" he asked boldly.

"Nesta was a skilled healer," she began, "I've seen her bring people back from the brink of death. I don't blame her for Adwen's death, I blame her for robbing me of the chance to say goodbye to the man I loved."

Lady Elora stood in front of him with a small tear in the corner of the eyes that reminded him so much of Eilidh's.

"My sister lied to me about the severity of his fever. As a result my dear husband died alone in bed without my hand around his. I didn't even get to tell him that I loved him."

"I'm sorry again," Ewan said softly.

"As am I," Lady Elora told him, "though I granted you two questions not one," she said regaining her smile.

Ewan thought of asking her about Eilidh and Tristan, but then decided to heed Sir Darrion's warning. He thought of the King's twin brother Galvin and the trouble brewing south of the Fringe. Ewan could think of only one question to ask the mother of the two brothers with equal claims to the Kingdom.

"Why do you support Rhain and not Galvin?" Ewan asked her as he met her eyes.

"A very good question young Ewan, one that should have been asked of me long before now," said Lady Elora.

She returned to her seat at the end of Ewan's bed, in the same graceful manner as she had left. Resting her hands in her lap, Lady Elora looked out over the balcony and considered his question. A soft breeze picked up the silk curtains from where they hung; Royal Bay appearing to glow through the transparent soft fabric. As the breeze glided over them, Lady Elora turned back to Ewan, who was still standing in the open doorway.

"Rhain was the son that never wished to become King and only wanted his father's affection," she told him, "yet he never received the love he hoped for and in the end felt forced to become King anyway. Galvin on the other hand," she said as she smoothed out a crease in her gown, "only ever wanted to become King with his wife and one love by his side. Yet she eventually died and he never became King because of it."

"But that doesn't answer my question," said Ewan with courage that she seemed to appreciate.

"I love both my sons," she said with a hard stare, "but despite Rhain not wanting to be King, he is the one that should be."

Chapter Six

The Fox of Tarn

It was dawn as Sir Darrion crossed the courtyard in front of the Citadel of Kings; his polished greaves glinting in the morning sun as he walked, the blue cloak of the Royal Guard flowing behind him. He had dedicated his life to the protection of the King of Farreach, a commitment he proudly upheld. His position in the Royal Guard had required him to forsake his home and live in the capitol city. The knight had been born into the noble House Tarn that had long been Lords and Keepers of the Glades, to the west of the Eastern Realm.

As the eldest son of Lord Dale Tarn, it was his birth right to become Lord after his father died. Sir Darrion missed his homeland; his love for the Glades ran thick through his veins. It was considered by many to be the most beautiful part of the Kingdom. He yearned for the scattered woods that concealed hidden meadows, for the brooks and streams that laced their way through the trees.

As a child he grew up in Castle Grove, its high walls covered with vines and ivy, making it appear at peace with the lush landscape that surrounded it. He would forever lose himself in the lands that his Lord father held; meadows were his only battle fields and trees his only enemies. Sir Darrion would spend hours with his shortened child's sword, dancing with the static wooden opponents. Wielding a blade had come as easy and natural to him as water flowing downstream. By the time he was strong enough for a longsword, adversaries had become scarce and few. Though he never took pleasure in killing, he came to admire the graceful motions it entailed, a dance of steel and blood.

It was the day before the coronation banquet and Sir Darrion had risen early as ever. The King had entrusted him with the training of young Ewan, the boy had never danced with a sword and it was Sir Darrion that was to teach him the steps. He had grown to like the young boy, saving Princess Eilidh had tested his character but his virtues shone on their own. Sir Darrion had asked Ewan the night before to meet him in the training yard so he may begin his training; Prince Richard had eagerly offered to help. Sir Darrion did not hold the Stag Prince in the highest regard, but he was his Prince nonetheless and there was no doubt he was skilled with a sword.

As Sir Darrion entered the training yard behind the barracks, some of his men were already at work honing their skills. Two of his finest fought with long practice spears, the blades made of carved wood. Others stood by and watched as they sparred, cheering their favourite. The two knights kicked up dust as they fought; the spear shafts met with the clap of wood on wood, breaking the quiet morning air. To one side Sir Darrion noticed young Ewan practicing his archery, seeming at peace with the earliness of the hour. The grouping of his arrows was by no means perfect, but his marksmanship had certainly come a long way in two days.

"Good morning Ewan," he said as the boy loosed another arrow.

"Good morning Sir Darrion," he replied lowering his bow.

"I see Princess Eilidh's lessons were not unheeded."

"It was very good of her to teach me," Ewan replied, his green eyes all the more brighter with mention of the Princess.

Sir Darrion felt for the boy, he saw the way he and the Princess looked at each other across tables and as they passed in the halls, they caught each other's eye like glass catches the light. Yet neither were free to follow their heart, Sir Darrion had told the lad as much and hoped that he listened. The betrothal between the Princess and Lord Heir Tristan may be the only thing keeping the Western Realm from rallying to Galvin in the south. As innocent as their young love was, it had the potential to bring down a Kingdom.

"Are you ready to begin?" Sir Darrion asked.

"I am indeed," replied Ewan placing his bow to one side.

"Well first you'll need armour and a sword."

Sir Darrion dressed Ewan in a suit of battered steel plate, full of dents and scratches received in the training yard. It took a long time to fasten the armour and the knight finished with a quick tug of leather securing it all in place. Sir Darrion shed his blue cloak and precious family longsword from around his waist and placed them both carefully to one side. The sword's name was Reynard and had been the blade of House Tarn since its founding. The blade was not of black steel but every bit as lethal in the Sir Darrion's hands and kept safe within the knight's brightly coloured fox scabbard.

Sir Darrion fetched two sword belts from the weapon rack, on both hung a sheathed longsword. He handed Ewan his and they securely fastened them around their waists. Ewan admired his new attire; the armour creaked as he bent his legs and twisted his hips under the old steel frame. Once satisfied the boy reached for the hilt of his sword, he pulled it from the scabbard and Sir Darrion watched with a smile as the boy's eyes filled with disappointment.

"It's blunt as a spoon," said Ewan sadly.

"What did you expect lad?" Sir Darrion asked him, "to fight the Captain of the Royal Guard with edged steel?"

"Fair point," said Ewan.

"This is tournament steel young Ewan," the knight told him, "the edge has been dulled so no one will get hurt."

"And by no one you really mean me?" asked Ewan with a smile.

"Precisely," replied the knight.

"Won't we need helmets?"

"Not right now, we won't be sparring until the Stag Prince arrives later, I just wanted you to get used to the weight and feel of the armour whilst I teach you the basics."

They made their way over to one of the training circles painted on the ground of the yard, both with swords drawn.

"Now place two hands on the grip between the crossguard and the pommel," he explained.

Ewan did as he asked but still looked very unnatural holding the sword.

"That's good," said Sir Darrion, "now place your left foot forward and slightly bend your knees."

"Like this?" asked Ewan as he mimicked the knight.

"Yes like that," he replied with encouragement, "now this is your basic fighting stance, from here you can hold your sword in a number of guards."

As the morning went on Sir Darrion found Ewan to be a very good student, he listened well and learned quickly. But more than that Sir Darrion could see a desire in the boy's eyes that reminded the knight of his own younger self; he strove to better himself simply because he believed he could. Ewan was in no way a knight in one morning, but Sir Darrion knew, as with his archery, the ability was there, it was simply a matter of discovering it.

The knight walked Ewan through the steps of swordsmanship, the water like motions and footwork he loved. If Sir Darrion had not been a knight he would have been a dancer, though his Lord father would not have been nearly as happy. Their dull blades slowly acted out what their more deadly brothers would put into practice. They stepped back and forth as Sir Darrion instructed Ewan on where to place his feet, their swords slowly met above as their eyes attentively looked below.

"What a lovely couple," said Prince Richard as he approached.

Sir Darrion lowered his sword and turned to the Stag Prince.

"My Prince," he said with a bow, Ewan quickly following suit.

Prince Richard had the light brown hair of his father accompanied with boyish features; he was old enough to be considered a man yet did not look it, nor did he act like it. Under his arm he held his helmet, a gift from his future brother by law Tristan. Sir Darrion admired the work; the young Anvil lad was a gifted blacksmith. It was a marvel made of black steel, decorated with a pair of large metal antlers so he truly looked like the Stag Prince.

"When do I get a taste of the boy?" the Prince asked looking at Ewan.

"You are here to help him learn my Prince, not hurt him," Sir Darrion replied placing a hand on Ewan's shoulder.

"If I were you Sir Darrion, I wouldn't presume to tell a Prince what to do."

"He is your father's guest," the knight said angrily, "and he has trusted me with Ewan's training and protection."

"Fine, fine," Richard said waving his hand, "I promise to be gentle."

The Prince put on his antlered helmet and made his way over to one side of the training circle. With the helmet on it was the first time the Stag Prince did not look like a boy, he stood menacing and gleaming beneath a face of black steel, the antlers towering overhead. Sir Darrion led young Ewan over to the other side of the circle and placed his helmet over his head.

"Try not to scratch his pretty new antlers," he said to Ewan with a smile as he closed the boy's visor.

Sir Darrion made his way out of the circle but stayed close; the two young men raised their dull swords and prepared to fight.

"Now this will be a slow fight lads, you will listen to my commands and it ends as soon as I say it does," he told them both.

The knight did not like the idea of young Ewan sparring after only just holding a sword for the first time, especially not against someone as skilled and without heart as Richard. But he was his Prince, it was just a shame he was not his father. The King was the best man he knew, it had been his life's honour to fight beside him and serve as his squire and Captain. Sir Darrion only wished that his son had been gifted with the same qualities.

"Now slowly attack my Prince," said Sir Darrion, "Ewan, you parry as I taught you before."

Prince Richard attacked slowly as he had been told, swinging his sword lightly towards Ewan who met it well with his own and parried.

"That's good," he told them, "now this time Ewan attack and Prince Richard parry the strike."

Ewan's attack was slow but well placed, his feet finding the ground it was meant to. Prince Richard met the strike with some force, their blades sending out a ring. Ewan seemed surprised but held his ground, until the Prince hit him hard with his armoured shoulder, causing Ewan to lose his footing and stumble backwards.

"My Prince he is not ready for this!" shouted Sir Darrion.

The Stag Prince did not listen; he followed up with a hard overhead strike that although parried, brought Ewan to his knees. Sir Darrion's hand fell to the hilt of what was now his own sword, not tournament steel, but a finely edged blade that had already taken lives.

Sir Darrion watched as Ewan stumbled to his feet in the heavy armour, only just raising his sword in time to block another heavy strike. Ewan was not quick enough to counter and the Stag Prince skilfully struck his blade across his breast plate, the metal rippling as it absorbed the blow, sending him back to his knees. The wind went out of young Ewan and as he struggled for breath, his sword falling from his hands to the ground. That obviously did not concern Prince Richard as he raised his sword high overhead to strike his unarmed opponent kneeling before him.

The Prince's sword was met in mid air with the edged steel of Reynard, Sir Darrion's hands at home around its hilt, the pommel on the handle shaped to form a fox's tail and the rain guard the creature's head; the blade rising from its mouth. Another ring echoed through the training yard as all eyes fell on the Captain.

"You may be my Prince, but I will not have you harm him," said Sir Darrion with rising anger.

"How dare you cross swords with me!" exclaimed Prince Richard as he pulled off the antlered helmet.

"How dare you attack an unarmed man!"

"I am your Prince!"

"But your father is my King," said the knight, regaining his easy tone, "this is *his* Royal Guard and I am *his* Captain. Now lower your sword."

The Stag Prince regrettably complied, throwing the dull steel to the ground.

"My father will hear about this Sir Darrion!" the Prince shouted behind him as he stormed out of the training yard.

"I hope that he does," the knight said under his breath.

The yard was deathly quiet as all eyes were still on Sir Darrion; he sheathed Reynard and before he had the chance to look around, his men promptly went back to their training, ending the awkward silence. He breathed a deep sigh and turned to young Ewan who was kneeling on the ground. Holding out his hand, he helped him to his feet.

"Thank you Sir Darrion," said Ewan as he removed his helmet.

"Don't thank me yet lad," he replied, "our Prince doesn't like being made a fool and will not soon forget it."

"Thank you all the same."

"Are you hurt?"

"I need to catch my breath," he replied clutching his breast plate, "but no I think I'll be fine."

Sir Darrion helped Ewan over to a nearby bench and sat the boy down. The knight handed him a skin full of water.

"Have a drink and catch your breath."

The knight sat down beside Ewan, watching him as he quenched his thirst. The boy deserved a drink he thought to himself, he had worked tirelessly all morning without question or complaint.

"Have you ever fought in a real battle Sir Darrion?" Ewan asked him handing back the water.

"Aye I have," he said taking a drink, "I squired for King Rhain during the Southern War, back when he was a Prince."

"Sister Margret told me about the war. It lasted a whole year didn't it?"

"It did," Sir Darrion told him, "but the southern force was finally quelled and like most rebellions, it eventually failed."

"You obviously haven't seen Star Wars," said Ewan with a smile.

~ 72 ~

"I don't understand," replied the knight slightly confused.

"Nothing," said Ewan quickly, "how long have you been a knight of the Royal Guard?"

"I've been wearing the blue cloak since I was seventeen, not much younger than you are now. But that was when we were at war; it makes quick work of turning boys into men."

Sir Darrion remembered the Southern War well; Lord Wolfrick had covered the entire Kingdom in conflict. As a young boy he had fought by Prince Rhain's side as his squire. It was only after the battle of the Fringe that he received his knighthood and the blue cloak of the Royal Guard. The Prince, who was now a King, had knighted him there on the battlefield, only fifteen years old. There were tales of younger boys being made knights, but none had ever received a blue cloak at such an age. He bent his knee on the blood soaked ground as the sword lightly touched each shoulder. It was the happiest moment of his life; he had become Sir Darrion of the Royal Guard and the Fox of Tarn in the same day. When he returned home with his knighthood and new title, Reynard was gifted to him by his father; the ancient sword only making him an even deadlier fox.

It was not until eight years later, at the age of twenty three, that Sir Darrion made history again and became the youngest Captain of the Royal Guard. It was the day of a large tournament in the southern stronghold of Castle Hilt on the edge of the trees of Heartwood. Sir Darrion was watching the then Captain joust. His name was Sir Jon of House Stokeworth, uncle to the Lord and Keeper of Fisherman's Bay. With the tournament held at his home, his people cheered and favoured his victory. Sir Jon was not a young man but well loved and still a formidable fighter. He had held the prestigious position as Captain for over a decade, fighting for his King throughout the Southern War despite his family ties beyond the Fringe.

Sir Darrion was also competing in the tournament but had taken the time between opponents to cheer his Captain. Sir Darrion watched as Sir Jon appeared at the far end of the lists, upon his horse he was a shining beacon in the polished armour of the Royal Guard. On his left arm he wore a large shield, decorated with the winged fish heraldry of House Stokeworth. In his right was his lance, the tip fashioned into a clenched fist.

His opponent was also a southerner, a brute of a knight in the service of House Larke, Lords and Keepers of the Sea Shield Mountains. Sir Jon kicked his heels into his horse and spurred it down his side of the tilt. The opposing knight joined him in the charge, kicking up sand from beneath his horse. Sir Darrion watched as the two knights pointed their lances and raced towards each other. He held his breath just before they collided, hoping his Captain would unhorse his opponent with the fist of his lance.

Sir Darrion watched as Sir Jon's lance remained unbroken as it glanced wide, just as his opponents splintered through his Captain's neck. Sir Jon was knocked from his horse, all eyes watched as the sand of the tournament ground soaked up the growing pool of blood. Sir Darrion could see the splinter of the lance still embedded in Sir Jon's throat as he coughed his last bloody breath.

Despite the death of the Royal Guard's Captain, the tournament had continued. Sir Darrion rode well throughout and made it into the final two. His opponent was the brute of a knight that had killed Sir Jon. Sir Darrion sat atop his horse and weighed up the knight; he was a large man, his surcoat embroidered with the moon and mountain of House Larke. Lances were tilted and horses were spurred. Sir Darrion watched as his opponent drew ever closer, a mountain of dark steel that he sought to bring crashing down.

The young knight felt the wood of his opponent's lance scratch by his helmet, the sound resonating inside the metal. Sir Darrion plunged his lance into the knight's chest and watched as he fell from his horse. Sir Darrion was declared the tournament's champion and King Adwen had seen it fit to also declare the knight his new Captain. He was the youngest by over a decade, no one of his age had earned such a prestigious position in the history of the Kingdom.

"Well thank you again," said young Ewan next to him, bringing Sir Darrion back to the present.

"You're welcome Ewan," Sir Darrion replied, "now I think that's enough for this morning; let's get you out of that armour."

Sir Darrion helped him out of the tough steel frame that imprisoned him and hung up his dull sword.

"What do you intend to do with the rest of your day?" the knight asked.

"I'm having lunch with Princess Eilidh later."

"Well tell the Princess I bid her good day, for now I have some business to attend to."

"I appreciate your time Captain," said Ewan politely.

"I appreciate a good student."

Sir Darrion gathered his blue cloak and left the training yard. He passed back through the barracks and when he stepped out into the courtyard, morning was giving way to midday. The sun was high in the sky and the white stone of the Citadel sparkled beneath it. The knight crossed the courtyard to where the stable lay at the southern end. Inside the air was hot and close, it smelt ripe with the dry scent of hay. Sir Darrion passed through the long corridor with the many stalls on either side; he knew one always lay empty at the far end. As he approached Sir Thomas

Gillain stepped out, the knight sent from the west to protect Tristan Anvil; his white cloak flowing behind him.

"You're late," Sir Thomas said to him.

"We missed you in the training yard," he replied.

"*We* or *you*?" Sir Thomas asked him with a smile.

Sir Thomas lent forward and planted a kiss on Sir Darrion's lips. He recoiled and pushed Sir Thomas back.

"What are you doing?" Sir Darrion demanded.

"What do you mean?"

Sir Darrion looked around desperately, searching for prying eyes.

"Someone might see us," replied the Captain.

He pushed the knight back into the empty stall before returning his kiss. The two men helped each other out of their armour and made love against the soft hay.

Chapter Seven

Old Friends

"That cannot be your decision my Lords," said King Rhain.

It was the morning of his coronation banquet and the King sat in the Crested Concave, the two Lords of the Western Realm sat across the table. Lord Torin Anvil, Tristan's father and Thane of the west, looked very much like his young son, though with a grim face and less hair. He was older than the King by over a decade and it showed in his features. The second man was Lord Farris of House Gillain, father to Sir Thomas. He was even older than his Thane, yet his temper had not succumbed with his elderly age.

"The Western Realm cannot and will not commit to a war that is sure to cripple it," replied Lord Torin.

"The aggrandisement of your trade should not outweigh the responsibility your Realm has to the Kingdom," said Rhain sternly.

"We would ask that peace be made with your brother my King, nothing more," replied Lord Farris.

"And what if no peace can be made with Galvin or the south? What will the west do then my Lords?"

"We do not wish for war on any front my King," said Lord Torin.

"War may be upon us whether you would wish it or not."

"Then the Western Realm wants no part in it!" shouted old Lord Farris.

The King rose from his seat and leant over the large table. The morning light shone through the different colours stained on the four windows, making the fury rising in his eyes easy to see.

"I would caution you my Lords," he told them, "I may not be my father, but I am still your King."

"And the west supports your claim," said Lord Torin.

"Just not enough to fight for it," added Rhain with an angry smile.

"We feel that peace is the only option," said Lord Farris.

"My brother did not seek out the support of House Fyrth or the south so he could bring about peace."

"We do not believe it will come to war," replied Lord Farris.

"Then I would call you a fool!" shouted Rhain quickly, showing the soldier inside him not the King.

Lord Farris also stood up from the table, his short temper boiling beneath his old skin. His Thane pulled him back into his chair and silenced him with a hard stare.

"The marriage that will soon bind our two great Houses still stands my King, but we will not support action that leads the Western Realm into war," said Lord Torin.

The King was furious as he descended the stairs of the Crested Concave. He could not understand the arrogance the western Lords showed towards the rest of the Kingdom. The King had every mind to strip them of their lands and titles, but he knew such drastic action would only send the west into the arms of his brother and Lord William.

The relationship with the west was a fragile one, the marriage between Eilidh and Tristan was the only thing keeping it together. Tristan was not just Lord Torin's only son, but his only child. He and his wife were unlucky in their attempts to have children. They were almost past their time when his wife, Lady Gwyn, gave birth to Tristan. The prospect of marrying into the royal family was not one Lord Torin would likely throw aside. Threatening an end to the marriage would only cause more harm. Rhain had to find some way of bringing the west back into the fold, for though he was currently without their support, the King could not afford to gain yet another enemy.

As Rhain reached the ground floor of the Citadel a very familiar horn blasted through the halls. It was the sound of the Northern Realm and House Dunharren. It had been a long time since Rhain had seen Lord Michael, his best friend and brother by law. Excitement welled up inside him and a very boyish smile spread across his manly face. Lord Michael and the King had known each other since they could walk and had remained good friends ever since.

Rhain tried to remain as kingly as possible as he hurried through the Citadel and out into the courtyard. The men of Forest Isle flowed across Greyfell's Sword, with Michael, their allieged Lord and Thane, at the forefront with his wife and three sons. He wore bronze coloured armour and a long brown cloak. The banners at his back were decorated with the roaring bear of his House. The bear had represented the Dunharren's for centuries, for they once had the power to change into the fearsome creatures.

During battle the ancient men of House Dunharren could shed aside their skin and emerge a mighty bear. However, this magical gift which had been passed from father to son for generations, was now lost from the world. The last skinshedder of Michael's great House was far back in their noble lineage.

The bears of Dunharren were from a time long forgotten; they had passed from living memory into legend. Not that his friend Michael needed his ancestor's gift, he was already a bear amongst men. He was only a few years older than the King but a giant of man with thick black hair, dark skin and a large beard. His hairy arms were knotted with muscles and his legs were the size of small trees. He dismounted the large horse that accommodated him and made his way over to Rhain standing on the steps of the Citadel.

"My King," his voice boomed as he approached, "can your royal self spare an old friend an embrace?"

"He can on occasion," replied Rhain with a smile.

His friend wrapped his huge arms around him and the King was smothered against his breast plate. The past few weeks had been long and troublesome. Rhain was very glad to have Michael by his side once more.

"I'm sorry about your father," Michael said to him pulling from the embrace, "he was a noble King and a good man, the world will miss him for both."

"Thank you Lord Michael," replied Rhain, "now where is your beautiful wife?"

Lady Thea stepped forward, her hair as black as her husband's. She was the daughter of Lord Peter of House Rowen, born in the Old Forest and married to the Thane. Rhain had always liked her, he admired the way she quelled some of his friend's less suitable behaviour.

"My King," she said with a graceful curtsy.

"Lady Thea," Rhain replied with a kiss on her hand, "I hope the journey wasn't too long."

"It was my King," she told him, "but I'm sure your banquet will more than make up for it."

"I don't have it in me to disappoint a lady. Though would it be quite all right to borrow your husband?"

"I expected nothing less my King," she said with a smile, "I'll go and greet Queen Bethan whilst you and my husband try and feel young again with your old war stories."

Rhain led Michael through the great doors of the Citadel and past the vast halls to where his chamber rested. They went to the balcony and sat down at a small table, the open sea air filling their lungs. With the doors shut the King felt as though he could converse with his old friend without the formalities that were required of their stations.

"So how is our *new* King?" asked Michael in a mocking tone.

"Still bedding your little sister if that's what you mean?"

"Just the one thankfully."

"Speaking of which, did Ellyn not travel down with you? I didn't see her in the courtyard."

"No the journey would have proven too much for her at the moment."

Ellyn was Michael and Bethan's younger sister, currently with child at home in the Northern Realm, not wanting to risk the long journey to the capitol.

"Being constantly reminded of you marrying one of my sisters is bad enough," continued Michael with a grin.

They gave each other a familiar smile. If there was one person that would not treat him like a King it was his friend Michael, and he was happier because of it.

"I see old age hasn't stolen your sense of humour."

"Not around you my old friend," answered Rhain with sincerity.

"Oh you eastern men are a soppy bunch aren't you?" said Michael with a booming laugh.

"Indeed we can be," he replied, "your sister still believes I show more love for you than I do her."

"Don't be absurd," said Michael, "there's no doubt about it. I've known you longer."

"Don't tell her that," replied Rhain only partially joking.

"How is my sweet Bethan?" asked Michael.

As children they would tease and pick on Michael's younger sister. It was only when they became of age that Rhain changed the teasing to courting. Bethan was the most beautiful young girl Rhain had ever seen. He was visiting the Northern Realm one summer when he was but a Prince. It had been a whole year since he had seen Michael and he was very much looking forward to it. When he arrived he did not recognise Bethan as the young woman she had become during that past year, she was tall and slender and her black hair danced over her dark skin.

"She misses the north from time to time," replied Rhain.

"Of course she does," said Michael in defence of his Realm, "so would I with all these fields that cover the ground. Where are the trees overhead that never end?"

"We walk in Beachwood from time to time," Rhain told him, "but I fear it doesn't compare to your northern forests."

"Speaking of which," said Michael, "I heard Lord Peter represented us northerners well at the meeting. What of the western Lords?"

"I spoke with Lord Torin and Lord Farris this morning."

"What did those frozen old men have to say?" asked Michael as he removed a hand axe from his belt and placed it on the table.

Michael was a soldier the same as he was. He disliked the bitter old men of the west that thought more about their gold than their oaths. The loyalty of the Northern Realm was unwavering in their devotion to the King and his royal House.

"They will not commit to war out of fear that their trade with the south will suffer," replied Rhain angrily.

"Damn their fish and steel Rhain," said Michael as he removed yet another hand axe from his belt and placed it on the table.

"They hope for peace with my brother and the south."

"And they think you don't?" asked Michael as he shifted in his seat and pulled out a throwing axe from behind him.

"It would appear not," replied Rhain grimly.

"You remember war as I do, no man that has seen battle wishes for it again," Michael told him as he placed the axe with the rest.

By the time they were finished talking the table was littered with every type of axe imaginable.

"Must you carry so many?" Rhain asked him, "you only have the two hands."

"When it comes to the fighting I like my options," replied Michael honestly, "our wives have their dresses and gowns and I have my axes."

Rhain remembered Michael during the Southern War, huge and gleaming in his bronze armour. His helmet was fashioned into the shape of a roaring bear, his black bearded face visible behind the open jaws. The woodland Realm of the north had two main trades, hunting and timber, both skills crossed over into their army. The hunters, lean and deadly with a bow, made up their archers, the woodcutters, axe wielding and muscular, formed the ranks of their infantry.

Michael had always been the latter, carrying a giant battle axe called Mane, an ancient blade forged of black steel. Rhain remembered he could barely lift the weapon but his colossal friend swung it with ease. He was a towering force on the battlefield and ripped through the enemy lines like his bear ancestors of old.

The two childhood friends stayed out on the balcony and talked on every subject. They did tell old war stories to try and feel young again, as Michael's wife had teased they would. Ale was brought to them and they drank a toast to Rhain's father.

"To King Adwen," Michael said as he lifted his cup.

They both drank and poured some ale out over Royal Bay so his father, where ever he may have been, could share in their toast.

It was near midday when they felt obliged to show their faces to their wives. The two men made jokes about them clucking like hens that they were too afraid to mention in their presence. The King was glad to have his friend back; he had missed the bear of a man and was glad they could still act like young men despite neither of them being able to live up to it anymore.

As they entered the hall outside the King's chamber, his daughter Eilidh was passing by with young Ewan by her side. The two were laughing quietly together and Eilidh teasingly pushed Ewan. The young friends noticed they were being watched and their behaviour immediately changed.

"Uncle Michael," said Eilidh as she ran into his big burly arms.

"Why if it isn't my favourite niece," he replied, "you truly are a young woman now aren't you? Rhain how did you create such a beautiful thing?"

"I believe it was Bethan's doing."

"You're probably right," replied Michael, "and this young man must be Ewan."

"It's an honour Lord Michael," the boy said with an outstretched hand.

"The honour is mine," replied Michael as he firmly shook the boy's hand, "I hear I have you to thank for saving my niece, though I'm quite sure you're almost sick to death of hearing it by now."

Ewan smiled as Michael's huge bear paws released him from the handshake.

"I'll take that as a yes," Michael told him, "will I be seeing you at the banquet tonight?"

"You will," replied Ewan, "it's a privilege to continue being the King's guest."

"Good," said Michael with a hearty boom, "now try to keep my niece out of any more trouble."

"I'll do my best," replied Ewan with a smile.

"Now to the wives!" shouted Michael as he pointed a huge hairy arm down the hall.

Eilidh and Ewan continued their laughter as they went in the other direction down the hall. He was happy that his daughter was taking care of Ewan and making sure that he felt welcome. He just hoped that his young daughter would not forget her promise to Tristan. Sir Darrion had told him the night before that he had spoken to the boy about the importance of the marriage. The King hoped that their affection would not grow past friendship.

"They seem to make a lovely pair," said his bear like friend in a tone the King knew all too well.

"Don't joke Michael."

"Old friend," he said, "I'm afraid I wasn't joking."

Chapter Eight

Feast and Fealty

The banquet hall was full of music and people, Eilidh could see the countless faces of Lords, their families and their subjects through the many candles that lit the large room. She sat with her royal family at the top table, raised higher than the rest at the far end of the room. To her right sat her brother Richard, the young Stag Prince. To her left was her betrothed, Lord Heir Tristan. The other members of House Anvil sat below with the rest of the Western Realm. Eilidh could not deny that he looked very handsome in his black and gold tunic, his curly auburn hair slightly falling over his face. Though the only person she wanted by her side was Ewan.

She looked across the large hall to where Ewan sat with House Dunharren. Her uncle Michael had invited him to eat with his family and he sat next to her cousin Ardal. He was the eldest of Michael's three sons. His younger brothers, Logan and Bowen, sat with their mother. Ardal was not built like a bear as his father was, he was tall and lean with slender shoulders, his amber eyes glowing amidst his olive skin. Like Eilidh, he favoured the bow over other weapons and he drew his with extraordinary skill.

Eilidh saw that Ewan and Ardal seemed to be getting on well. They drank and smiled amongst the loud and hearty cheer of the hall. The Princess felt guilty for wanting to spend time with Ewan over Tristan, the young Lord Heir had been nothing but kind to her. He understood that they were still strangers and was doing his best to make her feel comfortable. Though with Ewan, feeling comfortable had come naturally. From the very first day he had pulled her from the Sea of Glass she had felt at ease with him, she could be her herself around him without the pressures that being a Princess could bring.

The day she had taught Ewan how to fire a bow, her heart had pounded when their hands intertwined. The touch of his skin against hers made her legs quiver and her mind race. Ewan made her feel like a woman where Tristan approached her as if she was made of delicate glass, a fragile pretty thing. She was once excited by the prospect of marrying Tristan and giving him sons and daughters. Now every moment she was with him she only thought of Ewan.

She knew her father would never allow it, not only was he not of noble birth but he did not have any power over the western armies. It seemed very unfair to the Princess, she knew her father loved her but she could not understand why he was free to follow his heart and not her. The King had married his Queen under the great Older Oak on Forest Isle. He had married her for love, not some army.

"Has Ewan regained any of his memory?" asked Tristan seeing that she was staring at him across the hall.

"He has not," she replied.

"It's very odd isn't it?" he said to her, "I've heard of people losing parts of their memories but never all of it."

Sometimes Eilidh would think that Ewan knew more about the manner in which he arrived on that beach than he owned up to. Every morning he returned there alone, never explaining his need to walk the beach. Eilidh had followed him one time, seeing the lost look on his face as he looked out upon the waves. There was no doubt that he was a stranger to these lands, but wherever or however he came to save her, all that mattered to the Princess is that he had.

Her father the King sat in the middle of the top table, her mother the Queen by his side. Behind him hung a large banner of azure, rippling with the prancing white stag of House Greyfell. The crown of antlers was atop her father's head, the jagged gold glinting as he rose from his seat.

"My Lords and friends!" the King shouted through the hall as everyone fell silent, "I welcome you! Please eat and drink your fill!"

The room cheered and roared as servants brought out mountains of food on countless large platters. Each table was a feast of its own, they were covered with whole pigs adorned with apples and large joints of ham smoked and seasoned with salt. The ale flowed all the more to wash down the mouthfuls of succulent meat. Eilidh had been allowed a few cups of wine, she preferred ale but apparently it was unbecoming for a Princess.

The feast lasted a few hours, with many more courses of food in between. The sun had gone down over Royal Bay by the time the Lords began to swear fealty to her father one by one. First came Sir Darrion's father, Lord Dale of House Tarn. He was older than the King by some years, but still stood tall and strong. He wore a long purple cloak with a fox dancing across the fabric. He approached the top table and knelt before his King.

"I, Dale of House Tarn, Lord of Castle Grove and Keeper of the Glades, do so swear fealty to King Rhain of House Greyfell, Lord of Gleamport, Keeper of Royal Bay, Thane of the Eastern Realm and Ruler of the Kingdom of Farreach."

Eilidh had forgotten the true length of the titles her father now held as King. Something she knew he never wished for, those titles had always been meant for Galvin. Her father had wished for a simple life as the soldier he had always been; now he controlled the Kingdom.

After Lord Dale returned to his seat the Lords of the Western Realm took to the floor. Tristan's father and Lord Farris bent their knees and said the words one by one, yet there was a tension in their voices that Eilidh could not quite understand. It was subtle enough to go unnoticed, even Tristan did not seem to detect it, but the Princess keenly caught a brief glimpse.

Next came the Lords of the north, first was Lord Peter of House Rowen and then his Thane and son by law, Lord Michael. The bear of a man kneeling was almost as tall as those standing. He was dressed in brown leather with a black bear pelt draped over his shoulders.

"I, Michael of House Dunharren, Lord of Oakenhold, Keeper of Forest Isle and Thane of the Northern Realm, do so swear fealty to King Rhain of House Greyfell," his voice boomed through the hall as he completed the titles of his friend and King.

By the time all oaths has been sworn, it was night and the candles had burnt low, their dim flickering light catching the last of the melted wax. Her father stood up from his seat and addressed the hall once more.

"I thank you my Lords for your oaths, I hope we can bring about the same peace my father once did. I wish to be as good a King as he ever was."

"Hail the King of Farreach!" roared her uncle Michael as he stood up.

"Hail the King of Farreach!" the rest of the hall shouted as one.

The music was struck up once more and cups were refilled. The tables were cleared away and a dance started in the centre of the large hall. Men bowed to maidens and they curtsied in turn. The dance was graceful and elegant as people glided from partner to partner across the floor.

"May I have the honour of this dance?" asked Tristan standing by her side, holding out his hand.

Eilidh wanted the hand in front of her to be Ewan's but she stood up and offered hers to Tristan anyway.

"It would be my pleasure my Lord Heir," she said to him.

"Please call me Tristan," he replied with a kind smile, "if we are to be married we can't rely on titles forever."

Eilidh could not help but smile as Tristan led her from the top table towards the middle of the dance. That night she wore a gown with a long pale white scarf draped around her neck, it was made of soft silk and adorned with blue stitching; a gift from her grandmother Lady Elora. She was worried she may tread on it whilst dancing, so before she reached the crowd she hung it over the back of an empty chair.

Free from the scarf they took their places amongst the dance. Tristan bowed low and long with his hand placed across the golden anvil that decorated the front of his tunic. Eilidh curtsied to the young man that was to be her husband; she could feel all the eyes of the large hall burning in her direction. The music struck up and her hand instinctively met Tristan's, she had always been a good dancer and knew the song well. The motions and steps came swiftly back to her as Tristan led with effortless grace.

She smiled and laughed as the young pair danced their way through different partners, she was surprised when she found herself counting the steps until she was back in the arms of Tristan. It was the first time he had truly made her feel that way. Though, however appealing, they could not dance their way through marriage forever.

Dancing with some knight she did not know, Eilidh caught a glimpse of the empty chair where she had carefully laid her white scarf, it was no longer there. Her eyes broke from her partner's as she looked about the room, distracted by the need to find it. The Princess continued the steps that she knew off by heart, though her heart was now far away from the dance and the man she danced with.

Eilidh saw the white tail of her scarf disappearing through an open door and she broke away from the dance after it. Partners shifted once more and Eilidh never found Tristan, his awaiting arms caught nothing but air. She cut through the crowd, not even looking back to see Tristan standing alone as partners danced around him.

The young Princess made her way through the busy hall to the door where she had seen her scarf vanish. Through the door was a thin corridor dimly lit with torches along the walls. As she peered down its length, Eilidh saw her scarf disappear around a corner at the far end. She ran down the corridor, all the while bemused by the seemly possessed white fabric. As Eilidh rounded the corner, she was shocked to see Ewan casually leaning against the wall, silk scarf in hand.

"Ewan?" she blurted out.

"I thought I could convince you to escape the banquet," he said as he handed her the scarf.

"Oh you did, did you?" she replied with a smile.

Ewan held out his hand and Eilidh took it without hesitation. She felt bad for leaving Tristan alone in the middle of the dance, but he was soon forgotten as Ewan led her away from the banquet. They half ran and half skipped their way down the long corridor, the noise of the large hall slowly falling into the background, along with any thoughts of her betrothed.

Behind the Citadel of Kings, at the very tip of Greyfell's Sword, there was a small garden terrace that looked out over Royal Bay. The moon was high overhead as they emerged out into the night, its light shining with a silver glow. Eilidh was led by Ewan to the far end of the garden, where it came to a thin point at the very end of the Sword. They both leant against the small white wall that ran around the edge of the terrace.

The waters of the Sea of Glass lived up to their name that night. The moonlight danced over the still surface, every star was visible as it reflected a second night sky. The young Princess looked at Ewan and he seemed deep in thought as he looked out over the bay. His eyes glowed green as they caught the softness of the light, they looked like emeralds speckled with small flakes of gold.

"Did you enjoy the banquet?" he asked turning to face her.

"I did, I always love to dance."

"I saw that," he said with a smile.

"What did you make of my uncle?"

"He and his family made me feel very welcome."

"I noticed you laughing with my cousin Ardal."

"He seems like a good man," he told her, "I'm looking forward to getting to know him better on the hunt the day after tomorrow."

"Not much can beat roasted venison," she said to him, "so make sure you bring down a stag."

"I'm still worried the stag will bring me down."

"Well be sure to watch out for Highthorn then."

"Who's that?"

"The White King, a majestic snowy stag, the largest in all the Realms," Eilidh told him, "Highthorn has lived for hundreds of years ever since the founding of House Greyfell, he is the stag depicted on our royal heraldry. Each King has sought to bring the elusive beast down yet none have ever succeeded. My grandfather, King Adwen, hunted him for years but the stag would always get away. He promised to mount Highthorn's head in the banquet hall, but died before getting a chance."

"Let's hope the White King and I don't cross paths then."

They spent an hour talking and soaking up the fading moonlight. Eilidh was so happy just to be alone with him on such a peaceful and clear night.

"You look very beautiful tonight Princess," he said to her suddenly.

"Thank you Ewan," she said as she felt her cheeks turn red.

"It's also a very beautiful scarf," he said as he ran his hands down the soft silk, lightly brushing her shoulder through the fabric.

"My grandmother made it for me," Eilidh replied as her skin tingled under his touch, "other than Kimber it's my favourite thing."

"Well I'm sorry I had to steal it from you."

"Yes that was a very clever trick," she said as she gave him a playful push.

"Well it was the only way to get you alone."

"And why would you want to do that?" she asked as she held her breath for the reply.

"Because there is no one I'd rather be alone with Eilidh."

It was strange to hear him say her name. Ewan would always call her *Princess*, but she loved the way her name sounded in his voice.

"That's the first time you've ever called me just *Eilidh*," she said with a smile.

"I'm sorry Princess," he said as he realised his mistake, "it won't happen again."

"No Ewan I liked it," she admitted, "I mean we're *friends* now and there's no one else here."

The word caught in her throat and seemed to hang in the air. She did not want to be *just* Ewan's friend, she wanted to kiss him and not be afraid who was watching. But she knew it could never be, it would be Tristan's lips that shared her first kiss, not the young man that stood disappointed before her. It was obvious on Ewan's face that the word had stirred in him as much as it did in her.

"We best be getting back," he said to her with a sad voice.

"Are you sure?"

"Yes," he replied, "Tristan will be waiting."

Chapter Nine

The White King

It was the morning of the hunt and Ewan was stirred from his dreams just before dawn. Sir Darrion, who seemed to never sleep, came to his chamber and woke him up whilst it was still dark. The young Captain instructed him to quickly get dressed and meet everyone in the courtyard. Being very agreeable in his sleepy state, Ewan blindly nodded and Sir Darrion took his leave. He pulled himself out from underneath the many warm furs that lined his bed, forcing his body to respond to his commands. Ewan's feet found the cold stone floor and he slowly walked over to the clothes he had laid out the previous night.

Sister Margret had given him a white linen shirt with a laced up front, brown leather trousers and soft high boots. Once dressed, he strung his simple wooden bow and placed a quiver of arrows across his back. Ewan looked at himself in the mirror across the chamber, in the greyness of the early morning he smiled at the fairytale character that seemed to stare back at him.

By the time Ewan made his way out of the Citadel of Kings and into the open courtyard, he was finally starting to feel awake. The crisp chill of the morning air breathed against his face as he made his way down the steps. The courtyard was full of people and the morning sun was just starting to etch its way over the western horizon. Horses were being led out of the stable to take them down to the trees of Beachwood. Fortunately Ewan had ridden for a number of years as a boy and found that it had all come flooding back.

House Dunharren was the only one to remain after the banquet, the other Lords and their families had returned home the morning after the feast. Whilst the many guests departed, Ewan was in the training yard with Sir Darrion and the men of House Dunharren. The sparring had all been in good fun and no one had taken it too seriously. Ewan was thankful Prince Richard had not taken an interest this time. The first to take to the practice circle was Lord Michael's two youngest sons. Logan was barely a teenager and Bowen younger still. Despite the years between them, they were the same height and looked very much alike. They both had young faces and the black hair of the Northern Realm.

They were dressed in wooden armour and wielded wooden swords, too young even for dull tournament steel. Under the wooden armour Sir Darrion had clad them in layer upon layer of padded clothing, under strict instruction from their mother, Lady Thea. The young boys fought under Sir Darrion's instruction, their wooden blades clapped together as they danced around the circle. Despite being older, Logan could not best his little brother. They were equally matched and Ewan was impressed as well as embarrassed by their skill.

Most of that day he had spent talking with their older brother Ardal, the young man of the north was as cheerful as his father but not quite as blunt. Ewan had noticed a bronze pin that Ardal bore on his chest; the orangey metal had been finely crafted into the shape of a bear. Eilidh had told him stories about the ancient skinshedders of House Dunharren, of how they could turn themselves into giant bears at will. He knew that the bears of Dunharren had long been lost from the world, but this magical quality intrigued young Ewan.

"Who was the first skinshedder of your House?" he had asked Ardal as they sat and watched his brothers fight.

"They called him Benathor Blackmane," said Ardal, "hundreds of years ago the four Realms were yet to be united by House Greyfell and the north was a dangerous place. The Dunharrens were not a grand family as you see them now; they were humble people and lived a very simple life."

"So you didn't always rule the Northern Realm?" asked Ewan.

"No far from it," replied Ardal, "they lived in a small village that was one day attacked by a band of raiders. Benathor returned from a hunt to find his home in flames. The men of the village were brave but small in number and none were fighters."

"Did Benathor have a family?"

"He did," said Ardal, "Benathor was a young man at the time but the love for his wife ran deep. She was with child when the raiders attacked."

"Did she live?"

"If you let me tell the story you might find out."

"Sorry," Ewan had said smiling.

"I'm afraid to say that she didn't," replied Ardal, "though the baby did. She had given birth whilst Benathor was hunting just before the attack; she was killed trying to hide her child. Benathor found his wife dead and presumed the baby was also lost.

"That would turn most men into an angry bear."

"Indeed it would," agreed Ardal, "so Benathor tracked the band of raiders back to their camp in hopes of vengeance. As he screamed his wife's name at the top of his voice it turned to a roar and he emerged a ferocious black bear. Not one of the raiders survived that day."

"What of his child?"

"When the people of his village that had fled returned, they found a giant black bear cradling a newborn baby. The boy was sound asleep in the bear's paws. From that day onwards he was known as Benathor Blackmane."

"That's quite a story," Ewan said to him.

"It certainly is," replied Ardal.

"So what eventually happened to Benathor?"

"He reared his son but never took another wife," said Ardal, "when he was old and near death, Benathor Blackmane changed into a bear one last time, he wandered off into the forest and was never seen again. His son, who had received the same gift as Benathor, later married and gave the gift to his son, thus the bears of Dunharren continued."

"So why did it stop?"

"No one really knows Ewan. It ended many generations ago, where the skinshedders of old passed from living memory into history. Some now even say it was a myth to begin with."

"No I want to be Benathor Blackmane this time," said Logan in the distance.

"But you always get to play him," replied Bowen.

"Well I'm older."

"Doesn't mean you can beat me."

The young boys carried on fighting with their wooden swords, unclear who was playing the fabled hero.

"The tale is a fond favourite in the north," said Ardal as he smiled at his brothers' game.

The story had fascinated Ewan all that day and most of the night. His dreams were filled with an army of bears crashing into one of men. Tooth and claw collided with sword and spear. The bears of Dunharren along with the seemingly immortal stag Highthorn, added a magical and truly fantastic quality to the Kingdom of Farreach. Eilidh told of how the White King was one of a kind, passing through the ages, unchanged by time, though Ewan struggled to understand why the Greyfell kings wanted to kill the symbol of their royal House. His dreams of such creatures were interrupted by Sir Darrion as the knight woke him for the hunt.

"Good morning young Ewan!" bellowed Lord Michael as he stepped down into the courtyard, the sun still trying to chase away the night.

"Good morning Lord Michael," he replied.

"Are you looking forward to your first hunt?"

"I'm a little nervous," said Ewan honestly.

"Don't be lad," he boomed as he placed a heavy paw on his shoulder, "just make sure that when everyone is firing arrows and throwing spears, you're doing it in the same direction."

Ewan could not help but laugh, the bear of a man always made him smile. Ardal was also taking part in the hunt, along with the King, Prince Richard, Sir Darrion and four other knights of the Royal Guard. They all mounted their horses and made their way across Greyfell's Sword and through the gates of the city. Sir Darrion rode in the centre of the column beside his King; the other knights riding at the front and rear in pairs. The Captain's men held tall spears at their sides, blue banners decorated with white stags rippling from the shafts. The royal procession traced a line across the edge of the Falling Cliffs, slowly making their way down to the shore.

The morning was clear and peaceful and Ewan could hear the soft waves of the Sea of Glass as they moved further down the cliff side. Eventually they reached the sandy shore and Beachwood stretched out in front of them, a dense expanse of green and brown. The horses were left in the care of two of the knights, as the rest of the party made their way through the trees.

The morning light scattered through the leaves above causing thin rays of light to pierce through. Ewan remembered how he had first woken up on the floor of the wood, confused and face down in the grass. It seemed a life time ago to him, his entire world had changed in a blink of eye. In the quietness of night just before he fell asleep, young Ewan would think of his home and family. He had returned to the beach each and every morning, waiting for the green mirror to take him home. Yet it never came, making the world he left behind seem less and less real, just like the ancient bears of old.

Once the party had moved further into the trees bows were slid from backs and arrows were nocked in turn. Ewan stayed close to Ardal, trying to mimic his actions. The men of the Northern Realm were renowned for their skills as hunters, and though Ardal walked and spoke in a casual manner, his amber eyes were alive to the trees around him.

"My cousin tells me you've come far with the bow," Ardal said to him.

"Which cousin would that be?"

"Well it certainly wasn't me," spat Prince Richard without even turning his head to look.

"Indeed, it was *Eilidh* that was kind enough to say," replied Ardal.

The Stag Prince did not even turn to acknowledge them; he simply made his way to the front of the procession where he walked alone.

"How do you put up with him?" asked Ewan now the Prince was out of ear shot.

"He's my cousin," replied Ardal simply, "he certainly has his faults but he's family so I try and see the good."

"I'm sure you have to try pretty hard sometimes," said Ewan with a smile.

"You're right it's not always an easy task," answered Ardal, "but the Sword will fall before I give up on family, even one as arrogant as Richard."

The hunting party moved on in silence out of fear of scaring away potential game. Their footsteps softened as Lord Michael led them through the trees. Ewan did his best to walk as lightly as he could, though the harder he tried the more roots he seemed to stumble over. Ardal was eventually summoned to his Lord father's side to help with tracking, Ewan found himself alone at the back of the party. They followed the trail quicker with both father and son keenly picking up on the slightest detail.

Ewan was finally getting the hang of avoiding the abundance of stubborn roots when he noticed something out the corner of his eye, he stopped to look and the hunting party carried on without him. Far into the trees Ewan could have sworn he saw something move through the undergrowth. His bowstring drew slightly tighter as he ventured through the thick wood alone.

As he moved closer Ewan began to see the outline of a deer, it was an elegant doe with her head to the ground. Ewan knew nothing about being down wind but he presumed he was, for the deer was unaware of his presence. The doe peacefully ate from the forest floor as Ewan drew his nocked arrow until the feathers brushed his cheek. His heart pounded in his ears so loudly that he was afraid his prey might hear. He slowed his breathing and aimed the arrow just behind the deer's shoulder as Ardal had told him.

Just as he was about to loose the deadly shaft, the doe's head lifted from the grass and it immediately bolted away through the trees. Ewan relaxed the bowstring and sighed. As he did, the side of the small clearing erupted. A huge stag burst out of the trees. It was a giant blur of pale antlers and snow coloured fur streaked with silver. The creature could be none other than Highthorn, the White King, for it was as large as any horse and perfectly white. Ewan whirled around and drew the arrow meant for the doe. He let it loose and watched it strike into the stag, causing the white fur to blossom with red. The grand creature kept coming and with a sharp agonising pain, the large antlers pierced his left leg and Ewan's world went dark.

In the blackness he dreamt of the magnificent stag that had wounded him. It stood over him with those glistening antlers; weaving together in a jagged array of sharp points. Yet one side rose higher than the other; the tip lay snapped and broken. The stag's fur was pure white and the silver streaks glinted like shards of moonlight. Around its grand neck it donned a crown similar to that of King Rhain and his father Adwen before him. The majestic creature bent down and licked the wound on Ewan's leg, the pain suddenly lifted and he woke up.

Light flooded in through the crack of his eyelids as he slowly lifted them. The pain in his leg was dull but had not disappeared. His eyes gradually grew accustomed to the light and he took in his surroundings. Ewan had woken up in a small wooden cabin, the ceiling hung with countless dry herbs that filled the air with a potent smell. A small fireplace was lit in the far side of the room and the smoke gently rose up a simple stone chimney.

Ewan looked down at his left leg to see that it was bound in clean white fabric. To his left on the bedside table he noticed a needle and thread lying next to a long pale shard of antler. It had three sharp prongs leading from the shaft, the longest of which was red with blood.

"I see you're awake," said an elderly woman as she walked in from outside.

She was well past her youth yet the gentle glow of the fire showed the graceful beauty of her features. Her hair was a dull reddish grey and her eyes were an icy blue that seemed familiar.

"Who are you?" he asked.

"My name is Nesta Mason."

"You were the sister of the once Queen Elora."

"*Were*?" she asked, "boy my sister may no longer be Queen but I am still by all rights her sister."

Lady Elora had told Ewan of how she had blamed her sister for King Adwen's death and that she had fled from the capitol. Ewan never thought he would run into Nesta in the middle of Beachwood.

"How did you find me?" he asked.

"I was out foraging when I came upon you," she told him, "lucky for you I hadn't found much and had an empty sled."

"And my leg?"

"Again you were lucky," Nesta continued, "it was a grievous wound and if it were not for me you would have bled out soon enough."

"Thank you Lady Nesta," said Ewan.

"Just Nesta," she said, "my sister was always the one with the titles not I."

"Thank you Nesta," he repeated.

"You're welcome my child, and your name is?"

"Ewan Anderson," he told her, "I'm a guest of House Greyfell."

"As was I as I'm sure you well know," said Nesta.

"Yes, until you..."

"Let the King die," she interrupted.

"I'm sorry I didn't mean to..."

"It's all right young Ewan," she interrupted again, "I may live in the woods but I still know what people are saying about me, especially when it's not true."

"So you could have helped him?" asked Ewan.

"No," sighed Nesta, "the fever that took him was swift and sharp; it was well beyond the realms of healing."

"Why didn't you tell your sister that?"

"I foolishly granted the last wish of a stubborn old man, who also happened to be a dear friend."

Ewan remembered the pain in Lady Elora's eyes when she told him about how she only wanted to say goodbye her husband.

"Your sister only wanted to let him die knowing that she loved him."

"And I am truly sorry she never got that chance."

"I'm sure in time she will see you're not to blame."

"Time will reveal a great many things," she said placing another log on the fire, her dull hair reignited to the flame kissed colour of her youth.

"Now about your leg," she said as she examined her work, "it may be stiff for a few days but the wound will heal nicely."

"It doesn't hurt much," he replied with relief as he remembered the brief but sudden pain from the antler.

"Not a happy coincidence I'll have you know," said Nesta as she reached into the folds of her gown and produced a small vial of clear liquid, "do you know what this is?"

Ewan silently shook his head.

"This is a mixture known as dreamlock; it is procured from a rare white flower only found in these woods, so think yourself lucky."

"What does it do?" he asked.

"Once refined a single drop will dull even the strongest pains and two drops will bring a dreamless sleep."

"And three drops?"

"Any more than two and you would be in a far worse state than when I found you."

Throughout that morning Ewan continued to receive care from Nesta. She gave him countless herbal remedies to drink; the thick and steaming broth had tasted horrible but brought life back into his broken body. They spoke about how he had met Princess Eilidh that morning on the shores of Beachwood and Nesta too thanked him for what he had done. The woman was kind as well as a gifted healer. Later that day when he was strong enough to walk, she helped him out of her house and pointed Ewan in the direction of where she found him.

"Thank you again," he said to her softly.

"It's been nice to have someone to talk to," she said with a smile.

"I have no way to repay you."

"There's no need, though I thought you might want this as a trophy," she said as she handed him the shard of antler.

"Thank you Nesta," he said quietly as he took the gift, "will we meet again?"

"War is afoot my dear," she said placing both hands gently on his shoulders, "I feel as if we both still have parts to play."

Ewan set off in the direction he had been pointed in. He was happy that he had met Nesta Mason, not just because he would be dead otherwise, but because it was nice to know whose room he had been sleeping in all this time. His leg was a little stiff as he walked through the trees, although he was remarkably unhindered by the wound. He held the antler tight in his hand; the smooth bone was soft against his skin. Ewan walked for some time before he returned to the small clearing where the great stag had charged him. As he broke through the last of the trees he found the rest of the hunting party standing over a small pool of blood, the leaves were stained red though the white stag was nowhere to be seen.

"Ewan!" some of them shouted in chorus and they came hurrying over.

"Are you all right?" asked Ardal as he reached him.

"Where have you been?" asked Sir Darrion in turn.

"You'll bury the lad with questions before he can answer," said King Rhain.

"I saw a doe and broke away from the party," he said.

"We had gone almost a mile before we noticed you missing," said Lord Michael.

"The doe got away before I could bring it down and then I ran into a bit of trouble," said Ewan presenting the shard of antler, "or should I say trouble ran into me."

"My dear boy," said King Rhain running his hand over the flawlessly white shard, "there is but one stag in the entire Kingdom that posses antlers such as this. In the hundreds of years that timeless creature has decorated my family's heraldry; no one has ever obtained a single trophy. Wounded or not, my father would have given anything to have come face to face with the White King and return with such a token."

That night Ewan was the hero of songs as he retold his battle with Highthorn, embellishing the details and brandishing the shard of antler to a host of merry cheer.

Chapter Ten

The Sweet Sister

The afternoon sun hung high in the vast skies above the Southern Realm. A sea of cloudless blue it stretched like a long pale cloak draped over the world. The island city of Black Stone stood alone amidst the expanse of Lake Titus, surrounded by both water and sky. Its high dark rocks rose up from beneath the surface of the lake; the walls of the large city were rooted deeply into the stone and were as black as the island they guarded.

In the fortress that lay in the centre of the city, Drusilla Greyfell looked out from a high window towards the north. Somewhere beyond the endless waters of the lake and the large Southern Realm that lay after it, stood the Citadel of Kings, the palace she had grown up in and the same place where her brother Rhain now wore his crown. Drusilla was younger than her twin brothers and like them, had not been gifted with their mother's fiery red curls; yet she retained a darker beauty.

The wind blew through the open window and Drusilla's long hair took flight. The city of Black Stone lay beneath her, the rows of buildings stretching out over the rock. From the high walls she could see the banners of House Fyrth, the red osprey flying over a field of yellow. The bird of prey had been chosen to decorate their heraldry due to the amount of them nesting in the rocks of the large island. Drusilla often saw them swooping low over the waters of the great lake, fresh fish wriggling in their sharp talons.

House Fyrth had long been Thanes of the Southern Realm, the largest and most powerful of the four. Drusilla remembered the days of the Southern War, watching her brothers ride off to face Lord Wolfrick and his rebellion. Though after his throat fell on Rhain's sword, his younger brother, Lord William, inherited the south. Her father made peace with the new Thane by promising his daughter will one day become Queen. The day Lady Caitlyn married Galvin, Drusilla lost her brother, but now in the south, after many long years, they were together again.

Drusilla knew that Lord William would support his once son by law at a chance to regain some of the power his older brother had once fought for. When the rest of the Realms had voiced their support for Rhain, she knew fleeing south could grant them an army. She had been right. There was a meeting taking place where her brother and Lord William were to talk of war. She planned to interrupt it.

Turning away from the window she looked about her new room. It was just as grand as the one she had left in the capitol. House Fyrth were well known for their wealth as much as their power. The enormity of the Southern Realm was controlled by five large Houses, the Fyrths at the head of them all. She had been gifted with dozens of new gowns by Lord William, made of fine silks and the best velvets. They had left Gleamport in a hurry with but a few belongings and only a handful of loyal men.

Drusilla wore a long yellow dress with many small gilded feathers sewn into the soft fabric; creating a lavish array of glinting gold. She left the room in a blur of bright trails. As Drusilla walked through the halls she traced her hand over the smooth stone of the walls, they were a dark charcoal colour and cool against her fingertips. The meeting was being held in Lord William's chamber; her brother had spoken to Drusilla about it the night before but in no way invited her.

Outside the grand double doors there was a single knight standing watch. His name was Sir Stefan Barron, the Captain of Lord William's armies and brother to the Lord of Southbank Point. Sir Stefan was very tall with broad shoulders and muscular arms; his age written in scars. He wore the armour of House Fyrth, red steel plate with golden chasings and clasps. The long cloak that fell behind him was yellow trimmed with more red, though it was held around his neck with a clasp fashioned into the howling wolf that represented House Barron.

"I'm here to see my brother," she said.

"The *King* is in council with Lord William," his voice as gruff as his face.

"Precisely why I'm here."

Without another word Drusilla briskly walked past the giant of a knight and pushed through the door. Inside she was met with the startled face of her brother and the angered one of Lord William. Galvin had the likeness of his twin though they were not identical; the death of his wife had almost aged him. His features had grown bleak and his eyes distant. Lord William on the other hand still looked strong. Youth was behind him and his blonde hair had partially receded yet frailty was far from claiming him.

"You do understand the meaning of a *private* meeting don't you?" asked Lord William.

"I do indeed my Lord."

"Yet I can't seem to separate you from the King even when *he* is called to one and *you* are not."

"Lord William I would not be here for you to call me King if it were not for my sister," answered Galvin.

"So be it," he conceded impatiently, "please have a seat my Lady."

Drusilla sat in the chair next to her brother, across from Lord William. His chamber was large with intricately embroidered banners of his House lining the dark stone walls.

"As I was saying my King," continued Lord William, "your brother will work to consolidate his Kingdom before..."

"You mean *my* Kingdom," interrupted Galvin sternly.

"Not yet," replied Lord William quickly, "first you must defeat your brother in the field."

The table that lay before them was littered with maps and old leather bound books. Drusilla cocked her head to read the title that ran down the spine of the largest. It read *'Strategies and War Tactics'* in grand gold writing. A second smaller book was titled *'The Great Battles of Farreach'*. The topic of the meeting so far was abundantly clear. Drusilla had little understanding of the ways in which wars were won, despite possibly being the main instigator of the one that loomed on the horizon.

"I stole my father's love so he feels fit to steal my crown. He's a usurper Lord William, nothing more," said Galvin bringing her mind back to the meeting.

"A usurper with an army dear brother," she said placing her hand on his, "the people will not know your strength until you show it to them."

"The people?" spat Galvin, "the people chose my weak brother over their true King."

"We have our own armies," said Lord William, "with your rightful claim behind us they will muster to our cause."

"My father was able to beat you back once," said Galvin, "who's to say it won't be you this time to fall on my brother's sword?"

She had been young when the Southern War had began, probably in the process of avoiding another marriage proposal put forward by her father, for there had been a great many over the years. Drusilla remembered the smell of blood and sweat on Galvin each time he had returned from battle; she also remembered how much she had liked it.

"Wolfrick was bold enough to rebel, yet greed was his only claim on the Kingdom," said Lord William as his lips curled with anger at the mention of his brother's death.

"Long have the south wanted the respect they deserve," said Galvin, "a second rebellion might lay waste to the kingdom I mean to rule. I say we let my brother have the other Realms and I rule the south as a kingdom of its own."

"I will not grant you my armies so you can become a glorified Thane in my stead, we will claim everything north of the Fringe, as my brother once did, or nothing at all."

The meeting went on for several hours, but Lord William had made it very clear that he planned to use her brother as a puppet to suit his own desires for power. Yet Drusilla knew they had no other choice, Lord William was the only one that could carry them back to the capitol and grant Galvin his crown. The matter of his lust for power would have to be addressed after he had won them the Kingdom.

Drusilla let the heavy wooden door shut behind her, the voices of Lord William and her brother still ringing with talk of war. The hall outside the Thane's chamber was deathly quiet, Sir Stefan remained at his post; a towering and loyal statue. The knight must have been angered by her abrupt entry into the meeting, for he did not even grace her with a glance. Drusilla had never liked knights; they believed themselves to be loyal wolves at their master's side, though she only thought of them as sheep. Despite being a very large and deadly sheep, she knew Sir Stefan was no different.

She briskly walked past the knight in the same manner she had done earlier, not even looking back to see the silent growl that must have been spreading across his ugly face. Drusilla walked through the halls with a cheerful skip in her step. War was brewing, her brothers were fighting and yet the sweet sister wore a smile. She might have been hundreds of miles from home, though as long as she was with Galvin, the problems of the Kingdom seemed just as far away.

"Ouch!" she exclaimed as someone turning the same corner bumped into her and tread on her foot.

The young man was Lord William's son, Stewart Fyrth. He was slightly younger than Drusilla and although he was incredibly shy, his handsome features outweighed his coyness. Stewart did not have the chiselled looks of his father; his face was soft and full of youth. It was well known throughout the Kingdom that Lord William's wife, Alva Fyrth, had died giving birth to Stewart. It was she who had gifted him with her likeness and Lord William hated him for it.

"I'm sorry Lady Drusilla," he said nervously as he scrambled around on the floor to retrieve the pile of books he had dropped.

Stewart had not only killed his mother as she brought him into the world, but also proved to be utterly useless on the battlefield. The grand and noble heir that Lord William had hoped for was replaced with a dead wife and a son that spent more time with books than he did with swords. Drusilla pitied him, despite his many faults; the death of his mother should not have given his father reason to hate him.

"Its fine Stewart," she said rubbing her sore foot, "you're lucky I was born with two."

"I'm afraid I didn't see you as I rounded the corner."

"In this bright dress I can't possibly fathom how."

"You look very lovely today my Lady," his eyes not meeting her own.

"Only today?" she cruelly teased

"No every day," he blurted out as his face turned red.

"Well perhaps I should dress brighter still, to draw your eyes out from those books."

"I have read many books my Lady," his eyes still fixed to the floor, "and few words could capture your beauty."

Drusilla was touched by Stewart's remark but before she could reply, the shy Lord Heir had already begun to hurry away down the hall. She continued towards her chamber with a small smile across her face. Inside one of Lord William's many servants had lit the large fireplace, its warm glow filling the dark corners of the room. Drusilla lay herself down on the long plush chair that sat beside the fire.

The flames licked at the stone of the chimney, struggling to be set free. Drusilla kicked off her shoes and closed her eyes; the room was silent other than the faint crackling of the fire. She gently pulled up the bright yellow dress and as her fingers continued to wander, she thought of her brother Galvin.

Chapter Eleven

A Brother Lost

The sound of steel rang out underneath the morning sky as King Rhain stood and watched his Royal Guard train. They were at the tip of Greyfell's Sword with the early western sun stretching out over the city and Citadel, the marble parapets standing as glistening vigils overhead.

"A fine morning," Rhain declared to his Captain.

"Indeed it is my King," replied Sir Darrion, "good for the lads to get some training done."

"Nice to see them working hard."

"Twice as hard with you here," his fox said with a smile.

"Do they no longer fear their mighty Captain?"

"I'm not sure they ever did."

"That's because they've never had to fight you."

The two men laughed as they continued to observe the knights spar, dull swords clashing as wooden spears clapped. Rhain cherished Sir Darrion as a friend and Captain for the countless deeds over the many years, yet he respected his men just as much. Each and every one vowed to give their life for the King and his family, guarding them both in battle and as they slept, day and night. Their dedication made Rhain ashamed he did not know them better; though their number made it rather challenging.

Since the start of the Greyfell dynasty there had always been exactly one hundred knights of the Royal Guard, with only the most talented young men entering their service and it was one for life. Each time one knight fell another would take his place, coming from throughout the four Realms, forever keeping their ranks full. The blue cloaks they donned were worn by the first members of the Royal Guard, a symbol of their promise to House Greyfell, and had remained with them to that day.

The cloaks flowed from their shoulders even now, a bright azure that danced in time with the wearer's steps, a reminder of all the knights that had worn the noble colour before them. The King and his Captain continued to watch the men train, though any cheering, no matter how wishful, fell before the perpetual feet of propriety.

As morning gave way to midday, the Citadel's tall towers were now flooded in bright sunlight. Beads of sweat appeared on the brows of the knights as they grew warm in their heavy armour; sword strokes and spear thrusts slowing beneath the heat.

"That will be enough for today," commanded their Captain, "I believe you've all earned some rest."

"I agree," added Rhain, "fine work lads, some cold water and cool shade is rightly due."

The knights quickly relieved themselves of their armour, shedding the heavy steel frames and letting them fall to the floor, their undershirts showing dark patches of sweat; proof of their commitment to the morning's training.

"What now my King?" asked the young fox.

"I think I'll take in a bit of the sea air, clear my head."

The King left the training yard and passed back through the barracks, his loyal Captain at his side. They continued on through the courtyard and over Greyfell's Sword with a soft breeze flowing through their hair as they crossed. From the edge of Gleamport there were steep steps cut into the cliffs that led down to the north side of the Sword, where the city's port lay sheltered by the length of its blade. Rhain and Sir Darrion made their way down, passing fishermen and traders carrying their catch and goods from their ships below.

As they descended into the port a large wooden dock stretched out before them, countless sailed ships moored up below the capitol to trade. Gleamport was always rife with goods coming in and out, acting as the heart of trade within the Kingdom. Even so Rhain found it both strange and comforting that with the Kingdom on the brink of war the people went about their daily lives as if the Realms were not about to plunge into conflict.

People greeted and bowed as they passed, offering the King and his Captain free pickings of their goods. Rhain enjoyed walking amongst his people, hopefully letting them see he was simply a man as a well as a King. Seeing them carry on about their business blissfully ignorant of the politics of the Citadel above, Rhain longed for the simplicity of the lives they led, free of the crown's weight that bore down on his head.

Later that day Rhain found himself alone in his chamber, running an oiled cloth over Sable's black blade. The walk had indeed cleared his head for a time but solitude once again made his mind wander. The sword felt at home in his hands as he cleaned the ancient sword. It had been in his family since its noble beginning, carried by Falen Greyfell, known as the Falen the Forger, the founder of their royal dynasty.

As he continued to clean Sable, Rhain thought of his brother Galvin in the south. He reminisced about the times they had shared as boys, running about the Citadel together, long before adulthood, war, politics or even women had come between them. Rhain's brother had not always been the cold fortress of malice he now was, he was once full of life and spirit, showing a love and compassion for all things. Virtues that only grew stronger with his marriage to Caitlyn Fyrth, to then die along with her.

He saw his reflection in the now gleaming black blade before him. Rhain told people that it was gifted to him by his father but the truth, as it often is, was far more complicated. Years before the south had started their first rebellion the Kingdom had seen a generation of peace, untouched by war or hardship. Rhain and Galvin were young princes in their teens, attending a tournament held by Lord Peter Rowen beneath the walls of his castle, Wood's Horn, in the Northern Realm. Lords, knights and people had come from all over the Kingdom to see the blazing heraldry of the noble Houses clash on the field.

Rhain and Galvin had always been close, though despite being equal in age, they seemed not to be in talent. Rhain had grown up watching his brother surpass him in everything they were taught. Where he had to practice and persevere, Galvin would excel in no time at all. Hence why their father and the Kingdom favoured his brother, and why he was competing in the tournament and Rhain was not.

So there Rhain was, a young Prince watching as his brother battled on the field in front of the Kingdom and their father. It was the evening of the final day of the tournament and the sun was starting to fall behind the trees of the Old Forest. Galvin had battled well throughout the long contest and was now competing in the penultimate fight, against a northern knight in the service of the tournament's host; his bronze armour covered with a surcoat of dark green, embellished with a golden oak leaf, wielding a two handed axe.

Galvin in his silver armour decorated with a blue sash, skilfully danced in between the heavy slashes of the axe, parrying with his longsword when needed. Both weapons had been dulled for the competition; rumour had it the axe more so, to save the King's favoured successor injury. This was not meant to be, for although Galvin won the fight, the northern knight had dealt the Prince a heavy final blow before defeat. As his arm was raised as champion, even from behind his full faced helmet, Rhain could see his brother wincing at the pain.

Galvin was able to keep his composure and left the field without others noticing his agony. Rhain met him at the edge of the field, taking his sword before he dropped it and hurried him back to their tent before the final fight.

"Dear brother!" cried Galvin once they were alone in the tent, collapsing to the floor in pain, clutching his right arm.

"You're slipping," smiled Rhain as he helped his him into a chair.

"Still better than you brother."

Rhain's smile did not go away for he knew Galvin did not mean it, he never held his talents over his brother's head. Their mother used to say that as soon as Galvin had learnt to walk, his first act was teaching his brother. This had always been their way, Galvin learnt something first then helped Rhain, never leaving him behind.

Rhain helped him out of his armour and carefully assessed his right arm. The armour and dull steel had saved him any broken skin but his forearm was heavily swollen and bruised. Rhain slowly straightened the arm, Galvin recoiling in pain.

"The bone is definitely broken," said Rhain.

"I can't fight without my sword arm!" his brother shouted in frustration as well as pain.

"I'll go tell father you can't fight," Rhain said as he got up to leave.

"No," replied Galvin as he caught him with his good arm.

"Surely you know you can't face Sir Walter like this."

"No, of course not," he said as he looked down at his armour, "but you can."

The walk to the tournament field felt long and slow as Rhain heard his own heart beat thunder around the inside of his brother's helmet. Through the narrow slit in the visor, the Prince could see his father high in the royal stand in the distance, thinking that for just once, the King was going to see Rhain in the way he had always wanted to be seen by his father, the way he saw Galvin.

Concealed behind his brother's helmet, Rhain stepped out on to the field to meet his opponent. The crowd cheered as they saw their Prince standing ready to fight; even if it was the *wrong* Prince. Being twins they shared a similar height and build so even their father the King was fooled. Across the field stood Sir Walter Anvil, older brother to Lord Torin Anvil. He had forsaken his birth right to the Hammer Hills and the Western Realm, staying true to the soldier in his heart and claiming only their House's ancestral warhammer in place of titles.

Sir Walter set the hammer to one side, the mighty black steel weapon was known as Hoarfrost, one Rhain was happy not to face. In its place Sir Walter picked up a similar hammer, though forged of regular steel and its points dulled the same as the Prince's sword. The men of the west wielded their hammers both in craft and combat as skilfully as the northerners and their axes.

Sir Walter approached in black and gold armour, his breastplate decorated with the Anvil of his noble House. He was known to be a very skilled fighter, winning a number of tournaments over the years. Rhain had seen him fight a number of times, not envious of the men beneath the fall of his hammer. The two men drew closer and the crowd fell silent as they anticipated the first strike. It was so quick the Prince nearly missed it entirely, his sword parrying the heavy blow just in time. The crowd erupted again as the two opponents met, the dull steel doing nothing to dampen their cheers.

The shaft of the hammer was long enough for two hands so Sir Walter switched between heavy two handed strikes and quick one handed swipes; the heavy head of the weapon narrowly missing Rhain each time. The Prince may not have been the swordsman his brother was, but he was in no way unskilled. Rhain returned with a series of slashes that brought the crowd's cheer to new heights. He knew they cheered Galvin but it felt like just for once, they were cheering him.

The fight continued back and forth as each opponent attempted to gain a winning hit, with Rhain holding his own against the more experienced fighter. The western knight advanced with a high single handed swipe, one that Rhain skilfully ducked beneath, leaving Sir Walter's chest exposed for but a moment. The closest weapon was not the Prince's sword but his armoured foot, which he swiftly brought up to meet his opponent; kicking Sir Walter back hard and off balance. The weight of the knight's armour made it impossible to recover and he went crashing down to meet the field. The crowd's cheer reached a climax as Rhain's sword tapped against Sir Walter's breastplate, forbidding his opponent from getting up and winning the fight.

Rhain could not long revel in the victory for he dashed off the field and returned to Galvin, out of fear of being discovered beneath the helmet. Though once in the safety of the tent the steel was shed to reveal the large smile on his face. His brother embraced him despite the pain it caused him, wincing as he helped Rhain out of his armour, completing the rouse.

Galvin had Nesta tend to his arm in secret once they had returned to the capitol, for both Rhain and he thought it best not to let their father find out of their deception, despite the fun they had had with it. It was only when the King had later gifted Galvin with Sable that he told the truth of the fight, refusing to take the victory away from his brother, encouraging their father to gift it to Rhain instead.

"The Kingdom thought it was their *favoured* Prince that won the fight and will continue to think so, now accept the sword and I'll hear no more on the matter," their father had said to them both.

Despite Galvin's plea to their father, the King would not listen. Rhain had always sought their father's approval; he died before he found it. He was always a good King, though not always the best father. It seemed Rhain could not escape the same fate, for he did not know where he had gone wrong with Richard, his son's failings only highlighting his own as a father.

The day after Galvin was given Sable by their father, he then gifted it to his brother; the black blade reflecting their strong and seemingly unbreakable bond. That was the brother that Rhain remembered, the one that was always there for him. He watched the light in his brother's eyes only grow brighter with age and the arrival of Caitlyn in his life, to then watch it fade as he darkened after her loss.

Tears dropped from the King's eyes onto the black blade that had once been the symbol of their brotherhood, now only a cruel reminder of the brother he had lost. Wiping the tears away, Rhain took one last look at Sable before returning it to his scabbard. His story was only one contained within the ancient sword, many had come before and many would come after, along with new blades all together.

Chapter Twelve

Everleaf

More sparks flew as Tristan brought the hammer down hard against the white hot steel. The searing metal was trapped between both anvil and tool, each hit forcing it to take on the desired shape. Tristan wiped the sweat from his brow, even the cool sea breeze could not lessen the heat bellowing from the open furnace. The forge where he worked his craft lay within the barracks of the Royal Guard, high upon the blade of Greyfell's Sword.

Tristan had been taught the ways of metal ever since he could lift a hammer, the men of House Anvil had long been the greatest blacksmiths in Farreach. Tristan had grown up in Mount Steel, a large castle high in the peaks of the Hammer Hills. It was built upon a waterfall, part of the Brittle River that came through the mountains from the north, down to the Rift in the south. The water ran straight through the heart of the castle, tumbling out in a great stone archway where it cascaded down the side of the mountain.

Tristan remembered the stone halls of his father, Lord Torin Anvil the Thane of the Western Realm. He was his only child and heir. Tristan's mother, Lady Gwyn, had given birth to him when hope for her was almost lost. As a result she smothered young Tristan with affection and rarely let him out of her sight. This soon became too much and he longed to see what lay beyond the reach of the Hammer Hills.

When King Rhain had proposed a marriage between him and his daughter, Tristan relished the opportunity to escape the walls of Mount Steel and journey through the vast Kingdom that surrounded it. When his father had agreed to the match, his mother had been reluctant to let him go. Finally she conceded under the condition that a knight of her choosing travels with Tristan to protect him. Many came forth for the position, but it had been Sir Thomas Gillain that had fought the most fiercely.

Tristan remembered the long journey to the capitol by Sir Thomas' side. They travelled down the Hammer Hills for many days, following the roots of the mountains to the town of Hillfoot. After spending the night in an inn, they turned southeast along the road that would take them to the Eastern Realm.

Sir Thomas told many stories as they rode of the men he had fought and the women he had loved, both were too high to count. They travelled into the Eastern Realm a few days later and crossed the Gilded River over a large stone bridge. The river was given its name for the water ran gold and green with the leaves of the Glades. Tristan asked his protector about the Southern War and the story of how had gained his knighthood.

"I was a barely a man when the war began," the knight had said, "only a squire at the time. As you know I served your father's older brother, Sir Walter."

"Were you a good squire?" asked Tristan.

"Let's just say I made a far better knight. I was always getting in the way, though your uncle was kind to me despite it. I served him throughout the war, learning the ways of battle. 'It's not the numbers you have at your back,' he'd always say, 'it's how you put them forward.'"

"And you were with him when he died?"

"I was," said the knight in a saddened voice, his long white cloak flowing over his horse, "in the final months of the rebellion Lord Wolfrick had pushed as far north as Stagsdale. Castle Grove lay under siege and he was gathering strength before advancing on the capitol. Your uncle attacked Stagsdale in an attempt to retake the town, whilst your father had taken the majority of House Anvil to break the siege at Castle Grove."

"My father told me about the siege; Lord Dale held the castle for weeks before he arrived."

"He did Tristan, not a single southern man set foot within his walls. It's said that he gave up his Lord's chamber for the wounded and slept on the battlements, his ancient family sword by his side."

"But what of Stagsdale?"

"We attacked from the south of Beachwood, hidden within the trees. Though we were too few and the battle took a turn for the worst. I watched your uncle get struck down by a crossbowman, the bolt pierced right through his plate armour. He died in my arms with his mighty warhammer still in hand."

"I wish I remembered more of him, he seemed like a brave man," said Tristan quietly.

"He was at that," replied the knight, "as good on the battlefield as he was on the tournament grounds. But there I was, a mere squire in the middle of a leaderless battle."

"But you won."

"We did, your uncle had taught me well Tristan. I led his men and won the battle."

"That's quite an accomplishment for a young squire," he said.

"Your father thought so, for he knighted me on our return."

Once across the Gilded River the pair passed Stagsdale on their way up to the capitol, all sign of battle washed away by time.

Back in the forge Tristan continued to pound the metal against the unrelenting anvil beneath it. The steel would eventually be forged into a longsword for young Ewan. A week had passed since he had returned from Beachwood after his encounter with Highthorn and his leg had regained all of its strength. He would not say how his wound came to be healed or who by, but his story of how he battled the grand white stag made such talk trivial.

That morning Tristan had gone in search of Ewan, hoping he could have the broken piece of antler that he brought back as a trophy.

"What are you going to do with it?" Ewan had asked him.

"It's about time someone forged you a sword, I thought the antler would make a fine addition."

Ewan's face had lit up at the mention of his own sword and he relinquished the antler eagerly. He saw how quickly Ewan and Eilidh had become friends, and Tristan desperately wanted to please the young Princess. Forging her new friend a magnificent sword would certainly put him in her good graces.

Blacksmiths from the Hammer Hills were not just the best forgers in Farreach because of their skills with metal work, but because of their unique ability to create black steel. This was done with a rare substance only found deep within the mines below the Hammer Hills, known as shadow ice.

This extraordinary mineral got its name from being black as a starless night sky and as smooth as glass. When mined it could be melted down and coated over ordinary steel in its liquid form, once cooled the steel took on the same black shine. Once regular steel was bound with shadow ice, it became stronger and never needed to be sharpened; forever keeping its deadly edge.

Black steel blades were rare and few, the most famous of which belonging to the four greater Houses, passed down to the Thanes that ruled them. Full sets of armour were rarer still; for the amount of shadow ice needed to coat armour was far greater than that of weapons. He had only brought a limited amount of shadow ice with him to Gleamport, most of which had coated the Stag Prince's helmet, a piece Tristan was very proud of. What was left was going to create Ewan's black steel sword.

The proud forgers of the west brought a new meaning to the word *blacksmith*, their use of shadow ice ringing the word with new truths. Despite the benefits that the dark mineral brought to ordinary steel, it was not the Hammer Hills' way to use the rare substance on nothing but the best of craftsmanship.

Tristan folded the hot metal and hammered it back into itself, purifying and hardening the steel with each turn. Countless times he did this, creating layer upon layer of fused metal. He then began to draw out the sword; beating and shaping the folded steel into a blade.

Once he had ground a basic edge and point, he cast the sword into the raging furnace, allowing it to regain its white hot flare. As soon as the fire's glow had crept up the entire length of the blade, Tristan removed it from the flames and plunged it into a vast tank of water. The burning metal spat and hissed as it lay beneath the surface, sending up bellows of steam. Rapidly cooling the sword was known as tempering, allowing it to be both strong and flexible but not brittle.

The blade then received its deadly sharp edge by slowly refining the steel with increasingly finer whet stones, bringing the metal to a thin razor point. Tristan then set about engraving the length of steel, demonstrating the fine detail of his art and craft. With this done the steel was ready to be bound with shadow ice. Tristan took out the last shards of the mineral and placed them in a small bowl sized crucible; placing it within the hot coals of the furnace. As the crucible began to soak up the unrelenting heat it too began to glow, the shadow ice blooming with small black droplets inside.

The rare and beautiful shards wept dark tears as they succumbed to the fire that surrounded them. The black liquid slowly rose up the sides of the crucible as the last of the shards slipped beneath the dark surface. It lay there bubbling as if it were a river of ink trying to escape being sealed into the words it would eventually form.

Tristan grasped the crucible from the flames using a pair of metal tongs in one hand and the ready blade in the other, both heavily wrapped to stop the heat reaching his fingers. In a very practiced and careful manner he slowly poured the now thick black liquid over the steel. Tristan constantly moved and rolled the blade as the shadow ice crept over the metal, for if it were to ever settle it would harden in such a way no amount of fire or skill could undo. It took years to perfect the process, to manipulate the rapidly cooling liquid to a degree worthy of the Hammer Hills. The shadow ice continued to run over the steel, filling every fine engraving in a perfectly even thin coat. As the last remnant of untouched silver was covered in darkness, it cooled before his very eyes, leaving a flawless shimmering black finish over the metal.

Tristan spent the rest of that day and most of the night completing Ewan's sword. Labouring over the intricate and final details that made the Hammer Hills so revered for their craft. By the time he left the forge it was the early hours and the sun had long set over the eastern horizon. He made his way back to his chamber, carefully wrapping the sword up in soft cloth and placing it on the table. The young Lord Heir then wrapped himself up in his furs and slept the few hours until morning. In his dreams he thought of Princess Eilidh.

When Tristan awoke he felt as if in the time it had taken him to blink, the sun had decided to come up. He rose from his bed and stretched his tired arms; they felt weak from wielding the hammer. He went to the window of his chamber and took in a deep breath of the fresh morning air, thankful that it was free from smoke and sparks. Tristan's room did not face out onto Royal Bay as Eilidh's did; his looked down upon Greyfell's Sword and the city of Gleamport that lay beyond.

The city was an expanse of glistening white stone, the western sun showering the capitol with light. It was built in a half circle, the straight edge lining the Falling Cliffs. It had once been a full grand circle, before part of the city had fallen into the Sea of Glass, leaving only the Sword standing strong. The Greyfell's royal dynasty had started with the making of the Sword. Legend told that when the sea reclaimed what it had missed, and the Sword fell, House Greyfell would fall with it.

Tristan got dressed and left his chamber, carefully carrying Ewan's wrapped sword under one arm. He had not seen Sir Thomas in over a day, the only time his loyal protector left his side was when he trained with his fellow knight Sir Darrion. The young Captain of the King's Royal Guard was one of the few to equal Sir Thomas' skill with a blade, and the knight said he relished the time spent with him.

Tristan descended the grand marble staircases to the garden terrace at the very back of the Citadel. There he had arranged to meet Princess Eilidh and Ewan. The small garden was lined with weaving paved footpaths with flowers and bushes growing in between. This created a lavish maze where stone and nature intertwined.

At the very back of the garden he found Ewan and Eilidh sitting on a bench talking to each other. A smile appeared across Tristan's lips as he looked upon the young Princess. He had been so happy when his father had accepted the betrothal, wanting nothing more than to escape the confines of Mount Steel. This had been nothing compared to the happiness he had felt when he first laid eyes on his wife to be. She was the most beautiful and delicate creature he had ever seen, and he was lucky enough to one day be hers.

"Tristan," she said as he approached, "we were just talking about you."

"Good things I hope," he replied.

"Nothing but," said Ewan, "I was saying that I'm honoured that you chose to forge me a sword."

"I thought that now you are starting to know how to use one, it's about time you were able to call one your own."

"It was very good of you Tristan," said Eilidh as she rubbed his arm.

"Well I suppose you'd like to see it," he said as he patted the buddle under his arm."

"Very much so," said Ewan with a smile.

Tristan unwrapped the cloth and held out the sword with both hands. He had crafted the scabbard from black rosewood and detailed it with silver along its shiny length. The hilt rose up from one end, the crossguard was polished steel decorated with silver leaves, the vines wrapping themselves around the metal. Tristan had decided to use the antler in the grip. The white bone made up the handle, gleaming like marble and fixed in place with more weaving silver. The pommel was also silver and shaped to form a tree; matching the leaves winding their way down the rest of the sword.

"It's beautiful," said Ewan in a whisper as he took hold of the sword.

"Wait until you've seen the blade," replied Tristan.

Ewan placed his hand over the smooth antler grip and drew the longsword from the scabbard. With a flash of black and a ring of steel, the blade emerged quickly from its sheath.

"I lined the inside of the scabbard with fur," said Tristan, "this allows for the quickest and cleanest draw."

They all admired the blade, its black gleam shining in the morning sun. It rose up long and sharp from the silver of the elaborate hilt. Down the centre of the blade's length Tristan had engraved more leaves, winding their way up the black steel.

"Here in Farreach Ewan," he said, "it's not the wielder that names the sword, but the forger."

"What did you decide on?" asked Ewan.

"I've named it Everleaf," he said, "let it protect and ever grow a part of you."

In the black reflection of the blade, Tristan saw that it was not him that held the young Princess' eyes, but Ewan.

Chapter Thirteen

A Stolen Night

The next day Ewan returned from the training yard in the late evening, he had practised with Sir Darrion and Ardal for as long as the sun had been overhead. When the rest of House Dunharren had returned north, Lord Michael had asked Ardal to stay in the capitol, acting as emissary in his father's stead.

They had been impressed with Ewan's progress and his new sword had only increased his eagerness. Everleaf was light as a feather and perfectly balanced. Every time the sword cut through the air, the light flowed along its gleaming black blade. He now knew why the Hammer Hills were so admired for their steel.

Ewan decided to go to the bathhouse before returning to his chamber, the training had not been easy on him and he wanted to soak his tired body. Like most of the Citadel's interior the bathhouse was made of marble, the smooth white floor cold against his feet despite the heat of the room. He hung his sword belt on the wall and let his clothes fall to the floor, before slipping beneath the steaming surface.

There were several pools around the large room, each one a square cut into the floor. Ewan lay back against the side, stretching out the aches and pains in his limbs. As he lifted his left leg, he noticed the long cut and the fine work of Nesta Mason. His story of Highthorn had made him a hero overnight, young Ewan could not help but smile each time he thought of the very unlikely collision with the White King. His wound had healed well and the secret of Nesta's hiding had remained untold. He thought it was the least he could do for saving his life.

After a while Ewan lifted himself from the water, watching the steam rise from his skin as he left the warmth of the pool. He dried himself with a soft towel and got dressed into a clean set of clothes, though Ewan still felt naked until he fastened Everleaf securely to his hip. The sword had indeed become a part of him as Tristan had said.

He made his way through the halls of the Citadel back to his chamber. Falling onto his bed, all he wanted was to see Eilidh, but the young Princess had plans to have a late dinner with Tristan. Ewan could not thank the young Lord Heir enough for forging him Everleaf, and he had shown nothing but compassion for Eilidh. Yet Ewan could not ignore his own feelings. He knew he should hide them and try to forget, but the young girl he had pulled from the water had never left his thoughts.

Sir Darrion had warned him not to interfere but it was proving hard, for each day it was more apparent to the young couple that their feelings went beyond mere friendship. In the last few days the words had been on both of their lips but neither had had the courage to say them. The choice to finally act did not take long for Ewan to decide; he leapt from his bed and left the room in a hurry. He hoped to find the young Princess still in her chamber before Tristan came to meet to her. He knew it was a mistake to interfere, though to him Eilidh was not some trophy to be traded; he was hers if he was lucky enough to be chosen by her.

When Ewan arrived outside her door he gave the wood a light knock with the back of his hand. It seemed that it was not just Eilidh he would have to convince but also Sister Margret. The elderly woman stood barring his path, a wall wearing a smile.

"Its Tristan we were expecting," she said in a suspicious tone.

"I thought I might have a few words with the Princess first."

"Words are fine dear boy," she replied, "but if you try to lead her away with a scarf again, I may just hang you with it."

"Consider me warned," he said as he heard Eilidh giggle from within the room.

Sister Margret opened the door and there stood Eilidh looking gorgeous as ever wearing crimson satin. Her long red hair was tied behind her head, showing off her perfectly round face.

"Ewan," she said as she gave a twirl, "how do I look?"

The dress caught the light of the fire as she turned in a circle making the fabric appear alive with licking flames.

"You look more beautiful each day," he said.

"Well I should hope so considering when you first saw me I looked like a drowned rat."

"Where will you and Tristan be eating?" he asked.

"In the garden terrace."

"How romantic."

"Yes, in fact Sister Margret would you mind checking if they have everything they need?"

"I will indeed my Princess, though you had better be here when I return."

When Sister Margret had taken her leave, the mood of the room changed and Eilidh spoke to him in earnest.

"I know what you're going to ask," she said.

"Only because you want the same thing."

"You know that I do, but I'm promised to Tristan."

"Not by your choosing," he said.

"That doesn't matter; I have a duty to my father and King."

"And what of to yourself?"

"Ewan please don't ask me to choose."

"But I am!" he almost shouted.

The room fell silent and they both looked at each other, sadness welling up in their eyes. He knew he should not have raised his voice, but it was frustrating to know the marriage was dictated not by love, but something much colder. Ewan drew closer and placed a hand delicately on her cheek.

"I don't want you to marry him."

"I don't either," she said as his hand caught a tear, "meeting you changed everything."

"So it's my fault?"

"Little bit," she said smiling through the tears.

"So can I convince you to escape again?"

"No scarf trick this time?" she asked, "I have to say I'm disappointed."

"You heard Sister Margret; I try that again and I'll be on the end of a silk noose."

"Just as long as I got my scarf back."

The young pair were not there for Sister Margret's return, they had left the chamber hand in hand and quietly made their way down to the stable. They had no intention of running away for good, just a stolen night. Ewan did not know what missing one dinner was going to accomplish, he knew the marriage was out of either of their control. Though he was just happy to be holding Eilidh's hand, nothing about it felt wrong.

As they quickly crossed the courtyard the sun had set and the faint moon was slowly growing bolder. Eilidh led the way with her hand still tightly around his, only briefly letting go to open the heavy door of the stable. The hinges stubbornly creaked as they swung the door aside as silently as possible, trying not to alert any of the Royal Guard on their patrols.

The many eyes of the horses in their stalls peered back at them, glowing soft colours in the growing moonlight. One pair, however, did not belong to a horse, but a man. Small shimmering circles glinting as brightly as his armour.

"Good evening Princess," said Sir Darrion as he emerged from the last stall, fastening his cloak around his shoulders.

"What are you doing here?" asked Eilidh.

"I might ask you two the same question," the knight replied with a smile, "only those seeking trouble would be lurking around a dark stable."

"We just wanted to go for a ride," she said.

"I gathered as much."

"Will you let us go?" asked Ewan hopefully.

"If you two can't stay away from each other, despite my advice, I suppose I can allow you this one night," said the young Captain with a sigh.

"Thank you Sir Darrion," said Eilidh.

"Just as long as you promise to tell the King nothing of me being here."

"Of course Sir Darrion," said Ewan honestly, knowing how much trouble the knight could get into for helping them.

With the young Captain's reluctant blessing, the two saddled their horses and rode across the Sword. Ewan was astride a large brown stallion, its muscular flanks carrying him with great ease and speed. Eilidh rode her own mare Willow, the Princess' red hair a dash of fire against the pure white horse. They sped through the city and curved round the Falling Cliffs, making their way down to the shore. By the time they had reached the white sand, the moon was out in full, the Sea of Glass softly rippling under its glow.

They both slowed to a steady walk as they rode side by side, the gentle waves running about the hooves of their horses. They dismounted at the edge of Beachwood, tying their horses up to a tree. Ewan took Eilidh's hand in his and they continued on along the shore. The pair removed their shoes to allow the feel of sand against their feet. This brought Ewan back to when he first arrived in the Kingdom, shoeless and unaware he was about to stumble across the young woman who would so quickly steal away his heart.

Eilidh had told him that in the hottest days of the summer months, the shore would be full of those living in the capitol, quenching their warm skin in the cool waters of the sea. Though that night, when the whole city lay quietly high above them, Ewan and Eilidh had the entire shore to themselves. Eventually they found the spot where they had first met and sat down in the sand. Eilidh lay back the way she had been when he had dragged her from the sea. No more than two weeks had passed since, yet his life before seemed a mere speck when compared to the time he had spent with her.

"Do you remember the last time we were here?" she asked.

"I do," he said, "I believe we kissed."

"We did?"

"Yes, when I breathed life back into you."

"Then *we* didn't kiss," she said with a playful nudge, "*you* kissed me when *I* wasn't even awake."

"I'm counting it," he said as he lay back in the sand next to her.

"Do you think you'll take part in the war?"

"I'm not sure there will be a war," he said honestly.

"If there is will you be afraid or brave?"

"Sir Darrion told me that being afraid is the only time a man can be brave."

"I'd be afraid for you," she said as her hand found his.

As they lay together in the sand, the stars came out overhead, sparkling as if someone had thrown a fistful of diamonds into the blackest sea. They spoke for hours as the night drifted away before their eyes, though Ewan still did not reveal his past to her.

His visits to the beach and his search for a way home had started to fade, thinking less and less about the life he had left behind; too caught up in the one he was already living. Even when he did allow his mind to wander home, he found it hard to recall. It was like trying to remember a dream; one reality seemed to drift into the other.

The entire night passed overhead as the two of them lay in the sand. Ewan found himself perfectly at ease next to her and never was there an awkward moment. The sun that began to spread over the western sky was all that interrupted them, forcing their stolen night to come to a close.

"We should be getting back," he said to her.

"The night passed far too quickly."

Eilidh was right, although the time he had spent with her was perfect; it had ended all too soon. The only thing that awaited them back at the Citadel was reality and angry faces. With great reluctance they found their horses and made their way back up to the city, the journey lacked all the speed and excitement it had started with.

As they entered the Citadel's courtyard they were not met with an ill tempered crowd as they both had expected. Knights and servants went about their business paying them little attention, save for wishing them a brief good morning. They dismounted and led their horses back to the stable, leaving them in capable hands.

They left the stable and made their way up the steps of the Citadel, though not hand in hand as they had done the night before. Eilidh stopped half way up and turned towards him, standing on the step above she was around the same height.

"Thank you for a wonderful night," she said.

Eilidh leaned down and placed a light kiss on Ewan's lips, it was soft but she lingered for some time, her red lips locked against his own. Slowly she broke away and climbed up the last few steps.

"Now *that* one counted," she said before she disappeared through the large doorway.

Ewan could not help but smile; it was a beautiful ending to a beautiful night. Though his smile did not last long, for as he looked up to the balcony above the doorway, Eilidh's father the King stared down at him. He was not smiling either.

Chapter Fourteen

A Father Knows Best

"How could you do this?" the King asked his daughter as she stood in tears in front of him.

The kiss had not just been a slight to him as her father, but also to her future husband. Tristan had come to him that night demanding to know where the Princess was. The King had planned a late dinner for them both, but the young Lord Heir was furious at being left alone by his daughter yet again.

"Father it was just once night," she pleaded.

"You mean just one kiss, at the end of a long line of recurring absences."

They stood in the King's chamber, it was still early morning and both were weary from a sleepless night. He could not understand how his daughter was so blissfully unaware to the possible repercussions of her actions.

"Mother, please you must understand."

"I agree with your father, this cannot continue," said the Queen.

Bethan stood faithfully by his side, her long black hair tumbling over her night gown. They both loved their daughter, but they knew the importance of her marriage and what it meant to abandon it. The allegiance with the western Lords continued to dangle by a thread, any offence could lead them straight into the arms of the south.

"Your mother is right," he told her, "this silly affair with Ewan must end."

"But..."

"There is no *but* Eilidh, you and Tristan will be wed."

"Father, please."

"You are young, so I know this seems unfair, but Tristan will make a good husband."

"I don't want to marry him," she said with more tears.

"Eilidh enough!" he shouted, "your marriage to Tristan could help prevent a war."

"Is that all you care about?" she asked.

"As King I'm afraid I have to."

"And what about as my father?"

"As your father you are confined to your chamber. Remain there until I say otherwise, whilst I try and resolve this matter."

Eilidh did not say another word; she left silently with tears still rolling down her cheeks. Rhain did not enjoy the harsh teachings a father is required to give, nor did being a King help the matter. He was forced to see the grand picture and put the needs of the Kingdom over others, including his own daughter. Rhain embraced his wife and held her close, taking in the sweet smell of her hair.

"Was I too hard on her?" he asked.

"No my love, you said what was needed."

"I want her to be happy, but the price cannot be the entire Kingdom."

"Tristan is a good man," said Bethan, "I know you would not let our daughter marry a man that would mistreat her."

The Lord Heir had done nothing to suggest he was not worthy of marrying his daughter. He had been kind and patient with her, though Tristan's blindness to her affection for Ewan was starting to wear away. Rhain would have to appease the young Lord Heir and convince him of his daughter's faithfulness. After the night before, he knew this would not be easily done.

"What is to be done with Ewan?" he asked his wife.

"The boy is harmless; Sister Margret assures me of that, she is very fond of him my dear."

"Well Sister Margret knows best, she certainly managed to straighten me out as a child."

"As a child? Don't try and pretend you're not still afraid she'll try and teach you a lesson."

"Well she had no trouble lecturing me as a Prince; I doubt being a King will make much difference."

Before Rhain had children of his own, Sister Margret had instructed Galvin and him as young boys. He remembered the woman to have a firm hand with a warm heart, though even now, as a grown man, his wife was very right about him still being afraid of her.

"As for Eilidh and Ewan," Bethan said, "they are just young. Do you remember us at that age?"

"We couldn't keep our hands off each other, though we were lucky enough to marry for love."

Rhain had married his northern bride at the roots of the Older Oak on Forest Isle, for Bethan had wanted the wedding to take place in the halls of her home. The Older Oak was a magnificent tree that grew inside the Carved Hall of Oakenhold. The roots crept down through the stone floor and its branches reached through the open roof, with a grand seat carved into the very trunk.

Bethan had stood before him in ivory satin as they had said their words to one another. It seemed only yesterday that he had taken her to bed for the first time. Back then he was only a Prince, not knowing that one day he would be a King. The cares of the Kingdom left to fall on someone else's shoulders.

"Tristan will be eased and Eilidh will be warned, troublesome children will be the least of our problems soon enough," his wife said to him.

"Give me a battle over parenting any day," he replied with a smile.

The King and his wife had been up all night worrying where their daughter had run off to. Though now that morning was upon them, neither of them could just crawl back into bed with each other, despite both wanting to. He decided to give Eilidh a day in her chamber as punishment and planned to speak with her and Tristan the following morning.

His wife got dressed and quickly left, breakfast and Rhain's mother awaiting her. Bethan spent a lot of time with Lady Elora, especially now that she was without her husband. Rhain's parents had been very much in love, still showing it even in their stubborn old age. Rhain had been granted with little time to mourn his father, the crown had quickly passed to him, along with the responsibilities it entailed.

He spent the morning dealing with many of them, most involving ink and parchment. The majority of battles were not fought with swords and spears but with quills and numbers, a reality that Rhain unfortunately became accustomed to. He found himself thinking why it was Lords and Kings that ruled the land and not philosophers and mathematicians, for their talents seemed far better suited.

Rhain sat at his desk, another piece of parchment requiring his signature before him. He wondered whether his father had hated being King as much as him. The crown that used to sit atop his father's head`, now sat on the desk in front of him. Rhain wore it as little as he could, when alone the golden nest of antlers was quickly placed to one side. His hand fell to the hilt of his sword Sable, his fingers brushing the gold of the pommel. The King tried not to forget the soldier he always believed he was.

Rhain placed his royal signature on the parchment in bold and flowing letters. He then took out a length of blue wax and held it up to the candle on his desk, as it began to weep under the flame he pressed it against the parchment. Before the wax had a chance to cool, the King sealed it with a stamp bearing the stag of House Greyfell. It was an order to increase the defences of the towns that lay close to the Southern Realm.

Rhain had received word that his brother and Lord William were indeed readying for war. The southern armies were being mustered but they would take some time to assemble, though that did not mean smaller raiding parties would not travel north. The Fringe was controlled by House Sayer as Lords of Gate Keep, whose allegiance was strongly held by Lord William. This allowed southern men to cross the border with impunity.

With the order signed and sealed, the King placed it on the ever growing pile of similar documents. His eyes hurt from peering at words all morning and he tried to rub some of the tension out of his temple. Rhain got up from behind his desk and made his way out onto the balcony. The fresh air cleared his head as he looked out over Royal Bay.

Whilst attending his responsibilities as King, Rhain's mind had not left the matter of the western Lords. He continued to try and find ways to bring them back into the fold. The marriage between Eilidh and Tristan was supposed to buy their support. However, even though Rhain did not receive it, now refusing to wed his daughter would only make an enemy of them.

The King, however, had another arrangement that could potentially regain the support he desperately needed, though he would require the help of his young Captain, Sir Darrion. The knight arrived as Rhain left the balcony, there was a familiar knock at the door and the King summoned him into the chamber.

Sir Darrion was never without the shining armour and blue cloak of the Royal Guard. He had served Rhain well as his squire and even better as his Captain, though he was sorry that it was his claim of House Tarn and the Glades that he would need use of.

"How may I serve you my King?" the knight asked as he entered.

"Sir Darrion come, take a seat."

Rhain took up his place behind the desk once again as his Captain placed himself in front of it, both lifting their swords as they sat.

"You know our relationship with the western Lords is fragile."

"I do my King, Lord Torin and Lord Farris made their position quite clear."

"They did at that," said Rhain sternly.

"Despite you offering your daughter's hand in marriage."

"Yes, but I thought a second marriage could regain their loyalty."

"Whose?" asked the knight.

"Your own."

Sir Darrion's expression showed the extent of his surprise, he could not understand what was being asked of him.

"I beg your pardon my King, but..." he started.

"I have been consulting with your father. Lord Dale and I believes it's about time that you take a wife of your own."

"A wife?" he said with more surprise.

"Yes, we both believe that your marriage to Lucille Gillain, the daughter of Lord Farris, could sway him into convincing his Thane to pledge their support."

"Lucille? The sister of Sir Thomas?"

"Yes, the very same."

"Would your son, Prince Richard, not be a more appealing offer?" asked Sir Darrion.

"Lord Farris has tried for years to wed Lucille to Richard, I shall not grant the west *that* kind of power. She may wish to become Queen but as long as I am King, it will remain a wish."

The daughter of Lord Farris was well known for her beauty throughout the Kingdom, as well as her ambition to one day become Queen. Rhain would not allow the west to have a claim on the Kingdom, though the prospect of Lucille's children eventually becoming Lords and Keepers of the Glades, could tempt the old western Lord into giving up her hand.

"And my father agrees?" asked Sir Darrion.

"Lord Dale believes it's a fine match, he would like to know that House Tarn will continue after he is dead and gone."

"But what of Lord Farris?"

"I have sent word to him along with your father's endorsement. If Lord Farris accepts he will agree to convince Lord Torin to pledge the entire support of the Western Realm."

"Have you told Sir Thomas?"

"No, but he should be pleased his sister is marrying such a fine suitor such as yourself. What say you?"

"I will do as my King commands," said the knight loyally.

"Don't look so sad Sir Darrion," Rhain told him, "Lucille is said to be the most beautiful woman in the Kingdom."

"It's just strange that this should come so soon after your father's proposition."

"What proposition was that?" he asked with confusion.

"You didn't know? Days before your father died, he asked if I would marry your sister."

"He asked you to wed Drusilla?"

"Yes, he said that your sister would make a good wife and that he had already spoken to her."

This was the first that Rhain had heard of such an arrangement; his father had tried for years to marry Drusilla off to another House, but for some reason she had always refused. It seemed that Sir Darrion was his last attempt, though his death had stopped it from going any further.

"Well with my sister in the south with House Fyrth, I think it's safe to say you're free to marry Lucille," said Rhain.

"Then I will do what is asked of me, for my Kingdom and House."

"You bring great honour to them both Sir Darrion."

The knight nodded but said no more.

"With that sorted may I ask where you were when my daughter turned fugitive?" Rhain asked with a smile.

"I apologise my King, I had some business to attend to."

"Well now it's over I guess we should think of ourselves as lucky."

"Why is that my King?"

"That it was only I that saw them kiss."

Chapter Fifteen

Fall from Grace

His footsteps echoed across the stone as Tristan stormed down the halls of the
Citadel. His anger burned as hot as the forging flames of his craft. The night before
Tristan had arrived at Eilidh's chamber to take her to a late dinner, only to be met
with an empty room and Sister Margret's hollow excuses.

The young Lord Heir had been looking forward to the evening all day, a
chance to spend the night with his bride to be. He had dressed in his finest tunic and
picked a handful of flowers to give to Eilidh. Sir Thomas had left early, wishing
Tristan the best of luck before departing.

"She is a lucky young woman," the knight had said, "I hope that she knows
it."

"You're mistaken," he had replied, "I'm the lucky one."

With Sir Thomas gone, the hour to call on his Princess soon came. He
gathered the flowers and made his way to her chamber. Tristan began to feel
nervous as he approached, hoping that everything went to plan, wishing only for
Eilidh to enjoy the evening. When he had learned she had left, before he was angry
he was only sad.

Tristan refused to cry in front of Sister Margret as she tried to explain or the
King as he tried to apologise. He left his tears for when he was alone in the garden
terrace, discarding the flowers where Eilidh should have received them. Tristan
threw them out over the sea and watched as the petals danced in the wind on their
way down. He knew in his heart why she had left him but more importantly who

with. Tristan had shown Ewan nothing but friendship, respecting the time that he spent with Eilidh. Ewan had stolen her away and she had let him.

After throwing away the flowers, Tristan retreated to the Citadel's forge, finding some comfort amongst the burning coals. He looked out over the Sword and moonlit water, knowing Ewan was out there somewhere, stealing secret moments with the woman promised to him. Tristan took up a hammer and pounded a piece of white hot steel, his heavy motions not driven by creation as usual, but destruction.

Again and again he hit the searing metal; he sought to drive his sadness away along with the sparks. Though it did not work, the strength in his arm broke before the steel. The hammer dropped from his tired hand and as he sunk to the floor, more tears ran down his face, cool droplets against his burning skin.

The night passed quickly in the forge, the sky beyond the Greyfell's Sword turning from a deep black to a soft red. The western sun reminded Tristan of his home. Atop the Hammer Hills in Mount Steel, the rising sun would break through even the thickest fog. The light shining off the snow covered Realm as if it were a jewel of the land. All Tristan had wanted was to escape those high peaks, though now sitting alone, he sorely missed them.

That morning Tristan left the forge and made his way back through the barracks of the Royal Guard. His eyes were red from tears and his hands blistered from the hammer, though as the steps of the Citadel came into view, he clearly watched as Eilidh pressed her lips into Ewan's in a long kiss.

The betrayal cut through Tristan like a knife, sharp and long it weaved its way into his heart. It consolidated all his anger and fears, replacing all naive notions with the cold truth. Eilidh had left him to be with Ewan for the last time and he would hear what she had to say.

Tristan had searched for Sir Thomas that morning but the knight was nowhere to be found, this only enraged him further. He had left his chamber slamming the door behind him as he muttered curses. He was soon outside Eilidh's room, his heart pounding in his ears. Tristan did not even grace the Princess with a knock; he simply opened the door and stormed in.

"Tristan!" Eilidh exclaimed as she sat up quickly from the bed.

Sister Margret was nowhere to be found and Tristan closed the door in the same manner that he had opened it.

"Sleeping were you?" he asked.

"Yes, I must have dozed off."

"Long nights will do that to you."

Eilidh was wearing a long white night gown, her slender body almost visible beneath the light fabric. She covered herself with her hands as he came towards her.

"Tristan you shouldn't be here."

"Yes well *you* should have been here last night."

"I'm sorry about our dinner."

"Where were you?" he asked knowing the answer.

"I wasn't feeling well."

"Is that the best lie you've got?" he said angered by the feeble attempt.

"What do you want me to say?"

"That you didn't leave me alone to be with him."

"I'm sorry but it just happened," she said with tears in the corner of her eyes.

"Just like *it* happened at the banquet, as the entire hall watched me dance alone."

"I never meant to hurt you."

"Did you think kissing him wouldn't!"

Eilidh took a step back; she had never heard him shout before. Tristan could tell that he had frightened her, though he did not care.

"Tristan I want you to leave."

"No," he said annoyed.

"Please just go."

"I said no. You are promised to me; it's about time that you acted like it. Now stop hiding yourself," he said as he pulled her arms away from covering her modesty.

This was met with a slap across his face. The hit was hard and loud. Though it did not match the one Tristan returned to her. He struck her with the back of his hand and the sound rang in his ears. Blood poured from Eilidh's lip as she fell sideways to the floor.

Tristan did not know how he came to be on top of her, but there he was, forcing himself upon her as she kicked and struggled on the floor.

"You are mine!" he said in her ear, "not his!"

Eilidh opened her mouth to scream but the sound was muffled by his hand, letting out only quiet pleads mixed with tears. She continued to fight beneath him, trying to escape, though he was too strong. Tristan's weight alone held her down, leaving one hand to cover her mouth and the other to untie his trousers.

His fingers struggled with the laces but eventually he managed to untie them and wriggle his legs free. He then placed his hand on the bottom on Eilidh's night gown and began to drag it up her legs. The change in her eyes was unmistakable as she realised what he meant to do. She fought all the more but to no end.

"This is your fault," he said in her ear, "you made me do this."

He felt the blade of the sword before he felt the touch of her skin. It was thrust through his back and came out his chest, a black gleaming point smeared with red. He knew the sword; his own hammer had forged the blade that killed him.

"And you made me do this," he heard Ewan say from behind him.

"Everleaf," Tristan whispered in reply as he fell to one side.

On the floor Tristan closed his eyes and once again thought of his home. He was sorry for his last action in the world, sorry for his fall from grace, though he did not have the strength to say.

"Ewan what have you done?" he heard Eilidh scream just before he died.

Chapter Sixteen

A Dark Crime

Gentle waves lapped at the small boat as it glided across the water. Drusilla sat at the back of the craft, beneath a large sun umbrella. Lake Titus lay all around her with the city of Black Stone still looming overhead. Lord William's son, Stewart, manned the rudder and sails, she had convinced him to leave his books behind and take her out on the water.

Galvin and Lord William would pore over maps and troop movements for hours, gathering their forces to launch an assault on the upper Realms. In truth Drusilla was bored, she had interrupted many meetings since and found each one less interesting than the one before.

That morning the sun had risen bright and full and Drusilla longed for the sky beyond the black walls of her chamber. Galvin had become consumed with overthrowing Rhain; it was as if he had retreated inside himself, far away from his sister's words.

"Come outside with me," she had pleaded, "these maps won't disappear but the sun will."

"The sun won't win me the Kingdom," he had replied sternly.

"You need a break dear brother."

"I need you to leave me be," he had said turning away from her.

"Perhaps you could convince my son to accompany you," Lord William had interjected, "Stewart is as uninterested by serious matters as you are."

"I might just do that my Lord," she had said, looking at Lord William but directing it at her brother.

Drusilla knew Galvin would not be offended by her seeking another man's company, but she did it to spite him regardless of whether he realised.

Drusilla found Stewart in the library; she had spoken to the Lord Heir a number of times but his coyness had not lifted. Rejected by his father, he found solace in the many books that he read, rarely speaking to anyone beyond their pages.

Stewart sat alone, the black wooden bookcases towering around him, his own fortress of the written word. His hungry eyes danced through the pages, taking in the mind of another.

"Lady Drusilla," he said lifting his head.

"Stewart, I thought I'd find you here."

"You were looking for me?" he said with surprise.

"Yes, now invite me to come out on the lake with you."

"My Lady?" he asked confused.

Drusilla understood that it was a blunt approach but she knew that there was a man somewhere behind that boyish mask of shyness.

"You want to take me out on the lake," she said.

"I do?"

"Yes you do."

"I do," he said obediently.

"Now, invite me."

Stewart's eyes returned to his book, his cheeks blushing under the situation she had forced upon him. Although teasing him certainly did amuse Drusilla, she found herself truly wanting to help him.

"Look at me Stewart," she said, "I'm not your father."

He looked up from his book, the redness in his cheeks retreating along with his nerves.

"Lady Drusilla," he began, "do you want to come out on the lake with me?"

"Women aren't fond of questions," she said with a smile.

"Come out on the lake with me."

"Too forceful."

Stewart stood up and considered what he would say next.

"Lady Drusilla," he started.

"Yes Stewart."

"I'm taking a boat out on the lake; I must insist I have the pleasure of your company."

"Much better," she said with a smile.

That is how they came to be on Lake Titus, the sun burning brightly over their heads. Stewart sat facing her, his hand on the rudder as he guided the boat. The sun shone off his golden hair as he steered them across the lake. Drusilla found him very handsome with his wall of shyness broken; for the first time she could see a glimpse of a fiery spirit.

Drusilla only wished that Galvin would lower his guard as easily as Stewart had. Long had she loved him more than a sister should love a brother, but he wore his resolve as if it were armour and would not put it aside long enough for her to show him.

Her mind was brought back to the present as Stewart got up to tend to the sails as they caught the wind; they were painted bright yellow and streaked with the red osprey of House Fyrth.

"Where did you learn to sail?"

"In a book," he replied as he secured the fabric.

"You know there are things in this world that you won't find within the pages of your books."

"You sound like my father."

"Well like I said before, I'm not your father."

"Neither am I," he said, "much to his disappointment."

Stewart was not the heir Lord William had hoped for, a truth he did not mind sharing with him. In his eyes, his wife's death did not justify his son's life.

"Does he ever speak of your mother?" she asked.

"No, he can't even look at me without seeing her."

"Many women die in child birth, what happened to her wasn't your fault. She gave her life so you could live yours."

"I know," he said quietly.

"Then don't waste it trying to live up to your father, you're already a better man."

The day passed quickly out on the water, the shadows were soon stretching their long dark fingers over the lake. Stewart guided them back towards the island city, sailing into the underground port that lay beneath. It was guarded by a large water gate that closed over the mouth of the cave. It was slowly drawn up as they approached, revealing the rusted and plant strewn half that often lay submerged.

Their small boat seemed even smaller inside the enormous cavern, the high rock ceiling holding the weight of the city that lay above. Once docked, Stewart held out his hand and helped Drusilla from the boat, her legs taking some time to adjust to the steady nature of solid ground. He then took the time to see her escorted back to her chamber, lightly kissing her cheek as they said their goodbyes.

"Thank you Lady Drusilla."

"I don't know what you mean," she said with a final teasing smile, "you're the one that invited me."

As she shut the door behind her, Drusilla gently touched the cheek he had kissed. She only wished Galvin had been there to see it, not that he would have cared. She had enjoyed helping Stewart overcome his shy nature, though the true reason of inciting jealously in her brother was entirely lost on him. She wished Galvin would look at her the way she did at him, with a longing in his eyes that only lovers share.

Something stirred within Drusilla, a strange determination to force her brother to no longer look at her as his sister, but a woman, beautiful and his to take. She waited until night fall before leaving her chamber. The black halls were dimly lit with candles, the flames flickering as she passed. Eventually she found her brother's room, a dull glow creeping out from under the door, telling her that he was not yet asleep.

Drusilla did not knock; she opened the door quietly and slipped inside, letting it close behind her. Galvin was wide awake at his desk, a candle burning low beside him. He was too busy pouring over another map to even hear his sister come in. Drusilla's hand found the heavy steel bolt on the door and she made a point of loudly locking it. Only then did Galvin look up from his desk and become aware of her presence.

"Drusilla?" he asked with surprise.

"Good evening dear brother."

"I wasn't expecting you."

"You never do anymore," she said angrily.

Galvin stood up from his desk and came towards her.

"We're not children anymore sister; there are other important matters that require my time."

"I know we're not children anymore," she said to him, "that's why I'm here."

"What do you mean?"

Drusilla was wearing a long silk night gown; she untied the laces at the front and let it fall over her naked shoulders to the floor.

"This is what I mean," she said.

Her brother's eyes took in her naked body, dancing over her skin. For a moment she glanced a longing in his eyes, but it quickly faded away.

"What are you doing?" he asked sharply.

"I want you to see me."

"I do see you," he said confused, looking at the floor.

"I want you to see me like this," she said turning her body, "as a lover."

"You are my sister!" he shouted as he turned away with disgust.

His words hurt but she knew he would not turn away if he understood what she had done for him. Drusilla had not been there for her father the morning he died; the fever had come too suddenly. She did, however, remember the night before.

The rain had lashed against the windows of the banquet hall as they ate their evening meal. She finished the feast with her family, masking her intentions under perfectly applied fake laughs and smiles. When the last of the food had been cleared away and many were retiring to their beds, Drusilla got up from her chair and went to kiss her father goodnight.

The King's jagged crown lay loosely on his frail head as she bent over and planted a light kiss on his cheek.

"Goodbye," she whispered to him, not goodnight, a last honest gesture amongst a final dishonest act.

She draped her long sleeve over the top of his wine cup and hidden within the fabric, lay the small vial of dreamlock. As she uncovered the cup, Drusilla saw the last of the clear liquid slip beneath the deep red folds of the wine.

Murdering her father had been surprisingly easy, though she supposed all things were in the name of love. She would often dream of being her brother's Queen, though her father did not die to ensure Galvin's claim, it was to prevent her marriage to another. Sir Darrion was the last in a long line of suitors arranged by the King. One she saw but one way out of.

Now her brother was all hers. She walked towards Galvin and felt his body shudder as she pressed hers naked against his back.

"Long have you been without a woman brother."

"I had a wife," he said sternly, "I loved her."

"And she died," she said wrapping her arms around him, "leaving you no children, no sons to carry on your name."

Galvin remained silent, refusing to look at her.

"I could give you a son brother."

She felt him shift uncomfortably under the words.

"A son?" he asked as he turned to face her.

"I promise to give you a pure Greyfell heir to the Kingdom."

"We would be condemned," he said with fear in his voice.

"We would keep it a secret."

The longing returned to Galvin's eyes as she watched him consider her promise.

"A son?" he repeated.

"A son."

Drusilla felt the forceful hands of her brother lift her up onto the desk, pushing all his maps and plans to the floor. She lay before him and blew out the candle, the room becoming as dark as their crime.

Chapter Seventeen

Duty over Love

There was a horrible sucking sound as Ewan pulled his sword from Tristan's back. The young Lord Heir lay dead on the floor, a large pool of blood growing beneath him, matching the slick red sheen that now coated Everleaf's blade. Ewan's grasp on the silver hilt of the sword trembled as the blood started to drip from the black steel.

Everything had happened so fast. Upon entering the room and hearing Eilidh's muffled cries for help, he had drawn his sword and thrust it through her attackers back without a second thought. There was no doubt in Ewan's mind about the reality of Tristan's intentions, the fear in Eilidh's eyes was all that he needed to kill him with conviction.

The young Princess lay on the floor beside the slumped body of the man she was meant to marry, her torn night gown stained red with his blood. She pulled at the fabric to cover what Tristan had thought his right to take.

"Ewan what have you done?" she screamed once more.

"I don't know," he said almost under his breath, realising the reality of it all.

He let his sword fall from his hand to floor, causing the steel to ring against the stone, the eerie sound lingering amidst the silence of the room.

"He was trying to..." Ewan began.

"I know," said Eilidh with more tears, "he hit me and at first I didn't know what was happening. Then he started to..."

Neither of them could say it.

"But he didn't," said Ewan holding Eilidh's face gently in his hands, "I stopped him."

"But now he's dead!" she blurted out, "you don't know what this means."

Ewan knew all too well what Tristan's death meant. The Thane of the Western Realm had lost his only son and Eilidh's father had lost his allegiance. Ewan knew that the Kingdom would suffer due to his actions, yet he did not regret them. Tristan sought to harm Eilidh, the women the Lord Heir would have later vowed to protect. Ewan would not apologise for driving a sword through his back when it meant the protection of someone as gentle as her.

"What were you even doing here?" she asked accusingly.

Ewan could not help but be hurt by the harshness of her question. He knew there would be consequences for killing Tristan but he was prepared to face them.

"I saved you," he said.

"I'm sorry Ewan," she replied, crying as she held him close, "I know you did it to protect me, I was just so frightened."

"It's over," he said as he wrapped his arms around her.

"Thank you," she whispered.

That morning after she had kissed him on the steps of the courtyard, Ewan had been far too excited to go to bed. They had spent the whole night together without a single moment of sleep, but that moment as her lips had pressed against his, he was filled with a joy that no dream could match.

Ewan sought out Sir Darrion so that he and the Fox of Tarn could practice the dance of steel. The sun had burnt brightly that morning, their swords glimmering in the light. Sir Darrion was a remarkable swordsman; Ewan had vastly improved and could not have hoped to learn the art from someone better. He was years away from besting his teacher but was now capable of putting up a fight against a lesser foe.

Tristan's back had not been the honourable and valiant first fight he had hoped for. Ewan had come looking for Eilidh after his time with Sir Darrion, hoping to perhaps chance a second kiss, only to kill her betrothed in front of her.

"What shall we do now?" she asked as the pool of blood continued to grow.

"We must find your father and tell him everything."

Ewan picked up Everleaf and helped Eilidh from the floor, only then did he notice the cut on her lip.

"It's nothing," she said when she saw him looking at it.

Ewan took her hand in his and led her towards the door. They both looked back before leaving the room, seeing Tristan's body sprawled out on the blood soaked floor in an awkward position. Ewan had very conflicting feelings about what he had done. He was not sorry for killing Tristan but he was sorry he was dead. It upset Ewan how easy it was to extinguish a person's life; the choice to make one thrust of his sword amongst a moment of chaos had not been a difficult one to make.

As they reached the hall outside they both heard footsteps coming from around the corner. Ewan knew that it was not wise to run, nor wise to try and explain with blood still on his sword. Before either of them could decide what to do, Sir Darrion and Sir Thomas appeared before them. Both knights looked at Eilidh's bloody clothes and then at Ewan's bloody sword.

"Ewan unhand the Princess," said Sir Darrion as he reached for the hilt of his own sword.

"No stop!" shouted Eilidh, "Ewan has done no wrong!"

"But the blood," said Sir Darrion.

"It's not mine."

"Then whose is it?"

Eilidh did not say another word, she simply looked at Sir Thomas and Ewan watched the knight's face grow blank with fear. Sir Thomas stormed passed them both and disappeared into Eilidh's chamber.

"What have you two done?" asked Sir Darrion as he too entered the room.

Ewan and Eilidh followed the two knights inside, to find Sir Thomas kneeling on the floor by Tristan's blood soaked body.

"It was my duty to protect him," cried Sir Thomas as he cradled the Lord Heir's head.

"There is nothing you can do for him now," said Sir Darrion.

"Yes there is," replied Sir Thomas as his sadness turned to fury, "I can kill the one who murdered him," he said as he stood up and drew his sword.

"We don't yet know what happened!" shouted Sir Darrion.

"He stabbed him in the back," said Sir Thomas as he looked at Ewan.

"To save me!" screamed Eilidh, "Tristan is the one that attacked me!"

"See Thomas," said the young Captain.

"It matters not," he replied as he advanced on Ewan.

"It matters to me," said Sir Darrion as he moved to Ewan's side, his hand returning to the hilt of Reynard.

"Stand aside Darrion," said the knight, "I'll kill him next to you if I must."

"You will do no such thing until we find out the truth of it."

"My ward lies dead on the floor with his blood smeared on this boy's sword and you wish to know the truth of it?"

"I will not let you harm him blinded by such anger."

Sir Darrion's words fell on deaf ears, Ewan watched Sir Thomas tighten his grip on his sword and raise the blade above his head. Before the strike could fall on him, Ewan saw a quick flash of steel as Sir Darrion flawlessly drew Reynard and buried it up through the overlap in Sir Thomas' breast plate.

The knight gasped as the sword went up through his chest, a look of disbelief spreading across his dying face. Just before the light went out of his eyes, he placed a light kiss on his killer's cheek. Sir Darrion withdrew his sword, the blade scratching on the armour it had so easily slipped beneath. Sir Thomas sank to the floor once more, though this time it was his own blood that gathered beneath him, his owl decorated white cloak, soaking up the redness that escaped him. Both sons of the western Lords now lay dead on the floor, both murdered to protect another.

The days that followed were a blur to young Ewan, accounting for the events that had transpired to more people than he cared to remember. His innocence was never questioned and he was thanked for saving the life of the Princess for a second time. By none more so than Sister Margret, she flew around him and Eilidh with uncontrollable amounts of tears and praise.

Though despite the gratitude, the only person that Ewan truly wanted to explain himself to was the King, yet he seemed to be the only person that would not hear him. Despite saving his daughter, Ewan knew that he had set the King on a path that would surely lead them all to war, and without the support of the Western Realm, it was one they may never win.

The bodies of Tristan and Sir Thomas were soon washed and burned, their ashes ready to be sent back to their Lord fathers in the snows of the west. Ewan knew that it was right to send them home, though he also knew the act of kindness would not lessen their fathers' vengeance. He had wiped the blade of Everleaf clean half a hundred times, though despite the black steel shining as brightly as ever, he could still picture it wet with blood.

One morning days later, he rose early and made his way to the garden at the back of the Citadel. The sun was breaking over the horizon; it stained the western sky a dark red as if it too was bleeding for its fallen sons. At the point of Greyfell's Sword stood Sir Darrion in his polished armour, tears ran down his face as he held the white cloak of Sir Thomas tightly in his hands.

"Sir Darrion," he said as he approached.

The knight turned but did not hide his tears; they ran from his eyes with a bold determination. Ewan came and stood beside him, the blue water of Royal Bay before them.

"I wanted to say thank you for what you did."

"Thank me?" the knight asked.

"For killing Sir Thomas."

"It's funny," said the knight with a forced smile, "we both killed someone to protect another, yet in your case you loved the person you were protecting, not the one you were forced to kill."

Ewan looked at how tightly Sir Darrion held Sir Thomas' white cloak in his hands and suddenly it all made sense.

"When you said that you understood hidden desire better than most, you were talking about Sir Thomas weren't you?"

"Now that you know, do you think of me as evil?" asked the knight as he forced another smile.

Ewan placed a kind hand on Sir Darrion's shoulder as he had so often done to him.

"I think of you as human."

Sir Darrion folded the soft white cloak over and over in his hands, showing the silver owl embroidered on the blood stained fabric.

"We were more than just lovers," he said with more tears, "we met as boys a long time ago, though we always had the entire Kingdom between us. We only saw each other every time our duties brought us together."

"That must have been difficult."

"It was," the knight went on, "though when Tristan was sent to marry Princess Eilidh, Lord Torin called all the western knights to challenge one another for the right to protect his son."

"And Sir Thomas bested them all."

"Yes, so we could be together."

"And you killed him for me," he said with sadness in his voice, now knowing what his life had cost Sir Darrion.

"Ewan there was one thing that Thomas and I loved more than each other, and that was our duty. In the end we both chose it over love."

Chapter Eighteen

The Fox and the Wolf

Smoke rose high into the night sky as they reached the top of the hill, Sir Darrion pulled at the reins of his horse and raised a fist, calling the vast company at his back to stop. The town of Helmsby lay below them; many of the thatched roofs inside the stone walls had been set ablaze, the flames licking at the darkness. Amidst the fire and chaos, Sir Darrion could hear the unmistakeable clash of steel.

It had been three months since Tristan and Sir Thomas had been killed, their ashes had long been sent back to their fathers. Sir Darrion also returned the knight's white cloak, knowing it belonged in his homeland in the west. The last night he was able to spend with Sir Thomas, was the night before he had killed him. Princess Eilidh and Ewan had almost caught them in the stable as they got their horses. Before Sir Thomas had quietly escaped, he placed a soft kiss on Sir Darrion's cheek, just as he had done when the Captain ran a sword through his heart, breaking both of them.

The western Lords had not supported King Rhain whilst their sons were alive; the death of them both beneath his roof was more than enough for Galvin and Lord William to secure their loyalty. The King had tried with all his power to bring the Western Realm back into the fold, though unless he could bring back their fallen heirs, they planned to take up arms against the Kingdom along with the south.

All the Realms were readying for the war that was now inevitable. Though their armies were yet to meet in the field, a number of southern raiding parties had already crossed the Fringe, burning and pillaging as they went.

Many villages and settlements had already been sacked, too small and too close to the southern border to receive support. However, King Rhain would not allow an attack on the town of Helmsby to go unchallenged. He had dispatched Sir Darrion and his company to retake the town from the clutches of the south.

The Captain commanded thirty mounted knights of the Royal Guard with a further one hundred and fifty men at arms on foot. The knights' polished armour created a glinting front line across the ridge of the hill. Beside him rode Ewan and Ardal, for them it would be their first battle, though Sir Darrion knew that there would be many more, far greater than this one, still to come.

Ewan wore Everleaf on his hip, the black steel blade already accustomed to the taste of blood. Ardal's belt held a pair of small axes with his longbow already in hand, an arrow nocked to the string. The men of the north wielded their bows as skilfully from horseback as they did on foot.

Set against the fire that raged through the town, Sir Darrion could see at least a hundred southern raiders, quelling any resistance they faced from the unprepared townspeople. Their surcoats and banners were decorated with a howling grey wolf on a blood red field; the colours of House Barron, men loyal to the Lord of Southbank Point.

Sir Darrion knew the brother of the southern Lord, the Captain of Lord William's armies, Sir Stefan Barron. He was cruel, without mercy and undoubtedly behind the attack. Sir Stefan had briefly served with him in the Royal Guard, though he was relieved of his position due to his brutal and violent nature.

As a knight, Sir Stefan believed himself to be above that of lesser men, a wolf amongst sheep he would always say; Sir Darrion had his own interpretation. In the world of knights and men, his brothers stood not as wolves but as shepherds, sworn to protect and guard the people. Though Sir Darrion was neither a shepherd nor a wolf, for with Reynard at his side, he was a fox.

He drew the blade of Tarn and rode down the hill towards the town, close to two hundred more gleaming swords at his back. His knights went in front of the men at arms, forming a line as they quickly rode towards Helmsby. The southern raiders had set up a small encampment between Sir Darrion's company and the town, with a few drunken men lying asleep by the fire. They woke at the sound of the knights hurtling towards them, though too late to warn the town.

"Prepare for..!" one tried to shout before Ardal quickly put an arrow through his mouth.

The rest were ridden down like grass beneath their horses, not even slowing the charge. Sir Darrion knew that they need not breach the walls of the town, for the main gate lay broken and burnt from the raiders. With their attack drawing near the element of surprise could not last. The knights closed on the town with the men at arms charging on foot not far behind. Southern archers appeared atop the walls, armed shadows against the flames rising from the town.

As the first few knights rode through the main gate, steel tipped rain fell down on the Captain and his men. Sir Darrion led his knights into the town, Ewan close at his side. The southern men had gathered their ranks inside the walls, meeting the mounted Royal Guard with a line of spears. The knights formed themselves into an arrow head, punching a hole through the centre of the southern ranks, creating a gap in the lines for the men at arms that now flowed through the gate behind them.

As Sir Darrion broke through the wall of spears he was separated from young Ewan, losing him in the battle that began to rage in the town. It was now clear to the Captain that the southern numbers rivalled if not bested his own, though Sir Darrion could see that they were not as disciplined or as well organised.

He rode through the crowd, cutting down the men of the south. As he pulled Reynard from yet another foe, his horse was struck by an arrow, throwing him from his mount to the ground. With an agile roll the Fox of Tarn kept his footing as well as his sword, continuing the fight without his horse.

The battle raged on in the town, the clash of steel all the more louder in Sir Darrion's ears. His mounted knights continued to ride through the streets, purging Helmsby of the raiders that sought to ruin it. Just as he thought the southern force was about to break, out of the crowd stepped the man behind the attack.

Sir Stefan was a giant amongst men, as Lord William's Captain, he wore the red and gold armour of House Fyrth. Though the clasp that held his yellow cloak remained his own, the howling wolf of House Barron that decorated the southern men around them. He wielded a large two handed greatsword, easily as long as Sir Darrion himself.

The two Captains stood across from one another; taking a calm breath before the storm. As Sir Stefan towered over him with his huge sword in hand, Sir Darrion could not help but be reminded of King Rhain as a young Prince, defeating the great Lord Wolfrick. The broad blade of Sir Stefan's sword was not made of black steel as his fallen Lord's had been, though it looked every bit as lethal.

"So we meet as Captains," said Sir Stefan.

"I guess Lord William so fit to promote you."

"He saw fit to recognise my talent."

"A talent for violence."

"One the south seems to appreciate."

"Then go back there!" shouted Sir Darrion.

"Let us see what a wolf does to a fox!"

Sir Stefan charged at him, bringing his heavy sword around towards Sir Darrion. The young Captain stepped back, as the large blade narrowly missed severing his head. Sir Darrion returned with a volley of blows with his smaller quicker sword, trying to pass the guard of his giant foe. Steel rang as each of his strikes were met, none finding the flesh that resided under Sir Stefan's armour.

The southern knight, though being far stronger, followed up with a number of heavy slow strikes, the likes of which Sir Darrion merely danced between. Speed was his ally, quickly moving around the large knight, forcing him to swing and miss and eventually tire.

Again Sir Stefan swung that heavy sword, a high overhead blow that found nothing but the stone beneath their feet, though this time he did not raise it quite as quickly. Sir Darrion saw his chance and slashed at the back of Sir Stefan's knee, Reynard's deadly point slipping between the joint in the armour.

The southern knight's giant leg buckled beneath the blade, forcing him onto one knee. Sir Darrion knew better than to give his foe time to recover and brought his sword in again. Before the Fox of Tarn could triumph as his King had all those years ago, Sir Stefan grabbed his arm. Held in the knight's strong grasp, Sir Darrion's speed and agility counted for nothing. As he tried to twist free the armoured fist of Sir Stefan met him square in the face, the metal knuckles sending his senses asunder.

Sir Darrion stumbled backwards into the crowd, knocking another southern man with him to the ground. The startled foe lay atop him but before he could bring his raised axe down on the Captain, Sir Darrion's dagger quickly slipped up through his throat. Throwing the dying man aside, he stood up and looked for Sir Stefan amongst the now retreating raiders.

The southern ranks had finally broken, their numbers counting for nothing against Sir Darrion's organised and well formed company. He watched as his knights chased the last of them out the rear gate, the wounded Sir Stefan limping somewhere amongst the crowd.

"Should we pursue them?" a knight asked from his side.

"No let them flee."

"But Captain, we have them on the run."

"The townspeople are still in need of help, see that they get it."

The night was spent putting out the fires that threatened to spread through the entire town. Sir Darrion later found Ewan and Ardal tending to the wounded. Though their armour was dented and stained with spots of red, both appeared to be unharmed. Ewan wiped the blood from his sword and Sir Darrion saw the empty quiver on Ardal's back, knowing every spent arrow and thrust of the sword had ended a life.

He had once told Ewan that war makes quick work of changing boys into men, it was all too true. They had both aged that very night, it showed on their faces. The poetic understanding of war had been dashed away by its true and grim reality.

He knew better than to let them dwell on it, giving them both tasks to carry out. Helmsby needed much repair; the southern raiders had left a path of ruin behind them. Sir Darrion first went about securing the walls. The main gate lay a pile of broken wood and scorched metal, not that the Captain had minded the ease of his men's entry into the town. They did not have the numbers or provisions to attempt a siege, Sir Darrion had made certain that their attack was swift, decisive and most importantly of all, victorious.

By morning the gate had been rebuilt and the last of the fire's smoke disappeared amongst the small wisps of cloud. The first of the summer's sky fell upon the world, an expanse of light blue that washed away the dark night that had come before it. Sir Darrion left behind the remaining men at arms to further garrison and protect Helmsby. He mounted a new horse and led his knights out of the town, a long procession of polished steel.

Ewan and Ardal again rode by his side, their spirits somewhat lifted by the fair summer morning, the battle, along with spring, now strangers to their bright new thoughts. They made their way out of the town, across the arrow stricken field that they had charged the night before. Sir Darrion led them northwest, along the road that had brought them to Helmsby's aid.

The journey was straight, cutting a line across the land, making a long ride even longer. Each night they set up camp where they could, nothing but open sky and stars above their heads. The chaos and thrill of battle was little when compared to the serenity of the calm that followed. They were the times that Sir Darrion enjoyed the most, the peaceful moments either side of conflict.

It was days before they reached the town of Stagsdale, sitting close to the trees of Beachwood. It was larger and more fortified than that of Helmsby, a stronghold with high walls and a keep at its heart. As they approached Sir Darrion knew that it would take more than a few hundred southern raiders to breach the town. The gatehouse itself was almost a small castle, the metal barricade rising as they approached.

Inside the streets were busy and narrow, the high buildings on either side almost looming in overhead, the sun trying to force its way through a canopy of slate roofs. Despite being crowded, the town accommodated Sir Darrion and his knights, welcoming their arrival and granting them access through the streets.

Flowers were thrown beneath their horses and some of his knights bent down to receive kisses from passing women. Ardal was one of the lucky few, leaning from his horse; he disappeared into the crowd, returning with a smile between his blushing cheeks. Ewan also caught the eye of many young women, though Sir Darrion knew that his lips were saved for another.

The Captain led his men to an inn where he planned to stay the night, sleeping beneath the stars was all well and good but rested horses and a warm bed were needed. As they rounded the corner of a busy market, the inn came into view. It was a large three story building with dark wooden beams set into the stone. Above the arched entrance hung a painted sign, decorated with the words 'The Jackdaw', along with a picture of the small black bird in flight.

It was nightfall by the time his men and horses were settled in the inn. Sir Darrion sat in the large hall surrounded by his knights, the drink flowing like water. The room was long and wide with tables reaching from end to end. In the centre of the hall there was a grand fire pit, the flames roaring along with the sound of song.

Sir Darrion knew his men had earned a night of cheer, they had fought bravely and well, doing their Captain proud. Across from him sat Ewan, not smiling and cheering as a young man should.

"How are you?" the knight asked.

"I'm fine," he said, though his face spoke otherwise.

"Are you sure?"

"Yes, I was just thinking about Princess Eilidh and I."

"Are the two of you not well?"

"No that's just it, we're perfect."

"Then why the unhappy face lad?"

"Despite Tristan, despite everything, we're closer now than before."

"And you feel guilty for killing him?"

"I do."

"Good," the knight replied quickly, "you should."

"But I did it to save to her."

"A man that kills without guilt is no man at all Ewan. Taking a life should always be difficult."

"But you've killed many men in battle."

"And I remember them all."

Sir Darrion knew that saving Princess Eilidh had come at a price for young Ewan. The killing of Tristan had not faded quickly from thought and Sir Darrion was glad of it, Ewan had done a terrible thing to save another and though being right, in no way should it have been easy.

"Ewan I think of you as a good and honourable man, please don't ever doubt it yourself."

"I just wish the King thought of me so."

"He does, you will see in time."

Eilidh's father had yet to see young Ewan, refusing to speak with him after he had killed Tristan. The King had said that it was due to the severed allegiance that Ewan had caused between the western Lords. Sir Darrion had served him a long time; he understood that the King simply did not know how to thank Ewan for saving his daughter.

"I know how to make my uncle come around," said Ardal as he sat down beside them, spilling ale over the table.

"And how is that my young northern friend?" asked Sir Darrion.

"You should speak with Sister Margret," he said turning to Ewan.

"What good will that do?"

"My father always says how to this day the King is still afraid of that old woman, thinking she'll sit him down and lecture him as she did when he was a boy," replied Ardal.

"I share his pain," said Ewan with a smile.

"That my young friends," said Sir Darrion raising his drink, "might just work."

Days later the capitol city of Gleamport came into view, its tall white walls shining in the afternoon sun, the Citadel of Kings a glinting beacon beyond. They entered the stone courtyard in front of the grand palace and dismounted their tired horses, Princess Eilidh rushed down the steps and threw herself into Ewan's arms.

At first it made the Captain sad, knowing that Sir Thomas was gone from the world. His love extinguished whilst theirs only flourished. But then as the smiles bloomed on their young faces he believed that his sacrifice, though terrible, had not been entirely in vain.

Chapter Nineteen

A Simple Plan

The morning sun flowed in through Ewan's open balcony, slowly creeping over his bed towards his sleeping face. The dreams and thoughts that played out on the inside of his closed eyes were quickly replaced by the bright morning light. Ewan opened his eyes, at first seeing nothing but the radiant field of the sun's glow. Though turning his head, he looked upon her.

Princess Eilidh lay asleep beside him, her delicate round face resting close to his. The nature of her spending the night in his bed had been an innocent one, both falling asleep still clothed after simply talking deep into the night. Motionless and asleep, Ewan watched her with a smile, hardly believing how truly beautiful she was.

The days he had spent away from the capitol were a blur of long roads and short battles, all the while wishing for a moment like the one he was now in. The death of Tristan had done little to hinder their affections. Despite still standing by his choice to kill Tristan, the price would be never forgetting it.

Placing all thoughts aside, Ewan simply watched as the sun moved from his face to hers, the morning light softly kissing her small lips. Eilidh awoke and their eyes met, each one reflected back at the other, capturing the moment in a never ending tunnel of fading mirrors.

"Hello you," he said to her.

"Hello yourself," she replied with a smile as well as a yawn.

"I think we might have fallen asleep."

"Really?" she said teasingly, "there was me thinking we blinked our way to morning."

Before he could reply the door of his chamber was thrown open and Sister Margret marched in, her expression even more stern than usual.

"Just as I thought the two of you couldn't get into any more trouble, you both decide to jump into bed together!" the old woman said as she shut the door behind her.

"My intentions were nothing but honourable," declared Ewan.

"They always are," scorned Sister Margret, "and thus far I have thanked you for them, though this will simply not do."

"It was an honest mistake," said Eilidh, "we merely fell asleep, as did you; otherwise you would have come sooner."

"Yes, well," stuttered Sister Margret, "that is inconveniently true."

"I promise nothing happened," said Eilidh.

"Be that as it may young lady, all this sneaking around brings us nothing but trouble and ill repute."

"It won't happen again," said Ewan.

"Make sure that it doesn't. Now come along Eilidh, before your father hears about this," said the old woman as she got the Princess out of bed and gave her a light push out of the door.

"Sister Margret," said Ewan as she too was about to leave, "before you go might I have a word?"

"Perhaps one or two," she replied as she closed the door, separating them for good.

"I was wondering if I could ask a favour," said Ewan.

"That entirely depends on the natue of it."

"The King hasn't spoken with me since the death of Tristan and Sir Thomas."

"And you wish me to put in a good word for you?"

"If you think the King would listen."

"My dear boy," said Sister Margret smiling, "the King still remembers me threatening to hang him by his toes."

"Like you threatened to hang me by Eilidh's scarf?"

"Well we teachers can still have our fun."

"So you'll speak with him for me?"

"Ewan if this is all you ask of me for saving the life of that young girl not once but twice, then I am more than happy to oblige."

"Why what else could I have got?"

"You'll never know," she said playfully.

It was not long before Sister Margret returned with Eilidh's father. Ewan was both amused and terrified of the seemingly ruthless sway such an old woman could have over a King. She marched him into Ewan's chamber as if he were still a young boy. He was dressed plainly with his crown of golden antlers atop his head.

"Good morning Ewan," he said.

"Good morning my King."

"Now you tell this dear boy what you just told me," said Sister Margret folding her arms.

"Ewan I wanted to say that I am sorry."

Sister Margret loudly cleared her throat.

"I wanted to say that I am *very* sorry."

"Go on," the old woman said.

"I should have come sooner," the King continued, "nothing can excuse the fact that I didn't, though I want you to understand why. I suppose thanking you would make a father realise the horror that could have fallen upon his daughter."

"My King..." Ewan started.

"No please let me finish," he said, "that day I was forced to think what it would be like to lose a child, to face the mortality of the one I love the most. How can anyone come up with words worthy of thanking the person that saved them?"

"I think you just did," said Ewan.

"Not quite yet," replied the King as he put both hands on Ewan's shoulders, "thank you."

"You're welcome, I care about her too you know," said Ewan bravely.

"I know you do lad, otherwise you wouldn't have done exactly what I would have."

"But the allegiance with the western Lords," said Ewan, "I brought it all down."

"Allowing my daughter to marry a man is very different from allowing what he intended to do to her. Despite the Kingdom, the Realms, despite everything, I would have killed him too."

"As would I," said Sister Margret.

"That is no secret," replied the King with a smile.

"Well, now that is all sorted," said the old woman, "I believe I shall take my leave. You boys behave yourselves."

"Yes Sister Margret," they both said in chorus.

She smiled at them before leaving the chamber, her role as mediator carried out perfectly. Once gone, the King turned to him once more.

"Ewan I was wondering whether I could ask yet another favour from you?"

"Anything my King."

"I have a meeting today to discuss the fight that is surely heading our way; I would greatly appreciate your presence."

"I'd be honoured but I don't really know anything about strategies or planning a battle."

"Precisely why I want you there, I believe you could bring a fresh perspective. Most of the time the best tactic is the simplest, one which is often overlooked."

"I can certainly do simple," said Ewan with a smile.

"Good," replied the King as he stood up to leave, "the meeting is at noon in the Crested Concave."

"I'll be there."

"Good," the King said again, "Oh Ewan before I go, I wanted to ask whether any of your memories have returned to you yet."

"No I'm afraid they haven't," he lied.

"Pity, based on your actions here, I'm sure you have a few stories to tell."

When the King also took his leave, Ewan was left alone with his thoughts. He had no stories to tell from his own world, no tales of courage or bold acts. He had become accustomed to lying about his past, the words slipping naturally from his mouth. He hated the deceit, though he knew the truth was far more dangerous.

Many a time Ewan thought of asking questions regarding the green mirror and his miraculous arrival in Farreach, though he was always stopped by the notion that such questions could be his undoing. He had invested more in this world than he had ever done in the last. He knew that the people of his new found home would never believe the true nature of his past, or how he came to be among them. The green mirror, as with his family back home, remained a safely guarded memory, his and his alone.

At noon Ewan made his way up to the Crested Concave at the very peak of the Citadel of Kings. As he rounded a corner he entered a long thin hall, a spiral staircase at one end leading up. The entrance was guarded by two knights of the Royal Guard, Ewan knew and had fought beside them both, their crossed spears parting as he approached.

As Ewan climbed the curved stairs, light eventually loomed overhead as he came up through the floor of the Crested Concave. He had been told stories of the chamber, though had never set foot inside. Each of the four windows stained with the heraldry of the greater Houses, looking out to the Realms that they ruled.

In the centre of the room lay a large square table, at the eastern end stood King Rhain, Prince Richard and Sir Darrion. To the northern end stood Ardal, speaking on his Lord father's behalf, the bear of House Dunharren at his back. All four men looked up as he approached, their faces glad of his arrival, except that of Prince Richard, who wore his disapproval clearly.

"What is *he* doing here?" the Stag Prince asked.

"*He* is here of my choosing," said the King, "and also being the saviour of your sister, I suggest you show a little more gratitude."

Silenced by his father, Prince Richard said no more.

"Ewan come join me," said Ardal.

He made his way over and stood by the Lord Heir's side, the mighty glass bear looming behind them. On the table lay a very large map of the Kingdom, stretching almost the entire length of the wooden surface. Placed around the depicted landscape stood what looked like chess pieces, though Ewan did not recognise their meaning.

"Lord William's troop movements suggest his forces will land on the coast of the Eastern Lowlands," said the King as he pointed to the map.

Ewan saw that the Eastern Lowlands were an expanse of open terrain between the Glades and the coast, uninterrupted by forests and scattered by rolling hills. The wooden pieces that had been placed along the coast were painted red, representing the south.

"The Lowlands would present a good battlefield," replied Sir Darrion, "as well as control of the coast."

"Then I say we fight them there," said Prince Richard, pushing the blue pieces, representing the King's forces, to the coast to meet the south.

"You would have us meet them on the coast?" asked his father.

"Yes, we could throw them back into the Sea of Sails before they even set foot in our Realm."

"And the Western Realm?" asked the King as he moved their black pieces from the west in behind that of his own, "meeting the south at the coast allows the west to flank us from behind, trapping us between two armies."

"It was an idea," said the Stag Prince.

"A bad one," replied his father, "we will have trouble winning this battle on one front, let alone two."

Ewan studied the map and the wooden pieces that lay upon it, the others continued to speak as he tried to find the simple tactic that the King had spoken of. Just as he was about to give up, he noticed a long row of hills on the map below the words 'The Eastern Lowlands', stretching from east to west, with a wide pass leading through the centre.

"Would it be possible to place your armies further inland?" asked Ewan suddenly.

"To what end?" asked the King.

"To draw Lord William away from the coast and give him time to join his forces with the west."

"Only to face a larger army," said Prince Richard, "what does this boy know of war?"

"Allow him to finish," said the King, "Ewan go on, why would we want them to rally together further inland?"

"These hills," said Ewan pointing to them on the map, "could we draw them there?"

"Yes," replied Sir Darrion who knew the land around his home well, "if we present a large enough force, I believe they would take the bait."

"Then we gather there," said Ewan moving the blue pieces to the hills, "using this pass to funnel their attack."

"The landscape would give us a distinct advantage and make it almost impossible to flank our position," said the young Captain.

"Speaking of which," continued Ewan, "with Lord William's forces joined with the west further into the Lowlands, would it be possible to ride behind their position?"

They all stared at the map for a moment, imagining the wooden pieces curving round the southern force to flank their enemy from behind.

"Simple," said the King with a smile.

"That's quite an idea lad," said Sir Darrion as his mind took in the plan, "indeed simple, but brilliant."

"So the majority of our armies will gather at these hills," said the King pointing to the map, "drawing Lord William away from the coast, causing him to join forces with the west."

"Whilst the rest of our men will ride behind their position and flank them, forcing *them* to fight on two fronts," said Sir Darrion with another smile.

"It might just give us the advantage we need," said the King, "Ardal, send word to your father of Ewan's plan."

"Ewan's plan?" interrupted Prince Richard, "you're actually going to listen to this fool?"

"How dare you call him a fool!" shouted the King, "Ewan's not helping for his own personal glory as you are. How your mother and I raised such an arrogant, cruel little boy I'll never know!"

"When I am King..."

"But you're not!" his father shouted.

The room fell silent as all eyes fell upon father and son, the Stag Prince trying to stop the tears in his eyes from falling. Without another word he turned and stormed out of the chamber. The King sighed and rested both hands on the table, staring at the large map before him.

"Ewan's plan," he finally said, "how long will it take you to prepare Captain?"

"Three weeks my King," replied Sir Darrion.

"Make it sooner."

Chapter Twenty

Three Gifts

Two weeks later Sir Darrion had gathered his King's armies, mustering as much of the Eastern and Northern Realms' forces as he could in such a short time. The morning the men were due to depart; Princess Eilidh had risen before them, intent on saying farewell before they left for war.

The great battle of her time was going to take place in the Eastern Lowlands, a grassy stretch of terrain that reached from the Glades down to the Sea of Sails. As a Princess and a young woman, she was deemed unfit to serve on the battlefield, forced to stay at home and watch men leave to defend a kingdom they loved no more than her.

The sun was yet to break over the western sky as Eilidh opened her eyes, a light mist had settled over Royal Bay, a grey cloak over the glassy water. She slipped out from underneath the warmth of her furs, the cool morning air biting at her pale skin. Her feet touched the smooth marble of the floor, the milky stone surface streaked with veins of bright blue.

Still not quite awake, the young Princess made an effort to find some clothes. She donned a satin gown of soft cream, placing her favourite silk scarf around her delicate neck. As she ran her hand over the fine material, Eilidh thought back to the clever trick that Ewan had played with it at the coronation banquet, leading her away with the fluttering white fabric. He had fallen into her life so unexpectedly yet he was never far from her thoughts, days upon days they had spent together, their fondness never waning.

The night before Ewan had left for Helmsby, the moments they had spent together felt as if they were their last, but when she was finally forced to say goodbye, she did not kiss him. Their lips had not touched since that fateful morning on the steps of the Citadel, despite the young Princess wanting nothing else. Now he was to leave again for yet another battle, far greater than the last.

Eilidh made her way out of her room, walking through the quiet halls of her great House. It was not long before she stood outside the King's chamber, lightly knocking on the strong doors. It was not her father that answered but his Captain, wearing his polished armour as usual.

"Good morning Princess," he said, "you're up very early."

"I wanted to see what it was like to be a fox."

"Tiresome," said the knight with a friendly smile.

He opened the door and gestured Eilidh inside. Her father stood by the open fire, he too was in armour, though not the simple steel she was used to seeing him in. He wore the armour of her grandfather, the armour of a King. It bore resemblance to that of the Royal Guard, though parts of the polished steel were gold, creating an array of glinting silver and gilded metal. The armour was embellished with a crown of antlers on his breast plate, matching the golden crown that lay atop his head, all of it shining in the light of the fire.

"Father," she said as she entered.

"Good morning Eilidh," he replied, "come to see me off?"

"Of course."

"Charming, though I suspect you've come for something else as well," he said with a smile, "daughters have a way of blending acts of good will with favours from their fathers."

"Well now that you mention it."

"Go on child, what would you ask of me?"

"I want you to promise to bring Ewan home safely."

Her father was clearly surprised by the bluntness of such a charge.

"You know that I'll do everything I can to make it so Eilidh," he said.

"I want you to do more," she said as she felt tears in the corner of her eyes.

Eilidh saw her father notice her sadness, the distress she felt at the thought of losing Ewan. The King fell silent for a moment before he smiled and looked to his Captain.

"Sir Darrion my good knight," he said, "would you bring me my sword?"

The knight brought forward the King's sword Sable, its dark red wood scabbard leading to the bright gold crossguard. Sir Darrion handed the sheathed blade to her father hilt first, the King took it and tied the leather belt around his waist, letting the sword hang by his side.

"Sir Darrion," her father said, "how about we make young Ewan your squire as you were mine?"

"It would be an honour my King," the knight replied, "the boy has much to learn but is capable beyond his years; I can't think of one who would make a better squire."

"Does that please you my daughter?" her father asked.

"It certainly does," she replied, the tears now retreating.

"Has it earned a father a goodbye embrace?"

"You need never earn them," she said as she folded into her father's arms, not minding the hard cold steel that fell between them.

Eilidh was too young to remember her father leaving for the Southern War. Now, wrapped in his embrace, she could not be more thankful for it. Saying goodbye to him once was harder than she had ever thought, if it had been the second time, she may have never have let him go.

"I love you," she whispered against his armour, her last words misting against the polished steel, imprinting her affection.

As she left her father's chamber, his Captain escorted her out, taking up his post outside.

"Please watch over them," she said turning to the knight.

"I'll see that they both return to you my Princess, you have my word."

Eilidh returned to her own chamber far more relieved than when she had left it, knowing that Ewan was under the young Captain's protection. As Sir Darrion's squire, he would carry out duties such as saddle the knight's horse, tend to his weapons and armour and stay close to him in battle. The latter of which Eilidh was most pleased about, for there were few in the Kingdom who matched Sir Darrion with a sword, Ewan would be well guarded by his side.

Back in her room, the young Princess picked up her bow, Kimber, and went out onto the balcony. The mist had lifted from Royal Bay, revealing the calm water that it had once covered. The white bow felt light in her hand, the smooth pale shaft held delicately in her palm. Eilidh nocked an arrow from a nearby quiver and drew the bowstring back, Kimber obediently bent into a tight curve.

Sister Margret was always lecturing her on firing arrows out over the water, partly because she may hit an innocent fisherman below, but mainly because she found the activity to be very unbecoming for a young Princess. Eilidh could see that the bay lay empty, no ships broke the stillness of the water. She let the arrow loose and watched as it sailed out from the Citadel, flying high and far, a piercing ship of its own, the clouds its only waves. As it started to look as if it would soar forever, it reached its peak and finished the long arch with a quiet and distant dip beneath the water.

The arrow disappeared below the surface, joining the many that Eilidh had fired over the years. She wondered what they all looked like, if she had created an arrow stricken sea bed, a silent battlefield beneath the waves. Turning away from the balcony, she tried not to dwell on battle, underwater or otherwise. It was nearing the time that the men were due to depart and Eilidh still had one person to bid farewell.

She found Ewan in the courtyard, the stone circle now busy with knights and horses; he was standing on the steps of the Citadel where she had once placed her lips against his. Ewan was not in full plate armour as her father and Sir Darrion were. He wore a coat of leather patterned with metal scales, his shoulders protected by steel pauldrons. Guarding his hands were a pair of gauntlets, the steel fingers gripping the white antler handle of Everleaf that hung by his side.

Eilidh found him very handsome in the armour, though she could not forget the reason for the steely attire. She made her way down the steps to him, his eyes all the more brighter at seeing her.

"Hello you," he said to her as she approached.

"Hello yourself," she replied as she smiled at their familiar nature.

"We'll be leaving soon."

"I know," she said as sadness made its way into her voice, "but first I have three gifts for you."

"Three? As in more than one?"

"Yes, as in more than one," she confirmed as the sadness was lifted by laughter.

"And there was me thinking I'd just get a simple farewell."

"You can have that instead of the gifts if you like."

"Well now I'm hoping for both," he said with a smile.

Eilidh loved the way Ewan made her feel; she knew that every simple joke and every single smile was just for her. She held up Kimber and offered it to him; the bow being her first gift.

"Eilidh," he said as he ran his hand over the white wood, "are you sure you want me to take it?"

"Yes, knowing that in some small way, I've helped keep you safe."

"Thank you Eilidh," he said as he took hold of Kimber and delicately placed it over one shoulder, the bow resting neatly against his back, "I couldn't have hoped for a better gift."

"That's just the first, the second is this," she said as she removed the silk scarf from around her neck and placed it over his.

"Eilidh I can't."

"You can," she said, "I want you to wear it as a token from me, to keep it until you return."

"Thank you," he said again, "I know you've given me your favourite two things in the world, I'll treasure them and you for as long as I'm able."

"And that brings us to my third gift," she said, "which is my heart."

She took hold of the silk scarf around Ewan's neck and pulled his lips to hers. The kiss was longer than the one they had shared before on the steps, full of everything a kiss should be. When their lips finally parted, their eyes fell upon each other, along with all the other eyes in the courtyard.

"You have always had my heart," said Ewan.

With their farewell soon stolen away, Eilidh remained on the steps as she watched them all ride across Greyfell's Sword, Kimber across Ewan's back and the long silk scarf flying behind him in the wind. With them gone, the young Princess ran back into the Citadel, making her way to one of the many high rooms that looked out over Gleamport. Through the open window she watched as Ewan and her father met up with the vast host that awaited them beyond the city walls.

Eilidh lost sight of them amongst the army of blue banners that began to ride southwest towards the Glades. In that moment she knew that Ewan did indeed have her heart, for she felt it break as she again watched him leave for battle.

Chapter Twenty One

A Field of Kings

Ewan was by Sir Darrion's side as they rode along the length of the hills that would be their defence, the grassy mounds rising high to their left. It was dawn as they reached their army's camp north of the hills, the morning light beginning to illuminate the vast sea of tents that housed their army.

The King and his son led the long procession through the camp, the banners of the Eastern and Northern Realms rippling as they passed. Sir Darrion had mustered all that he could in the few weeks he had been given, his efforts where displayed in each of the thousands of faces that had answered their King's call.

They made their way to a grand tent at the centre of the camp and dismounted their horses. Ewan stayed by Sir Darrion's side as they followed the King and Prince Richard into the tent. The ground was carpeted by furs and a table full of food rested to one side.

"I could get used to war if this is what it entails," said Prince Richard as he threw a grape into his mouth.

"War should never be this comfortable," said his father as he looked about the tent with a stern face.

"Your orders my King?" asked Sir Darrion.

"Situate our men at arms amongst the rest of the infantry; meet me back here when you're done."

"At once," replied his Captain.

"I see you trust your fox with more than the rabble you're having me lead," said Prince Richard.

"You have yet to prove yourself off the battlefield yet alone on it," replied the King, "I suggest you hold your tongue until you have done both."

Ewan and Sir Darrion left the tent with even less faith in their Prince, his childish and arrogant nature had somewhat worsened of late and his father's patience had not lengthened. Their relationship grew more fragile by the day as Ewan grew more afraid of the tyrant the Stag Prince was becoming.

As Sir Darrion's new squire, Ewan helped him organise the last of their forces, bolstering their outnumbered ranks. To serve the Captain of the Royal Guard at such a young age was an incredible honour; Ewan was just pleased that his dedication and worth alone had earned him the position.

Once the men had been seen to they made their way back to the King's tent as instructed. Prince Richard was nowhere to be seen, most likely sulking over his so called *rabble*, which Ewan knew to be a company of several hundred fine men at arms. The King stood outside silent and pensive, his silver and gold armour catching the morning sun as his light brown hair drifted in the wind under his crown. Three horses waited for them, saddled and ready.

"Shall we go meet my brother?" the King asked.

"How else would we accept his surrender?" replied the knight with a smile.

"I only wish it were that simple."

"Is the third horse for me?" asked Ewan hesitantly.

"It is my lad," replied the King, "I thought my Captain's new squire could bare our royal banner."

"It would be an honour," said Ewan.

The three of them made their way out of the camp towards the long row of hills, riding through the wide sweeping pass where they would make their stand. Looking back Ewan saw the hills at the entrance of the pass rising gently behind them. The King had improved on his *simple* plan by lining the bottom of the gentle slopes with rows of sharpened stakes, making the hills bristle with resilience, protecting the higher ground, where in addition he saw countless northern archers lining the top of the hills, set back against the entrance, making their preparations for the coming fight.

In front of him Ewan could finally see the enemy camp far in the distance, a blurred expanse of blood red, much larger than their own. He held the King's banner in one hand; on a bright blue setting it bore a stag as white as the scarf around his neck.

Eilidh's gifts were second only to the kiss she had granted him. The young Princess had stolen his heart away with those first few glances on the beach, now he had her heart in return. Ewan had left her for battle once more, though this time was different knowing her lips were his to kiss again when he returned.

As they approached the middle of the field, three enemy riders emerged from the other side to meet them. The King stopped his horse in the very centre of the Lowlands, Sir Darrion and Ewan on either side. As the enemy riders grew closer, Ewan could make out the banner that one of them carried. It was as red as the vast amount of enemy tents before them, embellished with a similar stag to the one Ewan carried, though this one was not white, but black.

The three riders stopped before them, the majestic creatures rippling on the two banners, convening their own silent council. The man opposite Ewan could be none other than the infamous Lord William, his features cold and unmoving. The man that held the enemy's banner across from Sir Darrion was also clearly a knight, his size as menacing as his features.

There was no doubt in Ewan's mind as to which one was Galvin; he stood in the centre and though he held a resemblance to his twin brother, looked more weathered with age. He wore armour made of black steel, bearing encrusted rubies on the breast plate outlining the shape of a stag. His crown was an exact match to his brother's, though it too had been treated with shadow ice, the black steel gleaming with an oily sheen.

"I see you've given up our father's heraldry as well as his memory," said King Rhain.

"So says the noble usurper," replied his brother.

"I did not cross this field to have you two argue like boys," interjected Lord William.

"True," replied King Rhain, "you came to invade our lands and bring ruin to the peace my father fought for."

"You mean *our* father," said Galvin grimly.

"Not since you disgraced his crown and had yourself forged another," answered his brother.

"Do you like it?" asked Galvin showing off the jagged circle of black antlers, "Lord Torin crafted it himself, after you were good enough to have his son murdered."

"That *son* attacked my daughter, you're own niece, I would have killed him myself and thank the man that did."

"I'm just thankful that you were stupid enough to grant me the entire Western Realm in one evening, not that we seem to need it."

"Our father taught us that over confidence will be a man's undoing."

~ 196 ~

"Our father never had the Southern Realm at his back."

"Then what are the south's terms?" asked the King.

"You may hide behind your hills but my scouts tell me that you have five thousand men where I have ten, you have no cavalry and I out number you two to one brother."

"So your terms?" asked the King again, this time more impatiently.

"I don't want to watch a massacre, so lead this army off field and none of your men need die."

"And what of the crown?"

"Step down and declare me the ruler of our father's Kingdom and I'll allow you to remain Thane of the Eastern Realm, keeping your family's place in the Citadel. I'll even pronounce you as my heir, until a son is born to me."

"Very reasonable terms."

"You have today to consider them, in the morning we shall have our war."

"You speak of it as if it's a game."

"With your numbers brother, it might just be."

With that said Galvin and his riders turned and made their way back across the field into the very folds of their army. The King led them back through the hill pass to their own camp, speaking no words over the heavy beat of their horses' hooves. Back inside the grand tent the King was neither angered nor nervous; he was steadfast in his iron resolve, hardened by many battles before the one that loomed.

"Sir Darrion we may just win this yet," he said.

"They put far too much trust in their numbers my King."

"Indeed they do, you will ride at once."

"My men are ready and waiting."

On their way to the Eastern Lowlands they had journeyed one thousand strong. The entire Royal Guard, all one hundred of them, glistening at the front of two hundred regular knights and a further seven hundred men at arms. Though once they fell beneath the shadow of the hills, their forces had divided, leaving their knights, save a handful of Royal Guard to stay with the King, concealed behind the hills' eastern edge. Though Sir Darrion was to lead these men, the King had made it very clear that he wanted his Captain by his side when he met with Galvin; to ensure no suspicions were raised.

"You are a cherished friend," said the King as he shook Sir Darrion's hand, "and an even finer Captain. Lead your knights behind their army and I'll meet you in the middle."

"Good luck my King."

"Good luck to you," he replied, "and Ewan, take care of my Captain," he said with a smile.

"I'll do my best," said Ewan as he followed Sir Darrion out of the tent.

The day was late when they finally reached the encampment and rejoined the host of knights. No fires were lit that night and no songs were sung, as they waited hidden and silent amidst the hills.

Sleep did not come for young Ewan, so he sat on the grassy banks over the camp, one of a dozen watchful sentries placed above the men below. As the stars shone out across the sky, Kimber rested gently across his lap, the bow reminding him of Eilidh.

"How are you feeling?" asked Sir Darrion as he came to sit beside him.

"Surprisingly calm," he replied, "though I'm sure tomorrow will be quite different."

"I'd call you a liar if you didn't, though fearing death only means you'll face it much later."

"Another wise proverb from our young Captain," said Ewan with a smile.

"You'll thank me for them one day," replied the knight as he pulled out a cloak, a colourful fox dancing over the fabric, "though I'd hoped you would thank me for *this* now."

The cloak was the dark purple of House Tarn, the fox finely embroidered onto the rich material. Sir Darrion threw if over Ewan's shoulder and let it fall over him.

"This is the cloak my father gave me to wear before my first battle," the knight said, "I know it's not a blue one, but I hope it will do for now."

"It's wonderful Sir Darrion."

"I know you're not a Tarn, but I've come to consider you a brother."

"Thank you," he replied as the night sky continued to pass overhead.

Ewan sat curled up warmly in his new cloak, his Captain at his side. He tried to wonder what tomorrow would bring; close to three hundred knights and their horses lay below, silent and ready to launch a mounted attack behind the enemy. He only hoped that it would be enough.

Chapter Twenty Two

The Witch in the Wood

That very same night, Drusilla was far from her new home in the south, travelling almost the length of the Kingdom, alone and in secret, whilst Galvin was away at battle. The War of Antlers, the people were calling it, a conflict between her two brothers each bearing different heraldry of the same beast, a war their sweet sister had brought upon them with the murder of their father.

The town of Stagsdale lay before her in the distance for she had ridden far into the Eastern Realm. The road would take her to the town's gate but Drusilla turned her horse off the stone path and into the trees of Beachwood. The stars shone brightly as she silently rode through the wood, a long dark hood casting a shadow over her face.

Drusilla had taken a great risk travelling so far alone and without the protection she was used to, though the importance of her journey outweighed the peril it entailed. It had been many months since she had promised Galvin a son, the first pure Greyfell heir to rule the Kingdom of Farreach. Though, despite lying with her brother often and well, her loins still bore no fruit of their dark act.

Long had Drusilla desired her brother's love, for him to see her the way she had always seen him, but she could not forget her promise, a son was the price of such affection and she grew ever fearful of her ability to make it so. The pressure of such a pledge was only joined by the risk of their actions being discovered. As brother and sister their love would be condemned, stripped from them as well as their very lives.

Drusilla continued to ride through the trees as the moonlight struggled through the branches above. Her journey through the Southern Realm had been long and tiresome, in each town and village she was forced to hide her identity out of fear of her true purpose being revealed.

She had stayed at an inn one night in Southern Cross, a town that rested at the heart of four roads not far from the roots of the Sea Shield Mountains. Drusilla sat alone and hidden under her hood, neither looking for trouble nor inviting any. Despite her attempts of concealment, a maid spilled a tray of drinks as she passed by and as she bent down, caught a glance of Drusilla's face in the wavering candle light.

With only that brief look, Drusilla knew that the maid had recognised her, but made no effort to inform those around them. Drusilla was happy with the maid's discretion but was in no way confident that she would keep it. She waited until the young girl left the inn and followed her out into the street as she drew her long dagger.

It was the dark of night and heavy summer rain fell upon the town, the streets were quiet as Drusilla pulled the young maid into an alley and held the steel blade to her throat.

"Do you know who I am girl?" she asked.

The maid nodded in reply, tears with no words.

Drusilla did not want to cut the young girl's throat in that dark alley but the fear in her eyes told her she did not have to.

"Then see that you forget it," she said withdrawing the blade and leaving the maid in the rain.

Drusilla continued to make her way through Beachwood, her horse following an old and overgrown track. Darkness crept beneath the trees as the moon was concealed by clouds, allowing shadowy fingers to lengthen and stretch forth from the gloom. When living in the capitol, Drusilla would often walk through the wood, though it was not as she remembered, now spent of all light, the trees took on new and menacing forms. Their gnarled bark faces and twisted knotted limbs seemed angered by her return, as if they had some unnatural insight into the depths of her betrayal.

The trees may have guessed her treachery but her brother had not, she had yet to divulge such secrets to Galvin. The murder of their father and other past crimes remained undisclosed. In her brother's eyes the King had died of natural causes, not at the hand of his own sister who he now took into his bed.

With Galvin now away at war, it was simple to escape Lord William's city of Black Stone. She travelled freely across the Realm and despite the little affair with the maid and dagger at Southern Cross; Drusilla's journey had been long but uneventful. Even passing through the great stronghold of Gate Keep at the Fringe had been easy. The road curved round the edge of Lake Meridian and the large castle came into view. It was a long thick wall that rose up from the very water of the lake, stretching across the land all the way to the shores of the sea.

From the high towers above her, Drusilla could see the banners of House Sayer flying in the wind, a grey gate on a field of pale green. She rode towards the castle, its tall walls reaching incredible heights. For the enormity of such a structure and how strongly it was garrisoned, it took but a small bag of silver to gain free passage. Both gates on either side of the long tunnel that bore through the heart of the castle, opened as she rode through to the upper Realms.

After crossing the Fringe, the road took Drusilla past the town of Helmsby and then into the trees of Beachwood before Stagsdale. The purpose for such a long and perilous journey resided within the wood, an acquaintance Drusilla believed she had long exhausted all use of.

Her aunt, Nesta Mason, had retreated to the safety of Beachwood after the death of King Adwen, being blamed in some small part by her sister. Nesta had taken up residence amongst the trees and it was her that Drusilla sought out. Her aunt had provided her with a means to death, in the form of the rare substance dreamlock. She had collected the deadly remedy the day before the King died, complaining of severe womanly pains, Nesta had been none the wiser to her plans. Though on this occasion, Drusilla required a means to life.

Galvin was growing ever more impatient for the son that his sister had so convincingly promised him but was yet to grant. Drusilla was fearful that she was unable to facilitate such a promise. She knew of a remedy given to her mother by Nesta, as a means to increase the chances of a woman procuring children, her mother later gave birth to two healthy sons.

Drusilla had travelled almost the entire length of the Kingdom to obtain such a remedy, knowing that her aunt was unaware of the part she played in murdering her own father. Nesta had granted Drusilla the means to take life away from Galvin and now she would allow her to grant it back to him in the form of an heir.

Drusilla had heard rumours of Nesta's whereabouts throughout the Kingdom, an old woman living in the woods, granting healing to those brave enough to seek her out. Nestled in amongst the trees, she came across a small wooden cabin, the round windows gleaming like hot coals, showing there was light from inside.

Drusilla dismounted her horse and walked towards the rough wooden door, all traces of paint torn away by time. She tied her mount to the side of the cabin and raised a fist to knock, though before it fell, the door creaked open and there her aunt stood, her dull red hair gleaming in the soft glow of the small fire.

"What do you want?" her aunt asked the hooded woman at her door.

"To seek your help," replied Drusilla.

"Who are you?" she asked recognising the voice.

Drusilla removed her hood and let her dark hair fall from under it, her aunt gasped as the light of the fire revealed her.

"Drusilla, child what are you doing here?"

"Like I said I need your help aunt."

Nesta studied her, trying to guess her intentions, though after a while she simply gestured Drusilla inside.

"Well come on in then," she finally said, "no point standing outside in the dark."

Drusilla walked inside as her aunt shut the door behind them. The cabin was but a single room with the fire at the far wall. The ceiling hung with all manner of herbs and made the small space even smaller. There were two chairs by the fire and her aunt beckoned her to one as she sat in the other.

"Have you heard what the people are calling you aunt?" asked Drusilla.

"The Witch in the Wood I believe is my preferred title now."

"When I heard I knew it could be none other than you."

"What skills of mine could possibly summon you across the Kingdom?" asked Nesta, "I shall have you know that I'll take no side in your brothers' war."

"I won't make you," she replied, "my coming is of a more personal nature."

"How can an old aunt help her niece?"

"I met someone."

"A southerner?"

"Yes a southerner but a good man regardless," she said sternly, defending her imaginary suitor.

"And you require my skills in what regard?"

"Regarding bearing children."

"I'm sure Lord William has fine people to help you with such problems," said her aunt.

"None that are family," replied Drusilla, "and none that are as skilled as you, my mother benefited from your help as I wish to."

"Your mother and I are not exactly on speaking terms," said her aunt as she pointed around her new accommodation.

"Does that lessen the bond you still share with me?"

"I suppose it doesn't," replied her aunt as she got up and went to a table littered with plants and herbs.

"The remedy I once gave to your mother is a proven recipe, although many can create forms of it, mine holds secret properties unlike any other."

"The exact reason why I journeyed so far," replied Drusilla, "my suitor is growing rather impatient."

"Such is the way of men," said her aunt with her back turned, preparing the remedy, "we women are far more diligent in our resolve."

"We certainly are that."

Her aunt returned to her seat by the fire with a small vial of dark liquid in hand.

"Cunning, some might say," she said as she offered Drusilla the vial.

She took it eagerly, removing the cork and lifting it to her lips but her aunt stopped her, staying her hand.

"You must wait until you next lie with your suitor," said Nesta, "drink it just before and I promise you'll be granted with children."

"Is that how my mother did it?"

"Indeed and she gave birth to twin sons, each strong and healthy even if they did later decide to go to war against each other."

"I still stand by Galvin."

"I know," replied her aunt, "you always have."

Shadow had truly taken hold of the land when she eventually left Nesta's cabin, the trees of Beachwood darker than ever. She bid her aunt farewell and collected her horse, riding back along the way she had come. Through the gaps in the branches above, Drusilla could see a maze of stars overhead, a blanket of studded brilliance. Hope filled her heart as she gripped the small vial in her hand. Pulling her hood back across her head, Drusilla broke free from the trees of Beachwood and steered her horse towards the south.

Chapter Twenty Three

Battle of the Lowlands

The next morning was cool yet beads of sweat still ran from Rhain's forehead, despite wearing a face of iron resolve for those around him, no man was immune to their own nerves, not even a King. He sat upon his horse on the verge of the battlefield as he had done countless times before, though this was the first time wearing a crown. It felt heavy on his head as he looked out towards the long row of hills, the wide pass straight ahead. Everything that morning was grey, the sky and the thousands of men under it were all darker shades of their former colours. Even his father's armour appeared dull, the bright mix of silver and gold muted with the shyness of the sun.

Beyond the pass in the hills lay his brother's host, Rhain hoped it was not a grassy gateway to his own armies' failure. Galvin had not lied about his numbers, the united force of the Southern and Western Realms stood ten thousand strong. Despite their superior numbers, they had indeed fallen into Ewan's plan and gathered further inland to meet Rhain's army.

"I see they came without cavalry," said Michael who was by his side, "though not without a shortage of men."

"Let us hope they think the same of us," replied Rhain.

"How is your young fox fairing?"

"I've had no word from Sir Darrion; we can only trust that he has succeeded, though if he has not, I'm afraid we'll learn of it far too late."

"Well we didn't come all this way for nothing," said Michael with a bearded smile.

At his back Rhain had five thousand men made up of infantry and archers, any knights that remained were on foot, merged within his army. The rest were in the hands of his Captain, a mounted assault that would hopefully break the far superior numbers of the south. Rhain trusted in Sir Darrion, though without his rear charge, the King's army would undoubtedly fail.

Michael was mounted by Rhain's side, he sat huge and gleaming in his bronze armour with his bear helmet tucked under one of his mighty arms. Arcoss his friend's back rested his mighty axe Mane, a huge and gleaming array of bronze and honed black steel. Also by the King's side were the other Lords of the Northern and Eastern Realm. Lord Peter was clad in bronze the same as his Thane. Despite his face looking old and weathered; Rhain knew he still had many years on the battlefield left in him.

Sir Darrion's father, Lord Dale, was also not a young man, though he was in no way frail and still filled the armour of his youth, with a cloak flowing behind him the deep purple of House Tarn. Rhain was lucky to have such experienced and battle seasoned men supporting him. He only wished he felt as grateful to have his son by his side.

Richard proudly held the antlered black steel helmet gifted to him by Tristan before he died. The work was indeed impressive, the dark metal finely etched with patterns that appeared to change and shift as they danced across the steel. Without the helmet on, Richard still looked like a boy, though it was his reluctance to scratch the black steel that confirmed as much.

Rhain turned in his saddle and looked out over his army; it was divided into four sections. The main bulk of the force lay in the middle, a large collection of infantry from the Eastern Realm. On either side of the centre attack were two smaller clusters of infantry from the Northern Realm, forming the western and eastern flanks. Atop the hills on either side of the pass, were the archers, a host of skilled northern bowmen.

"Lord Dale," said Rhain, "you will accompany me and help lead the men of the east in the centre attack."

"Yes my King."

"Lord Peter, you have the eastern flank, and Michael," the King said turning to the Thane, "Ardal has command of the archers, controlling the higher ground. You my friend will lead the western flank."

"Just like old times," said Michael with another smile.

Through the hills there came a rumble like a gathering storm, the ground seemed to shake as a rhythmic pound grew in the stillness of that grey morning. Far in the distance the enemy was on the move.

"Archers!" the King shouted as his words were repeated throughout the army like a wave.

He watched Ardal high above them as he nocked an arrow and drew the back the string, aiming high and far. As he did this hundreds followed; the hills bristled with row upon row of arrows standing ready, struggling to be let loose upon the vast host that advanced. The King raised his hand to signal the attack.

"What are you doing?" shouted Prince Richard, "they're clearly out of range!"

"You have much to learn about warfare," replied his father.

"And about northern archers," added Michael.

"Be careful to mind who you address uncle," said Richard angrily.

"Will you give the Stag Prince a slap or shall I?" Lord Peter asked Rhain.

"Be my guest," the King replied, not even turning around.

Behind him Rhain heard a mailed hand crash into the mouth of his son, it was a hard lesson for a father to allow but one he knew was long overdue. Richard did not cry or argue Rhain simply heard him ride away. As the sound of his son's galloping horse faded into the distance, he let his raised hand finally fall.

"Fire!" he shouted as the sky darkened with a sea of flying arrows.

The enemy were indeed out of range, at least for regular archers, though not the skilled bowmen of the Northern Realm, their arrows could fly further and with more accuracy than any in the Kingdom. Before the first volley had even fallen upon the enemy, Ardal had led a second. More arrows took flight and again the sky darkened.

The barrage rained down upon the enemy from the hills, with very few arrows finding the ground. Hundreds fell as they continued to advance, a third volley was fired and then a forth, relentlessly keeping up the hail of arrows.

"It is time," said Rhain to his commanders, "my northern Lords, when Lord Dale and I meet them with the centre attack, keep the eastern and western flanks hard against the hills, force their numbers to cluster in the entrance to the pass. Our archers will continue the volleys; their accuracy will spare them striking our own men. Hold your lines and do not press too far with the attack, let our arrows whittle down their numbers until Sir Darrion and our cavalry can charge them from the rear. Is that understood?"

"Yes my King," they all said together.

"Then get to your posts and good luck."

He watched his Lords ride out to their separate positions and then spurred his own horse down the frontline of his army as the enemy drew ever closer, arrows still flying from the hills.

"Men! The hour is upon us!" he shouted out over the ranks, "there will be songs of this day, of valour and heroism. The men beyond those hills seek to steal your names from them, are you going to let them?"

His men shouted and cheered as they beat their shields.

"The enemy has been waiting to wipe your deeds from the pages of eternity! I say we make them wait a little longer!"

Swords were drawn and shields were raised as the King's army swelled with a mighty roar.

Rhain dismounted his horse and readied his shield; joining the ranks on foot with a handful of remaining Royal Guard knights as his protectors. He would fight side by side with the soldiers that had gathered for his cause. Shoulder to shoulder he stood equal to the faithful men he had become proud to rule.

"For Farreach!" Rhain shouted as he drew Sable, the black blade pointing towards the now rushing enemy seen through the grassy hills.

The King broke into a run towards the pass with five thousand men charging at his back. The Battle of the Eastern Lowlands had begun.

Rhain dashed amongst a sea of swords and spears, he and his army filling the wide gap in the hills. The enemy too neared the pass, their broad ranks becoming narrower to enter. Just as they were about to meet, a well timed and precise volley of arrows cut through the entire frontline of the enemy, so near that Rhain felt the deadly shafts race just over his head.

As the first wave of enemies fell beneath the northern bows, the King's army came to a sudden halt just before the entrance to the hills, forming a crescent moon shaped line, beckoning the enemy into the pass. Shields were raised and lined with spears, as the unprepared second line of the south met nothing but a wall of steel.

The vastly greater foe broke upon Rhain's men like water on rocks, shattering themselves against the readied shields.

There Rhain's army held them, a well formed and united front, holding strong against the sea that longed to wash over them. The King pushed hard against his shield, driving the enemy back, using Sable to cut down those that made it through. The volley of arrows continued from high above, falling flawlessly close to the wall of shields.

To his left Rhain saw that his men had forced back the enemy, revealing a small pocket of open ground.

"Knights of the Royal Guard!" he shouted.

In front of the relinquished space, shields parted revealing a row of readied spears.

"Drive them back!" Rhain roared.

Spears took flight as their honed leaf shaped points crashed into the enemy lines, several cutting down two men with a single shaft.

This continued for several hours, the wall of shields holding strong as the arrows and spears continued to fly. Some southerners attempted to climb the hills on their flanks but in their heavy armour it was a slow and unwise effort, making it easy for Ardal's archers to pick off any who tried for their higher ground. Michael and Lord Peter had succeeded in forcing the enemy to cluster, leaving no room between their men and the hills. With the eastern and western flank pressing the sides of the enemy, Rhain's army formed a long curve within the pass, continuing to force the opposition to flow into their midst. He knew that it would not last; the hills would not protect them forever. It was only a matter of time before Galvin's superior numbers washed over Michael and Lord Peter on the flanks, when that happened Rhain's army would undoubtedly break.

Galvin was no stranger to a battlefield nor was Lord William, but Rhain did not see them amongst the thousands of men that they had sent against him. Perhaps Lord William thought that losing Galvin would mean losing his cause, the fight to claim the Kingdom would indeed prove difficult if the claimant was killed in battle.

House Fyrth had poured its wealth into the armies of the south; they were clad in fine armour and wielded well forged weapons, though despite their numbers and impressive arsenal, they seemed to lack the discipline instilled within Rhain's men. Their line was long but it lay scattered and unorganised, not able to make use of their numbers in the grassy pass. They broke upon the King's wall of shields not as one with the constant hail of arrows falling around them.

The battle appeared promising, though by the time morning was coming to a close, Rhain watched as the enemy began to concentrate on their flanks, rallied by none other than the colossal Sir Stefan Barron. Sir Darrion had told him of how he wounded the great knight at the Battle of Helmsby, though now revived he continued the assault to weaken the sides of Rhain's army.

"Inform Ardal to concentrate his archers on the flanks!" ordered Rhain, "they must hold until Sir Darrion brings aid!"

By the time the archers had received word, the flanks were already beginning to fail, their arrows only just holding back the tide of southerners led by Sir Stefan. Rhain heard their northern bows singing from the hills, the countless volleys barely stopping the advancing enemy, each sharp twang of their strings more desperate than the last.

With Michael and Lord Peter struggling to hold control of their flanks, Rhain's wall of shields was also beginning to fail. The once tight and impregnable line now showed gaps and weaknesses that were growing with every moment.

"Hold firm!" he shouted through the ranks, quelling the despair in his voice.

With the sun now high overhead, Rhain watched clearly as the line of their flanks broke under the enemy's vast numbers. The northern infantry had stood as two defiant bulwarks that had held strong against the rushing force, but no more. Their lines were scattered as the enemy host flowed further into the pass, gaining more and more of the higher ground.

The knight of the Royal Guard that stood by Rhain's side, whose shield had been defiantly locked with his own as he fought for both his King and Realm, gasped as a spear was thrust passed his guard and buried itself in his chest. Rhain was close enough to feel the dying man's last breath on his cheek before he fell, joining the many hundreds that had died for his cause that day. Hope left the King and before his men could close the gap in the line, the enemy broke through, knocking Rhain to the grass.

The ground hit him hard and he lay in a daze of despair, knowing that it had all been in vain. The light cracked through the clouds as he watched the enemy run over him, his army lay broken and he had failed. Though as his senses returned to him, it was not victory he saw in the southerners' eyes, but fear, they were not advancing but trying to flee.

The ground shook beneath him, a heavy beat ran through the earth that he was not sure was real. Rhain struggled to his knees and what he saw brought laughter to his broken heart. Crashing through the enemy ranks from behind came nearly three hundred mounted knights with the bulk of the Royal Guard leading the charge; their armour glistening in the sun, their lances long and sharp. The horses too were clad in steel, streaked with the colours of House Greyfell, a shining beacon of hope that tore its way towards the hill pass, riding over the surprised and unprepared enemy.

Rhain's army cheered and the welcomed arrival of the knights, his trust in his Captain had not been ill placed. His men were filled with new hope and a sudden surge of energy.

"For Farreach!" roared their King once more as they charged the now fleeing enemy that lay trapped between two fronts.

The battle ended soon after, the broken and fleeing enemy putting up no further fight. Those that were not cut down by Sir Darrion's cavalry fled west, Galvin, Lord William and his Captain amongst them. Rhain and his army had won the day, though not without great loss. The King climbed the walls of the hill pass, looking out over the blood stained Lowlands, there he was met by his old friend Michael, still clutching the shaft of his mighty axe.

"I see you're still alive," the bear of man said as he approached.

"It would appear someone beyond life has a sense of humour."

"Indeed," replied Michael as he panted heavily.

His large battle axe hung loosely in his hand. His bronze armour bore many scratches and his right arm lay bandaged. Rhain was overjoyed to see him alive and knew that his large friend would shake off such a wound in a matter of days.

"This time I thought I had finally gotten rid of you," Rhain said with a smile.

"It will take more than insurmountable odds and almost certain defeat to rid yourself of this old bear."

"In that case I'll have to plan something even more perilous next time."

"I heard it wasn't even your plan," said Michael returning his smile, "I hope you know it's only a matter of time before he asks for Eilidh's hand in marriage."

"Let's hope not too soon, as a father I try not to think about such things."

"I suppose I'm lucky to have had three sons," he replied with a booming laugh, "speaking of which, where did yours get to?"

"Nowhere near the battle I'm sure, I've sent a host of knights to go look for him."

"He's just young Rhain," said Michael, "he'll come around eventually."

"He certainly has a lot to learn before he becomes King."

"There's time enough yet for that."

They both looked out over the vast field where the wounded were still being gathered. Despite those that they had lost, it had been a truly great victory, one that Galvin and Lord William would not soon forget. The War of Antlers was in no way over, but for the time being they had gained the upper hand.

"What now?" asked Michael.

"Home old friend," he replied, "now we go home."

Chapter Twenty Four

Promise in the Rain

The high white walls of Gleamport grew steadily in the distance, rising out of the land like shimmering panes of marble as they had done when Ewan had first seen them, all those months ago. The midsummer sun hung over his head as he rode towards the capitol with the Lowlands now behind them. They had brought about a swift end to the southern force; arriving just when they were needed, for the King's lines lay on the verge of breaking.

Night was still upon them when they rode to towards the battle, staying within the rolling hills to avoid detection, only turning southwest as they neared the enemy, giving themselves a wide birth to attack the pass directly behind the southern force. They knew that they had to make haste in order to reach the Lowlands in time, though they also had to arrive with the energy needed for both man and steed to fight.

Ewan remembered the wind through his helmet and the roar in his ears as they charged the enemy from the rear. On his horse he galloped amidst the storm of mounted knights; they fell upon the opposition in a state of disbelief and fear as they rode them down. The enemy had fled to the snowy borders of the Western Realm, beaten but not defeated. The King and his army left the blood stained fields of the Lowlands behind and now they were returning home.

Ewan's *simple* plan had won them the day, before the battle his name was barely whispered outside the capitol, now it was shouted across the Kingdom. Though despite his new renowned fame, the only person whose face he wished to look upon was Eilidh's. Her bow had proved useful and her scarf had been a peaceful comfort amongst the turmoil of war, but it was her third gift that he now longed for, her heart.

Riding towards the capitol with Sir Darrion and the King at his side, Ewan watched as the white city filled his eyes. Behind them rode a small host of knights of the Royal Guard, escorting them to the safety of Gleamport. As the gates opened before them, the Citadel of Kings shone like a glinting jewel at the tip of Greyfell's Sword in the distance.

Crowds had gathered along the main street of the city, cheering their victorious King as they lay flowers across their path. The King and his Captain waved at the applauding host but Ewan noticed they were shouting his name also. He too raised his hand in a wave and it was met with smiles and more cheers.

Leaving the noise of the crowd behind, the gates of the Sword parted and they began to cross the length of its blade. The cool sea air kissed their faces as they made their way towards the Citadel, now towering overhead like a majestic white statue. At the base of the steps stood the Princess next to her mother, both women were dressed in fine blue silk, for Eilidh did indeed look like a woman, young, fair and the one Ewan loved. The battle had made him realise his feelings, for he knew what it felt like to know that he may never see her face again or kiss her lips. Now that Ewan knew he loved her it was hard to remember a time when he did not, as if it had always been so.

They entered the courtyard and dismounted their horses, Ewan and the King made their way across to the steps and both mother and daughter ran towards them and fell into their arms. Before any words escaped his mouth, Ewan kissed Eilidh deeply, his hand running through her soft fiery hair. How he had missed her, so much so that neither of them felt the eyes of her parents watching them as they kissed.

"If you don't mind," coughed King Rhain, "a father is still allowed some degree of modesty concerning his daughter."

"Sorry father," said Eilidh as she broke from the kiss and embraced him, "I've missed you both so much."

"I know child," said the King, "I've missed you also, but before you steal Ewan away from me I'm afraid I must steal him away from you."

"What ever for?" asked Eilidh.

"I require his council."

"You've only just returned," said his wife, "can't it wait until morning?"

"I'm afraid it cannot, this young man's advice has become quite invaluable."

Ewan had no notion of what further council the King required but it had to have been of some importance for him to leave his wife and daughter so promptly on their return.

"Come my lad," said the King as he wrapped his arm around Ewan, leading him up the steps to the Citadel.

"Find me later," whispered Eilidh before her father escorted him through the doors.

The King silently led Ewan through the halls of the Citadel, still not knowing what council of his was so urgent. Though as his firm arm remained around him, Ewan started to think that he was in trouble, perhaps for the long kiss he had granted his daughter. His mind raced over versions of the same apology, thinking of ways to quell a father's rage.

As fear set in they finally arrived outside the King's chamber, who opened the door and led Ewan inside, only then did he release him from his grasp. The King walked out onto the balcony and gestured for Ewan to come join him. Fear now overwhelmed him as he pictured himself being thrown out over Royal Bay.

"It appears we have a problem," said the King as Ewan stepped out onto the balcony, "one regarding my only daughter."

"Firstly I just wanted to apologise..." started Ewan.

"My dear lad," interrupted the King with kindness falling over his face, "there's no need to apologise, you love her don't you?"

The question took Ewan by surprise, he had told no one of his feelings for Eilidh, least of all her father.

"How did you know?"

"Believe it or not but I was young once," replied the King, "I can see it in your eyes; it's the same look I had when I fell for her mother."

"I do love her," said Ewan softly.

It was the first time saying it out loud and yet no words had ever come easier.

"I know you do lad, though after that kiss, I'm sure half the Citadel knows as well."

Ewan smiled and then something stirred in him that he did not expect, a feeling that gave no warning.

"I want to marry her," he said suddenly.

The King said nothing; he simply studied Ewan in silence. The gentle waves could be heard lapping on the Fallings Cliffs far below, a rhythmic sound that made the moment last an age.

"Lord Michael warned me this would happen," said the King finally, "though I didn't expect it so soon."

"The battle changed everything," Ewan replied honestly.

"War has that effect; it strengthens bonds and reveals unknown truths."

"I mean to wed your daughter but I will not ask your permission, I believe the decision lies with her alone," said Ewan with a sudden boldness, "I would, however, ask your blessing."

Again the King stood in silence, letting the firm statement set before answering. Ewan knew that they were bold words to speak to any father, especially one that was also a King. After a long pause the silence was eventually broken.

"Better words have never been spoken to a father," he said with happiness shining on his face, "I let Tristan betroth my daughter for the support of his father's Realm but love is a far more binding promise than that of any army Ewan. I will not tell Eilidh to marry you; you're right in that the decision lies only with her and you have my blessing to ask her for it."

"Thank you my King," said Ewan, "know that I cherish each and every moment with your daughter, I'll protect her for as long as I'm able."

"Well said lad, I can't think of a finer young man for Eilidh. You have proven yourself loyal to her time and time again."

"Thank you," said Ewan as he offered out his hand.

"No thank you," replied the King as he met the hand in a firm shake, "and not just for this but for everything you have done for Eilidh. It's rare in these days that people marry for love, I'm happy to see that my daughter is one of the few, that's if she does indeed say yes," he said with a final smile.

When Ewan had entered the King's chamber he could not have guessed he would ask for Eilidh's hand in marriage, for it was as much a surprise to himself as it was to her father, though it was indeed true. He had fallen in love with the girl he had met on the shore on that first fateful day, everything that had happened since had only brought him closer to her. Now, with her father's blessing, he intended to propose.

Ewan made his way to his own chamber without going to find Eilidh as she had asked. The King had told him that a third party may have something to help him with the proposal and would call on him later. The Kingdom was still very much at war but Ewan was only nervous about the question he would soon ask. He dared not see the Princess out of fear of raising suspicion; it was a hard choice for since his return they had shared but one kiss and fewer words.

Ewan found that his chamber was cool with a midsummer's breeze, though it did not reach him under his layers of leather and steel. He slowly shed his armour and after he carefully folded Sir Darrion's purple cloak, he let the rest of the battle stained attire fall to the marble floor. The air brushed over his skin and washed away the toil that had been trapped under his clothes.

A large bowl of steaming water lay by the fire alongside fresh garments, including the light green tunic that Sister Margret had made for him and Eilidh liked so much. The water was hot and refreshing as he washed, filling his skin with new life. Though his body was tired and sore, he had sustained no wounds from battle little more than scrapes and bruises; he knew that many had not been as lucky. Despite the cavalry charge winning the day, many knights had been unhorsed and killed in the attack.

Once finished washing, Ewan dressed in the fresh clothes laid out for him, the clean and light fabric feeling unnatural after many hard days in his heavy armour. Just as he lay down on his bed, seeking the softness and comfort that the ground had failed to grant him, there was a firm knock at the door.

"Are you decent my boy?" asked the voice of an elderly woman.

Ewan got up to open the door, bracing himself for the bustling nature of Sister Margret. Though as he pulled the heavy wooden door aside the King's mother stood waiting.

"Ewan," she said with a smile, "it's good to see you well."

"And you Lady Elora, please come in."

He gestured her inside and offered her a seat by the fire where he joined her. She too was dressed in fine blue silk, her reddish grey hair falling softly over one shoulder.

"I suppose you're wondering why us women are all dressed the same," she said as she saw Ewan notice the colour of her gown, "it's a tradition for the women of House Greyfell to welcome back the men wearing the colours of our family."

"Well you look graceful as ever my Lady."

"Graceful is simply a nice word for getting old," she replied with a playful scorn.

Ewan enjoyed the company of Eilidh's grandmother; old age had certainly not dulled her humour.

"You wouldn't happen to be a certain third party by any chance?" he asked.

"And if I wasn't? You could have just ruined your perfectly placed element of surprise," she said with a grin, "thankfully for you I am indeed said third party and have something very special for you."

From the many folds of her silk gown, Lady Elora produced a small ornate box made of pale white wood. She carefully opened the lid, revealing a delicate and beautiful ring. The band was of soft white gold and the single marquise shaped stone glittered a brilliant light blue.

"This is the very same ring that Rhain's father proposed to me with Ewan, it was meant for Prince Richard to give to his bride one day but seeing as my grandson is still sulking alone somewhere, I'd be honoured if you would give it to Eilidh."

"The honour would be mine," said Ewan as he took the ring and admired it, "the stone is beautiful."

"It's a rare water diamond from the Sea of Glass," she said, "there's but a handful in the Kingdom and it's said that there are enough faces on the stone to represent each and every wave. King Adwen wanted something very special for me and I think you'll agree that he succeeded."

A small tear fell down Lady's Elora cheek as she looked at the diamond her late husband once gifted her.

"Thank you Lady Elora," said Ewan as he closed the box, "I know that it will mean everything to Eilidh."

"My dear boy you're very welcome, such gifts are meant for the young and I know you'll make my granddaughter happy."

Lady Elora departed with a graceful flutter of blue silk, leaving Ewan alone with the ring. He stared deep into the many faces, almost hearing the waves as they crashed into each other with perfect brilliance. Holding the ring brought a smile to Ewan's face, it made everything seem far more real and his nerves were now matched with excitement.

He waited until evening before he went to find Eilidh, the ring concealed within its small box and stowed away in his pocket. He knocked on her chamber door and the friendly face of Sister Margret answered.

"Master Ewan," she said, "I see you thought you'd grace us with your presence finally."

"Well I know you simply can't get enough of me," he replied, matching her wit and placing a light kiss on her cheek.

Sister Margret blushed and let out a small giggle as she gestured him inside. By now Ewan knew that she was all bark and no bite and that she did in fact adore him. Though despite also adoring her, she was not the one he had come to see. Eilidh came in from the balcony and brushed back the hair the wind had blown across her beautiful face, her fair skin glowing from the summer sun.

"I was beginning to think I would never get to see you," said Eilidh, "only to find it's now Sister Margret you wish to kiss instead of me."

"Beauty is a cruel mistress," replied the old woman, "you can't blame me for that."

"Indeed you can't," said Ewan, "though I thought I could make it up to the young Princess by taking her out for an evening ride."

"I believe that should suffice," said Eilidh with a smile.

Ewan led her from the chamber and as he closed the door behind them, he saw Sister Margret wink and silently mouth good luck through the gap; it seemed nothing escaped her.

They walked hand in hand and spoke as if they had never been parted. A smile shone on both their faces as they made their way to the stable. They entered the courtyard and the sun hung low in the eastern sky, mirrored in the glistening waters of Royal Bay. Collecting their horses they rode out across the Sword. The couple slowed to a steady pace once beyond the city's walls and followed the line of cliffs down to the shores of Beachwood to their usual spot.

They sat down in the sand where they had first met, their horses left in the trees. Many times since their stolen night had they journeyed back to that special place. As they spoke and laughed, Ewan fondled the ring box in his pocket, wondering when would be the best time to present it. Though as the sun continued to die behind the gentle waves, that time never came.

As dusk fell into night, he finally came to the moment he had been circling for so long and reached for the ring, but as his fingers grazed over the smooth white wood of the box, the clouds above erupted in a shower of heavy summer rain, mirroring the suddenness and power of his feelings. They ran back to their horses and rode back up the cliffs to the city, Ewan cursing the untimely weather as they galloped through the downpour.

Back at the Citadel, with their horses returned, the rain had not lessened. Eilidh held Ewan's hand and ran across the courtyard, leading him up the steps. He knew that it was now or never so he pulled his hand from Eilidh's grasp and stood defiantly in the rain.

"Eilidh wait."

She stopped a few steps above, water running down her face, her wet hair still glowing a fiery red. He climbed up to meet her and took both her hands in his. He trembled though not from the rain, for it was a warm summer shower, he refused to cower under his nerves but their presence still lingered.

"All the time I was away I thought of you," he said, "it was here on these steps that you told me I had your heart, though you had mine when you first opened your eyes that day on the beach and I've loved you every moment since."

Ewan got down on one knee on the steps and brought out the box from his pocket, opening the lid to reveal her grandmother's glistening ring inside. Eilidh gasped as she suddenly realised what was happening.

"Will you marry me?" he said softly as he stared up at her through the rain.

"I love you too," she said as tears rolled down her cheeks, "yes! Ewan of course yes!"

Ewan slipped the ring over her slender finger and stood up to meet her lips. The kiss was longer than before and the rain applauded as it danced heavily around them.

Chapter Twenty Five

Bottled Hope

Months later, in the last day of summer, the wind blew swift and fair as Drusilla looked out over the southern fortress of Black Stone. Her journey to the trees of Beachwood and back had been long and lonely, though she had obtained what she sought. Her aunt's vial was clutched tightly in her hand, where it would remain until needed out of fear of losing what she had risked so much to gain.

From her high chamber the island city stretched out before her, the brisk wind scattering her long dark hair as she waited. Drusilla's gaze never strayed far from the great black bridge, hewn out of the rock that led to the mainland. She longed to hear the horn's call cut through the air as her brother returned to the city. He and Lord William had left for battle weeks before she had travelled north; it now seemed a lifetime since Drusilla had looked upon her brother's face.

The news of Galvin's defeat had spread across the Realms, disheartening those that had once supported their cause. It was but the first great battle of the War of Antlers but Rhain had done much to show his strength. Drusilla knew that Galvin would not be happy, he never took defeat lightly and the knowledge that his sister was no closer to providing the heir she had promised would only anger him further. Drusilla had spent many nights staring at the vial of dark liquid, placing all her remaining hope in the remedy her aunt had gifted her.

"You must wait until you next lie with your suitor," she heard as she remembered her aunt's words, "drink it just before and I promise you'll be granted with children."

So Drusilla kept the vial, waiting to be reunited with her brother. After the hardship of battle she hoped he would look for comfort in her arms, allowing her to make use of the remedy and finally fulfil her costly promise. After the defeat at the Lowlands, he and Lord William took refuge in the Western Realm to which they fled. There they had stayed for many weeks before starting their journey home across the Sea of Sails, making their way down the coast by ship to the shores south of Black Stone.

Drusilla leaned forward as a horn's long bellow rose up and through the city. She saw a host of riders approaching the bridge, smiling at the sight of many red banners depicting proud black stags. The glistening white portrayal of Highthorn had forever been the heraldry of Drusilla's royal House. She had chosen to leave the white halls and blue banners of her family behind, all for the deep love she bore her brother.

Amidst the roaring black stags, also flew the bloody osprey of Lord William and the western banners of House Gillain, a silver snow owl flying over an ice white field. As Drusilla watched the host of rippling colours make their way through the city, she knew that Lord Farris must have travelled across the Sea of Sails alongside Lord William and her brother. The old Lords of the Western Realm rarely left their snowy wastes unless their own interests were in peril. After the death of their sons, Lord Farris and his Thane committed to the side that could grant them vengeance alongside a profit, believing the south would undoubtedly win. Drusilla knew that the defeat at the Lowlands may have lessened their certainty.

As the banners disappeared out of sight into the depths of the keep below, Drusilla left her window and hurried out of the chamber. She half walked and half ran down the halls, the anticipation of seeing Galvin growing with every second, all the while tightly clutching the small vial in her hand. As she entered a long corridor, Drusilla's wealth of excitement fell to the very bottom of her heart.

Towards her walked her brother Galvin, looking bold and handsome in his newly forged black steel armour. He was in no state of defeat, no need of comfort, for a smile spread over his lips but it was not from the sight of her. On his arm there was a beautiful young woman that walked beside him; her hair was golden and her face full of youth. She was a lot younger than Drusilla and fair as the morning sun. Her eyes were a deep blue and in them lay the likeness of Lady Caitlyn, Galvin's departed wife.

In the time since her death, Drusilla had never succeeded in making her brother smile as he did now. The young woman was none other than Lucille Gillain, daughter of Lord Farris and said to be the most beautiful maiden in all of Farreach. Drusilla had met her on several royal occasions, often by her brother's side, Sir Thomas, her beauty growing with every year. The Kingdom knew of Lucille's desire to one day become Queen, it appeared she had now found her King.

Galvin and his party walked right past Drusilla without even gracing her with a glance. Her brother was too busy staring into the beautiful young eyes that reminded him so much of his wife, that he did not even realise his sister was standing there, eagerly awaiting him. A single tear fell down Drusilla's face that went as unnoticed as herself with the group disappearing around the corner.

Rage built up inside her and she clenched her fists to save from screaming, a small crack of glass echoed through her tight fingers. Fear ran through her as she remembered the vial in her hand. As she opened her fist she let out a breath of relief, a hairline crack had appeared on the neck of the glass but the vial remained intact, safeguarding its precious content.

Drusilla was used to being ignored by her brother and having to fight for his attention and love, though never at the hands of another woman, one far younger and fairer than she. Galvin had lain with Drusilla, reciprocating the love she had always felt for him. To be held close and then simply cast aside broke her heart. She had promised to grant him with a son, a pure Greyfell heir that she believed would consolidate their love forever.

Drusilla clutched the small vial once again, this time more gently. She walked down the corridor in silence, her shadow against the wall and the soft sound of her footsteps the only things keeping her from being a ghost. She too rounded the corner, her eyes fixed on the stone floor.

"Ouch!" she screamed as someone tread on her toe.

As she looked up it was none other than Stewart.

"We really should stop meeting like this," he said with a smile.

"You mean you should start looking where you place your feet," she replied sternly, still angered by her brother.

"I'm sorry my Lady," he said earnestly, "I meant no offence."

"I know you didn't Stewart," she said regretfully, "I just want to be alone."

He placed a hand softly under her chin and raised her eyes to his.

"Someone so beautiful should never be alone," he said without an ounce of shyness.

Drusilla did not see the coy and silent man he had once been, his eyes met hers instead of the ground or some dusty book. He looked at her then the way Galvin seldom did, the way she had always wanted her brother to. Drusilla held Stewart's head and pulled his lips towards hers into a kiss. She did it mostly because she wanted to, but a small part of her hoped Galvin was watching; to make him feel as unwanted as he had done to her.

The kiss was long but another tear ran down Drusilla's face as she parted her lips from Stewart's. All her life she had been a slave to the feelings she had for her brother, the lengths she went to in order to gain his affection never seemed too strong. Yet despite all she had done, all the lives she had ruined, she remained at the mercy of his love, ever struggling to have it returned to her. Stewart was not like his father, he was a good and honest man. However, she was not free to love him, her heart still belonged to Galvin and for better or for worse it always would.

"What's wrong?" asked Stewart as he caught the tear falling from her cheek.

"I just can't."

"You kissed me," he said with a look of confusion mixed with sadness.

"I'm sorry but I shouldn't have."

"Is there another?" he asked.

"There always has been."

Drusilla said nothing more; she simply turned and walked away. As she left Stewart standing alone, in that moment she both loved and hated Galvin. She knew that her brother never forced her to have feelings for him, she only wanted someone to blame and placing it on herself was simply too difficult.

She hurried back to her chamber and shut the door, leaning her back against the heavy wood to ensure the world was sealed behind. For the first time since she was a young girl, Drusilla wished she could embrace her father and hear his gentle words. By her own hand she had cast him from this life, all in the name of love. Suddenly, as remorse took hold of her, that simply was no longer reason enough.

In that moment Drusilla remembered that as a child all her problems and tears could be cured within her father's arms. She had loved him dearly and his only fault was trying to see his daughter happy. The marriage he had arranged with

Sir Darrion would have broken her, so she had murdered him to be with Galvin and now she lay broken all the more.

Her love for her brother had consumed her, laying waste to the lives of everyone she cared about including herself. It was then that she remembered her aunt's remedy; the vial still lay clutched in her hand. At the very edge of hope she still believed that giving Galvin a son would ensure it had not all been in vain, to bring a bright new life out of the wake of death and deceit.

Night came swiftly that evening, rushing in from the western sky to lay a dark starless cloak over the land. The waters of Lake Titus rested calm and cold, a soft mist kissing the still surface. By pale candle light Drusilla walked the stone halls, every bit of her resolve bottled in the small vial. Galvin's eyes may have wandered to another but Drusilla was intent on holding true to her promise of granting him an heir. She would not turn her back on their love after it had cost them so much already, whether her brother knew the price or not.

A dim flame lit the outside of Galvin's chamber, there Drusilla stood, holding the glass vial up to the light. She wondered how something so small could grant her the life she so desperately sought. Placing all hope in the remedy she opened the vial and put it to her lips, allowing the dark liquid to trickle down her throat. It was surprisingly warm but retained no taste, filling her with a vitalised and refreshed feeling.

With the vial empty, Drusilla placed her hand on the wooden door and pushed the metal hinges into submission. It slowly opened, revealing Galvin's faintly lit chamber inside. As usual her brother sat at his desk, pondering over many maps and scrolls. His head lifted as she entered, finally noticing her presence.

"Sweet sister," he said as he got up and embraced her, "how I have missed you."

"More than that pretty little thing on your arm?"

Galvin stood surprised, an awkward and embarrassed expression falling over his face.

"You mean Lucille?" he asked, "she's here at the request of Lord William not me."

"You certainly didn't seem to mind."

"Jealously doesn't suit you sister," he said angrily.

"And you don't suit her!" she shouted, "or have you forgotten our love?"

"Our love came at a price," he said sternly, "you told me you would give me a son. Where is he? Is my so called heir here?"

"I'm able to give you one now," she said desperately presenting the empty vial.

At that moment the dark room grew darker, she felt faint and all light faded as Drusilla began to fall. The stone floor came rushing towards her too quick for Galvin to intervene. The chamber was a blur as a rushing fever washed over her trembling frame. Galvin lay over her, though his words could not be heard.

She saw the empty glass vial roll from her hand where it had been clutched safely for so long. The fever took hold of her as the room continued to darken. Drusilla had been a fool but worst of all, as she lay trembling, she knew she deserved it. In that moment as summer died, so did she.

Chapter Twenty Six

A Journey North

Autumn had begun to take hold over the land of Farreach. Evening was drawing in as Ewan looked out from the great northern city of Oakenhold, the trees of Forest Isle stretching out far beyond the horizon. The city lay a stronghold amongst the trees, the walls rising from beneath the leaves. There Ewan stood, on the tall battlements, at the tip of the Northern Realm in the home of House Dunharren.

His proposal to Eilidh in the rain seemed a life time ago, for much had happened since. The days that followed their engagement were a blur of excitement that spread through the capitol. The War of Antlers was far from over and the prospect of battle had grown all too familiar. A royal wedding gave the people a reason to celebrate; the streets of Gleamport shed the heavy burden of conflict and rejoiced at their union.

The flawless water diamond sat perfectly on the young Princess' slender finger, glinting in the eyes of the many that asked to look upon it. His sudden choice to marry her had not been regretted, each breath she took only made his decision clearer. They had little time together once the planning of their wedding began, stolen moments in quiet corners of the Citadel did not come often enough.

Eilidh had told Ewan of her wish to be married under the Older Oak in the north, as her mother and father had done. Though it touched the King that his daughter would make such a request, he was reluctant to endorse it. The victory of the Lowlands had won them little time and the threat of war still loomed over the land, undertaking such a journey could undo all their progress.

Eilidh soon got her wish; the King saw how their wedding brought a sense of hope to the Kingdom, uplifting the people's spirits with a vision of life beyond war. Preparations were made for the entire royal family to journey to the Northern Realm, to be guests of Lord Michael on Forest Isle. Ewan had seen much of the eastern lands of Farreach, though still longed to walk in the legendary forests of the wild north that lay above.

Their travelling company would also include the once lost Stag Prince, who had returned to the capitol not long after his sister's proposal. After hearing about him being struck by Lord Peter and fleeing the field, Ewan thought he would return worse than before, though this was not so. Despite not accounting for his whereabouts, Prince Richard was apologetic and almost humble, qualities Ewan never thought he even possessed.

The morning for their journey soon came, Eilidh had eluded the watchful eyes of Sister Margret once again and she had fallen asleep the night before in Ewan's arms. As the morning light fell upon the Citadel there she was still, wrapped in his loyal grasp. Ewan's eyes opened and let the room fill his sleepy gaze. Eilidh lay beside him, her fiery red hair dashed over the pillow. Her heavy breathing told him she was still asleep and he did not have the heart to disturb her dreams.

Placing a soft kiss on her cheek he gently left her in bed, though not without placing a flower beside her in his stead. He quietly made his way out of the Princess' chamber and into the hall, slowly shutting the door as not to wake her. The hinges creaked stubbornly and he winced at the sharp sound cutting through the silent morning.

"Subtlety is in no way your strong suit young man," said a voice from behind him.

Ewan turned around to the crossed arms and stern face of Sister Margret who must have been watching his entire escape.

"If you're going to continue to disobey by instructions then at least do it with a little astuteness," she said shaking her head.

"To be fair I was trying," he replied with a smile.

"Not nearly hard enough."

"I'll do better next time."

"Next time?" she asked, the sternness finally leaving her face, "my dear boy there won't be a next time until your wedding night."

"There are still many nights in between," he said boldly.

"You two may be able to out flank an old woman in these great halls but mark my words, the journey north won't provide you with such a luxury and neither shall I."

Ewan knew that Sister Margret was right, he would be able to see and speak to Eilidh on their travels but they would not be granted a moment alone. At first this made him sad, knowing how fondly he cherished the time they spent with each other, but then he drew happiness from the notion that their wedding night would be all the more special because of it.

With Sister Margret's lecture concluded, Ewan returned to his own chamber to get ready for their journey. He would be riding by Sir Darrion's side where Eilidh, her mother and Sister Margret would be travelling in a grand carriage. The Princess had pleaded with her father to take Willow, though despite the King understanding his daughter's wish to ride in the open air; it was expected of them to travel in such a way. Ewan was glad such confinement did not apply to him as well, for he wished to be cast into the very depth of the land, to take in every moment of their journey.

The morning was spent gathering the needed supplies and readying the horses. It was almost midday by the time they left the capitol, the white towers falling into the distance as the company headed northwest. Ardal, who had not returned to Forest Isle after the battle, was to escort them to the halls of his father, leading them across the rugged land of the Northern Realm. Ewan had met up with him on the fields of the Lowlands after the fighting was done. He had led the northern bowmen atop the grassy hills, tirelessly directing the storm of arrows that for so long, held back the enemy forces. Ardal had been among the many heroes of that day and Ewan was happy to see that he had survived.

The young Lord Heir was at the head of the company leading them towards his homeland. Ewan and Sir Darrion rode by his side, behind them followed the King and Prince Richard riding beside the grand carriage and a host of fifty mounted Royal Guard to ensure their safety. As the days went by the lands of the Eastern Realm began to fall behind them, making way for the wild region of the north.

One afternoon, with the town of Borderton now behind them, the pace was slow and Ewan rode ahead with Ardal. A soft rain filled the air as they galloped along the road, guarded on each side by walls of dense trees. They did not venture too far from the company, soon slowing their horses as they spoke, Sir Darrion's purple cloak shielding him from the rain.

"So tell me once more of your battle with Highthorn," said Ardal looking at the pale antler set in Everleaf's hilt, "how did you claim such a trophy from the White King?"

"I didn't claim anything and it was very far from a battle," replied Ewan with a smile, "more of an unlikely collision."

"All the best stories deserve a small amount of embellishment," said Ardal returning his smile.

"The true account is far less heroic trust me."

"Simply seeing the beast is worthy of a tale my friend, let alone an encounter like yours."

Ewan ran his hand over the smooth grip of his sword, admiring the snow white surface of the antler.

"He truly was an incredible creature," he said gently as he remembered the grand stag, "I'm only sorry he forced me to loose an arrow."

"I'm afraid you didn't render such a mighty beast to the past tense with a single arrow," said Ardal, "he has roamed the trees of Beachwood for hundreds of years, a stag such as he would not be brought down so easily."

"I hope so; I would hate to have killed the very symbol of House Greyfell."

"Fear not Ewan, I'm sure old Highthorn still has a part to play," said Ardal as the rain continued to fall, "at least the King's heraldry still belongs to this world. The bears that stand proudly on the banners of my House have long since passed from memory."

"Do you think the skinshedders will ever return?"

"The bears of Dunharren guarded my family and home for many generations," replied Ardal with a look of sadness, "but no I think their time is done. Unlike Highthorn I believe they have played their part, such powers are gone from the world."

Though the bears of Dunharren had indeed left the Kingdom of Farreach, they certainly had not been forgotten. Many days of travel soon brought them through the vast expanse of the Old Forest to the shores that lay beyond. Forest Isle was separated from the mainland by the Northern Straits, a stretch of the Sea of

Glass that cut through the Kingdom. Passage across was granted by a colossal wooden bridge, there the bears of old were remembered.

The northerners' skill and craftsmanship with wood was mirrored in this vast structure, two mighty carved bears standing guard at either end.

"This is Bear Bridge," Ardal called back to him as they passed through the fearsome and ever watchful sentinels.

Ewan looked in wonder as they crossed, emerging from the trees out over the deep water of the Northern Straits. Forest Isle lay ahead of them, the land rolling with hills and dense trees. It was not long after that they reached the great city of Oakenhold, where Ewan now stood atop the high walls.

It was the day before his wedding and he sought the peaceful battlements to gather his thoughts. The sun was beginning to set and the dying light reflected off the soon to fall amber leaves. Though autumn would soon claim them, the leaves of the Older Oak would remain, remaining gold and glowing in memory of the summer sun. Ewan had seen the great tree that stood within the Carved Hall as it stretched through the open roof, its leaves shining like a million gilded shields, protecting the hall against the fast coming winter cold.

Ewan was not sure whether it was the beautiful leaves or his wedding that made him miss home. The world he was born to was one of logic and reason, absent of magical qualities such as the shimmering tree. The Kingdom of Farreach had quickly become his home, though he never forgot the one he left behind. Much had changed since he was cast from his family though they never strayed from his heart. The only thing he wanted more than to marry Eilidh was for them to be there when he did.

As the golden leaves continued to glow within their wooden hall, Ewan was joined on the battlements by Sir Darrion, his armour shining as brightly as the undying tree.

"No man should be left alone the night before his wedding," said the knight, "that can lead to them disappearing."

"Spoiling my plans as usual Captain," he replied with a smile.

"For the better trust me, Sister Margret would hunt both of us down."

"I don't doubt it, though she won't have to, for I very much plan on getting married tomorrow."

"Nervous yet?"

"Is it bad that battle scared me less?"

"It's funny that you mention that," replied the knight, "the night before the Lowlands I gave you a cloak of House Tarn, but now on the eve of your wedding, you'll be needing one of your own."

"What do you mean?"

"My dear lad" said Sir Darrion, "tomorrow you won't merely be my squire, you will be my Prince."

Ewan stood speechless and surprised, he had never realised the implication of marrying a Princess, he only thought he would gain a wife, not a royal title.

"A Prince?" he finally uttered.

"Yes Ewan," confirmed the knight, "and as such you'll require heraldry to represent House Anderson."

"House Anderson?" he said, repeating Sir Darrion again.

"Soon to be the twelfth noble House of Farreach."

Once more Ewan stood speechless, never thinking that his family name would gain such recognition in a distant and unknown land.

"What heraldry will be used?" he asked, wondering about the colours and depictions soon to embody his new House.

"That is entirely up to you," replied Sir Darrion, "many women have married into noble Houses, but in the history of the Kingdom, a man has yet to create his own, it's only fitting that you choose that which will portray it."

Ewan thought of the many beasts and strong symbols that represented the other eleven Houses, all decorated in their unique colours.

"Any thoughts?" asked Sir Darrion.

Ewan's eyes fell to the hilt of his sword, his fingers brushing over the silver tree that was the pommel and the leaves that wound their way towards the hidden black blade.

"A tree," he finally said, still staring at Everleaf, "a silver tree upon a field of black."

"A fitting heraldry," replied the knight, noticing his focus on the sword, "to a fitting blade. I shall have the design made by midnight."

With that the young Captain took his leave, his polished greaves glinting with the departing sun. There Ewan stood once more, alone with his thoughts, though now they were not sad. His mind no longer dwelled on the home he had left behind, but on the new one he had built. He wished his family could be a part of it, or at the very least have a chance to tell them he was happy. Eilidh was his family now and he no longer wished to leave.

The sun had long died in the eastern sky before Sir Darrion returned, though Ewan had not left the walls, finding comfort high above the trees. As darkness had crept over the north, the gentle glow of moonlight bathed the land in a pale silver light, a sea of stars spread out above.

Sir Darrion handed him a black cloak of fine fabric, the soft material bearing a large silver tree upon its back. The tree was littered with shining leaves, along with a score that fell from the branches over the darkness. The young Captain removed the purple cloak he had once gifted him, placing the newly made one over his shoulders.

Wrapped in the silver speckled blackness of his own heraldry, Ewan became lost against the starry sky, now ready for the day that lay just beyond the horizon.

Chapter Twenty Seven

The Elegance of Revenge

A cold autumn chill ran through the fallings leaves of the Southern Realm. The dark fortress of Black Stone stood as a menacing silhouette, blocking out the stars that shone high above. Lord William had been called from his bed in the middle of the night; the reason now lay before him, the body of Drusilla Greyfell, as cold as the autumn air outside.

She had died during the night, stricken by a sudden and powerful fever. Her body now rested in bed as if she were simply asleep, spent of the life that had once coursed through her mere hours before. Lord William stood over her, his old yet striking eyes searching her still young and beautiful face, looking for an explanation to her very abrupt fate.

He had seen her the day of their return to the city, showing no signs of anything other than jealously. Galvin's interest in Lucille Gillain had certainly wounded his sister, but Lord William had not seen her as the type to die merely of a broken heart. In truth she had shown him more strength of spirit than her feeble brother. Yet there she lay, stricken from the world only a day later. Lord William had been informed as soon as she had taken ill, seeing that she was tended to by his best healers. Yet no amount of skill seemed to lessen her ailment, as if the sickness had a will of its own, driven by a vengeance that nature simply did not possess.

The night was late and he had dressed quickly, arriving at Drusilla's chamber in a robe of red and gold. He was a few years shy of sixty and his blonde hair was growing thin. His deep eyes had grown darker with time but were filled with a resolve beyond contestation.

Across from him stood the loyal Captain of his armies, Sir Stefan Barron. Even at such a late hour, the knight remained in his armour, his greatsword resting across his back. Drusilla's body lay in front of them both, the colour fading from her cheeks with each passing moment.

"What shall I tell her brother my Lord?" asked Sir Stefan, his gruff voice cutting the silence of the room.

"Nothing for the moment."

"Shouldn't be a problem," said the knight, "Galvin's far too distracted with the Gillain girl."

"Good," he replied, "see that it stays that way, I have plans for them both."

He left Sir Stefan with instructions to deal with the body quietly; he could not afford Galvin to learn of his sister's death until he had no further use of him. Lord William had gone to considerable lengths to put a crown on his former son by law's head; he would not see it undone by Drusilla's death. He had invested too much in the War of Antlers for him to be on the losing side.

It had not always been so; there had been a time that Lord William did not desire the power he now reached for. Such dreams of glory and control had belonged to his brother. Wolfrick had been every bit of their father, tyranny ran through him thicker than blood and blood is what he sought. Wolfrick grew up with his eyes on the upper Realms, waiting for the day when he commanded the vast armies of the south.

Their father had lived long, Wolfrick's hunger for war growing with each passing year. Eventually his opportunity came; the Thane of the south left the world, passing his powers to his eldest son. It was not long before rebellion swept over the Kingdom, a conflict that came to be known as the Southern War. For a whole year Lord William asked his brother to end the campaign but he continued to push forward, ravaging the very land with his insatiable fury.

But he would not stop, even when King Adwen pushed their forces back beyond the walls of Gate Keep. There, at the Battle of the Fringe, young Prince Rhain put a sword through his brother's throat, a brutal end to a brutal endeavour. Soon after the dust had settled, the King proposed an end to the conflict, offering a marriage between his son and Lord William's own daughter, his sweet and precious Caitlyn.

She would be Queen of Farreach, as her father he could not deny his daughter the opportunity for such a life. He only wanted what was best for her and seeing as the decision would bring about the end of his brother's war, he found it folly to refuse. The agreement was made and he said farewell to his beloved Caitlyn, entrusting her life to House Greyfell.

Letting her go had been the hardest thing since the death of his wife, so many years before. Though the wound soon healed, knowing that in time his daughter was happy and safe, she had the life he always wanted for her. The wound, however, did not stay closed; it was later ripped open with her death, as unexpected and sudden as Drusilla's.

Lord William's world came crashing down when he received word, losing his beloved daughter was more than he could bare. Despite the insurmountable hurt of Caitlyn's death, she was not the reason he now sought power, a war would not bring her back. He fought for a far simpler motive that in time plagues all men, the fear of leaving the world with it never remembering your name.

As he made his way back to his chamber, Lord William heard nothing but his heavy footsteps on the stone floor. Age had certainly been kind to him, the years did not show in his stride but they were hard pressed on his mind. Time had started to fill him with fear, in his youth he had not cared for the glory his older brother fought and died for, to have his deeds echo across time. Now, with fewer years ahead than he had behind, his thoughts never strayed far from the notion of legacy and the manner in which he would be remembered.

The War of Antlers would be just the start of that legacy, he had used Galvin's claim as the face of the rebellion, yet he would not stop there. Lord William wanted to carve his name into the very rock of the land. He had only ever lived for his loved ones, yet they were all taken from him. He had done nothing in his youth worthy of remembrance, but no longer.

He eventually reached the grand double doors of his chamber, finding them warm against his hand as he pushed them open. The cold autumn air did not linger inside; the large fireplace filled the room with a glorious heat, keeping the shadows in their dark corners. Though morning was not far off, Lord William was now far too awake to fall back asleep. A large chair rested in front of the blazing fire, there he sat and watched his thoughts play out in the flames.

As the fire raged on in front of him, out of the corner of his eye, Lord William saw a shape emerge from the shadows. He quickly turned around to see an elderly woman enter the soft glow of the fire. At first he thought it was Galvin's mother, the once Queen Elora, but soon realised he was not far wrong.

"Nesta Mason," he said calmly, "few find their way into my Realm without me knowing, let alone into my own chamber."

"What age takes in strength it gives back in wits, as I'm sure you're aware," she said with a sly smile.

Unlike her sister, Nesta had always dressed plainly, unadorned by the trinkets befitting of a Queen. She stood just beyond the shadows, the darkness still lurking behind. Her once red hair that she shared with her sister, returned to its youth in the light of the flames. She did not approach nor did she seem afraid.

"So what do I owe the pleasure of having yet another Greyfell in my halls?" he asked.

"My Lord I am no Greyfell," she replied, "though I believe you are now short of one."

For the first time in many years, Lord William was surprised. Drusilla had just died with only a handful of his loyal subjects knowing of it. He did not want anyone finding out about her sudden parting and yet her aunt stood in front of him, stating it outright moments later.

"What would you know of such things?" he asked.

"One as skilled as I in such matters should be able to recognise my own work."

For a second time, not long after the first, Lord William stood surprised. He was speechless, the quiet crackle of the fire filling his silence.

"Drusilla is dead and by my hand," continued Nesta, "though the reasons are far more complicated than the act."

"Why would you murder your own niece?" he questioned.

"Because she murdered her father."

Lord William had long known King Adwen, speaking with him many times from the southern end of the Crested Concave. Despite his death granting him with the opportunity to seize the legacy he now wanted, he had always respected the King as both a leader and a fellow father.

"Even if what you say is true," he replied, "why would you go to such trouble to avenge King Adwen?"

"He may have been my sister's husband but he meant a great deal to me too," she said with sadness in her voice, "he gave my sister and I our lives back in more ways than anyone could realise."

"The King died many months ago, why now?"

"Unlike you men, we don't bring our heavy swords down on our foe's head so hastily," she replied, "a woman's revenge is far more elegant."

"But why would Drusilla want to kill her own father in the first place?"

"For the love of another, one she was not allowed to love."

Lord William remembered the hurt that had so obviously shown on Drusilla's face at the sight of her brother with Lord Farris' daughter. He now understood the love that Nesta spoke of.

"But Drusilla and her father died of a fever," he said, casting aside Nesta's elaborate tale, "my daughter was no different."

The words caught in his throat as it suddenly all became clear.

"My daughter was no different," he repeated quietly as the words washed over him.

"I'm afraid so," Nesta replied earnestly, "King Adwen's blood was not the only one on Drusilla's hands."

Anger and sadness consumed him, dreams of glory and legacy turned to ash in his mouth. The death of his daughter returned to him with more pain than when it had left.

"Why now?" he demanded, "why tell me now?"

Nesta came forth from the shadows, entering the full glow of the fire's light. She placed a gentle hand on his shoulder that he welcomed and did not have the heart to shrug off.

"You may be on the wrong side of this war but you were still her father," she told him, "you had the right to know."

Lord William was staring so deeply into the fire that he did not even notice Nesta's hand leave him as she shrink back into the shadows. Amongst the flames, as his daughter's death weighed heavy on his heart once more, he pictured House Greyfell burning, along with all their loved ones.

Chapter Twenty Eight

Vows and Golden Leaves

"Ouch!" exclaimed Eilidh as a needle poked her through the fabric.

She stood atop a raised platform in a round chamber made of many arches, through which beautiful gardens could be seen. It was the morning of her wedding and the sun had risen bright and full over the city of Oakenhold. Her mother and Sister Margret were busy at work around her, making the final alterations to her dress. She shifted her position to avoid one more needle only to find another.

"The more you struggle child, the more it'll hurt," said the Queen.

"Listen to your mother," replied Sister Margret, "we're nearly finished."

Eilidh silently winced as the needles continued to poke her, thoughts of it being by mere chance quickly diminishing. Also in the room were her two northern aunts, Lord Michael's wife, Lady Thea, and Lady Ellyn. The latter was her mother and uncle's younger sister. Her aunt Ellyn was currently with child, making it difficult for her to leave the Northern Realm, her stomach forming a round curve under her dress.

Seeing her aunts along with Sister Margret and her mother, all smiling as her dress began to take form, only made Eilidh miss her aunt Drusilla. She had always been kind to her, teaching her things that Sister Margret would not. Eilidh wanted her there, to be a part of her special day alongside her other loved ones. She never understood why Drusilla had chosen to leave them all to be with Galvin, Eilidh only wished she was safe and that her decision had brought her happiness.

"Ouch!" she said again as yet another needle found her skin.

Her cheeks flushed with annoyance but the Princess managed a strained smile. The two women continued to work, buzzing around her like bees over honey. As they did, Eilidh's mind wandered to her journey north. It had been long and hard, only made more difficult by how little she saw of her betrothed, the word replacing her fake smile with a real one.

A life time seemed to have passed since Ewan had proposed to her on the steps of the Citadel. She fiddled with the gleaming water diamond he had gifted her, remembering the rain on her face as he asked for her hand. The proposal had indeed surprised her, yet no answer had come more easily. Eilidh would be the first woman of the newly founded House Anderson, but all she wanted was to be Ewan's wife.

The prospect of marriage was only made better knowing it would be beneath the Older Oak as her parents had done. She could not thank her father enough for allowing them to travel all the way to Forest Isle. She felt terrible for stealing away the Realms' King but happy she had her father. The thought of him walking her down the aisle made her fight back a tear. When the time came, she only hoped the King would do the same, for without her father's strength, she would have none.

"You look wonderful," said her aunt Ellyn when Sister Margret and her mother had finished their work.

"You truly do," added Lady Thea as Eilidh stood in front of the four women, all smiling in admiration.

"Give us a twirl before we all start crying," said Sister Margret, the tears already visible in the corners of her eyes.

Eilidh obliged and felt the softness of the fabric as she spun atop the raised platform, the red of her hair and the ivory of the dress creating a blur of fire and lace. As she turned, the room became a mix of morning light and smiling faces, the Princess' lips forming one of her own, larger than the rest.

With her dress now finished and fitting perfectly, Eilidh stole a moment of seclusion in the gardens that surrounded them. She walked slowly through the trees, her head towards the sky, her eyes drinking the cloudless expanse of blue that loomed overhead. The early autumn day was bright yet cold, the chilling air breathing a sense of freshness over the land. Every year, Eilidh would find her favourite day; she would rise and simply fall in love with the clarity it brought her. It was never the same time each year but was always in autumn, bright yet cold as it was that day.

As she continued through the gardens, she did not mind the cold breeze brushing over her bare arms, for the sun warmed them soon after. That year, she was lucky enough to have her favourite day fall on her wedding, her happiness shining as brightly as the autumn sun. Eilidh's peaceful garden walk lasted long enough for her to breathe the fresh air and gather her thoughts. Ewan waited beneath the Older Oak for her and despite being tempted, she did not want him to wait long.

Sister Margret soon came to hurry her through the halls of House Dunharren, fussing all the while over the Princess as they walked. Eilidh did not mind, the old woman had brought her into the world and knew her better than most, teaching her to be the woman she was. Eilidh often got annoyed by her many lectures but she very much loved Sister Margret, knowing that she always had her young heart in mind.

The Older Oak rested in the Carved Hall, the grand chamber of the Northern Realm, where she would soon be married. Outside its large double doors and beneath a brilliant blue sky, stood her father, waiting as he gleamed in his bright armour. As he watched her approach in her dress, Eilidh saw a perfect blend of sadness and happiness fill his eyes. He took each of her hands and bent down to gently kiss her forehead, his golden crown brushing against her hair.

"You look beautiful," he said softly.

Sister Margret gave them both a quick smile and then left them alone. Eilidh stood by her father, holding his arm tightly, unsure of whether she was ready to let it go. He had forever been the one who protected her, the armour of her heart. Never doubting his love and always seeing it displayed in his actions, he had been there for her, all her life. Now he entrusted that care to another and though it made her sad, Eilidh knew that it was again because he loved her.

"Are you ready for this?" he asked her, not taking his eyes off the doors that stood before them.

"Are you?"

"Not in the least," he said gently, still looking ahead, "though you're a young woman now, you'll always be my little girl."

Eilidh held her father's arm tighter and looked up at him, his eyes slowly turning to meet hers.

"Make sure it stays that way," she said to him as both doors opened before them, holding each other's gaze, they slowly started to walk down the aisle.

The Carved Hall was full of people, all upstanding for her entrance, gathered on each side of the long chamber. Harps began to play as they walked, hundreds of faces looking her way. The ceiling was high with large oak beams lacing their way through the air, creating a floating wooden maze high above. Light streamed in from the windows that lined each side, scattering rays of sunshine through the room.

A light breeze began to flow through the hall, causing her crimson hair to gently dance as she walked. It hung loosely down by her waist, an elegant river of fire. The silk under gown of the bodice, which had a slightly revealing square neckline, was layered with the same ivory lace trim of the capped sleeves, and was brought in at the top of the waist by an embellished brooch, showing off her slim feminine figure. The skirt of her dress, which flowed seamlessly from the bodice, featured the same lace detailing, trailing subtly on the floor behind her, as she slowly made her way down the aisle.

Before her, resting atop a flight of stone steps, lay the Older Oak, a giant tree that stood within the Carved Hall. Its thick trunk formed a wooden seat; its long roots buried into the very floor and weaved down the steps. High up its branches rose, littered with thousands of golden leaves that never fell.

Beneath the mighty tree, waiting beyond the steps, was Ewan, standing handsome and bold in shining ceremonial armour, his new cloak streaming from his shoulders. She had waited so long to see him standing there, watching her as she slowly made her way towards him. His expression did not disappoint, his eyes alone told Eilidh that he loved her.

At the bottom of the steps, her father gave her one final kiss before going to stand beside her mother. She made her way up the steps alone, leaving her old life behind, rising towards her new one. Eilidh hesitated at the final step, not out of fear, just from the vastness of the moment. But all doubts were soon forgotten as Ewan held out his hand; she welcomed it and was soon facing him.

Her uncle Michael stood before his mighty wooden seat of the Older Oak, facing the still upstanding crowd below. He donned polished bronze that covered his mighty frame and his shoulders were trimmed with thick brown fur. He gave them both a reassuring wink, revealing a smile beneath his black beard that only they could see. He gestured to the crowd to be seated as his voice began to boom through the hall.

"These are dark times," he said, "since the death of King Adwen, rebels and raiders have troubled the borders of our lands and war has beset our Kingdom, forcing us to pull more on the strings of bows than that of harps."

The crowd remained deathly quiet as he spoke, knowing the truth of his words.

"Though let this marriage be a glimmer of hope amongst the shadow," he continued, "a chance for new life to grow and lead us from darkness."

Lord Michael reached behind him and produced her white silk scarf, his amber eyes shining brightly as he watched her smile. Eilidh had no idea that Ewan had brought it north with them but she was very pleased that he had.

"Take each other's hands," he told them as their fingers entwined.

He wrapped the scarf around their joined hands, the soft fabric brushing her bare skin as it tied them together.

"Now as you stand here in unity, bound as a couple by silk and the love you share, please speak the words together."

Eilidh fell into Ewan's gaze as he fell into hers; matching each other breath for breath as the moment seemed to stand still. With their hands joined and their eyes locked, they both spoke in unison.

"Take, honour, hold, love."

Their words were a promise, a vow to love each other in that life and any after. The entire hall seemed to vanish along with the hundreds that watched them. Eilidh found herself alone with Ewan in a sea of golden leaves, he was hers and she was his.

"I, as Thane of the Northern Realm, join this couple in marriage," pronounced Lord Michael, his booming voice bringing them back to the hall, "you may now kiss the bride."

With their hands still bound together, they both leant forward and shared a kiss, not the longest or the most passionate, but certainly the most meaningful.

The ceremony was then followed by a feast, along with a line of congratulations to the newlywed couple, a string of faces and smiles too long for Eilidh to remember. Despite being forever by her new husband's side, the formalities of the day seemed to cast a distance between them, she saw on Ewan's face that he felt the same. Their guests were everyone that they knew and loved, but the young couple longed to be alone together.

The day passed quickly and darkness soon fell over Oakenhold, bathing the city in moonlight. The time to say goodnight to their guests and retire to their chamber had come. After saying their final farewells, they joined hands and left their wedding to continue on without them, the sound of music and laughter still flowing through the halls.

As they walked towards their chamber, Eilidh grew ever nervous; she was now a married woman and yet trembled as if she were a young girl. The thought her wedding night had always excited her, but now, when it was far more real than just a thought, excitement was quickly replaced with worry.

This feeling grew as Ewan's hand fell upon the door of their chamber, slowly pushing the heavy oak aside. Eilidh knew they had been granted a grand room for their wedding night, though she still did not expect what they found inside. As the door opened they were faced with the bright glow of hundreds of candles, covering the very floor of the chamber. Their flames formed a path across the stone, ending in an ornate bed surrounded by clear silk curtains. They both entered and closed the door behind them, which only furthered the beauty the candlelight created.

"Finally alone," said Ewan as he held her in a close embrace.

Eilidh hoped he did not hear how loud her heart was beating in her chest, for the sound resonated through her body. She had no idea she would be so terrified, Ewan had always made her feel so comfortable, yet now she trembled at his very touch. No doubts formed in her mind, she did not want the act any less, it only scared her.

Standing in the river of candles, they faced away from each other, slowly shedding their clothes to the floor. Eilidh heard the sound of Ewan's armour as he placed the steel on the stone, knowing each piece brought the moment closer. The last of her beautiful dress slipped from her body as the flames warmed her naked skin.

Ewan made no sound behind her; Eilidh's heart was the only noise she heard. She had never revealed herself to any man, yet there she stood, the flames exposing her womanly figure. Before she gathered the courage to turn around and face him, she felt Ewan embrace her from behind, his skin pressed against hers.

"Do you know if you loved any before me?" Eilidh asked as he gently kissed her cheek.

She held her breath, fearful of the answer he might give. Ewan's lips left her cheek, holding her close as he whispered in her ear.

"I know that you *are* and always *will* be the only one."

They stood silently for a moment as the candles flickered around them, causing shadows to dance about their embrace. Eilidh slowly turned around and kissed her husband as their bodies became one. Falling onto the bed they made the love they had always shared.

Afterwards they lay on the bed together, the candles burning low as beads of sweat glistened on their skin. Her head rested on Ewan's chest, listening to his heart beat faster than hers had done. She came up and kissed him, feeling every part of him pressed against her. Ewan held her head in his hands, a smile forming on his lips as he gazed at her.

"I want these eyes to be the last thing I ever see," he said gently, giving her one final kiss.

Wrapped in a close embrace, they softly drifted off to sleep. All of Eilidh's favourite days had eventually ended, releasing their hold to allow the next one to surprise her, and though this one had ended like all the ones before, it had ended ever so perfectly.

Chapter Twenty Nine

Beauty Deserves Royalty

A starless sky rested over the south, the moon heavily shrouded in a cloak of thick clouds. A light autumn rain fell over Lake Titus, the small droplets leaping over the calm surface. No boats sailed that night, leaving the expanse of water vacant, an oily reflection of the dark sky above.

Lord William stood on his balcony, ignoring the rain as it slowly seeped through his fine clothes. His thinning blonde hair was dripping wet as it clung to his head, yet there he stood, refusing to seek the warmth of his chamber. He was a statue, a watchful sentinel over the dark and quiet city that lay below. No amount of rain could lessen the fire in his heart, for it was fuelled by vengeance.

The words of Nesta Mason still rang in his mind, for they were the last ones he had heard. He had not left his chamber since she had shrunk back into the shadows; leaving the knowledge she had given him to plague his every thought. He could not sleep without seeing his daughter's face, forever tormented by her beautiful smile. Knowing that Caitlyn had been murdered only renewed her death in her father's heart.

Lord William knew her killer lay dead as well, though he took no comfort in it. Nesta had stolen the chance for him to seek his own vengeance on Drusilla; he wanted her to remember the daughter she had taken from him as the light faded from her treacherous eyes. The once seductive and cunning Greyfell Princess, now lay in an unmarked grave, unadorned of the grand remembrance she did little to deserve.

Lord William still kept her brother and lover as his guest, now aware of the secret affair that had started with his daughter's death. He held Galvin as responsible as the rest of House Greyfell, Drusilla was only the start. The Southern Thane would continue his support only to further his own retribution, he would see the fall of their royal dynasty, his legacy becoming the end of theirs.

The rain had not lessened, yet still he stood, hardened by his resolve. Lord William would continue to act as Galvin's loyal subject, concealing the knowledge that the Greyfell outcast had bedded not only his sister, but also his beloved wife's killer. He held no sympathy for his so called King; he would see House Greyfell in ashes, using their own to help with the burning.

Lighting streaked across the night sky, followed by a low and distant rumble of thunder, a prelude to Lord William's sinister plans, gathering alongside the autumn storm. He finally returned inside, only then feeling the chill that had crept through his bones. The fire still burned brightly, warming his chamber with a steady glow. As he was changing, Lord William quickly glanced at the dark corner from which Nesta had emerged, wondering if he was now indeed alone.

He had ignored many of his duties that day, shutting himself away from the world as the hours slowly passed by. His mourning had turned to hatred, his grief replaced with a desire for revenge, and taking Nesta's advice, his would be ever so elegant. It would start with Lord Farris, the head of House Gillian. The Western Realm had quickly changed their allegiance with the death of their sons; Lord William knew it would not take much for them to change it back. In the battles to come he would require their support, especially with winter drawing ever closer.

He had arranged a late meeting with Lord Farris to discuss their continued loyalty. The Battle of the Lowlands had taken them all by surprise, their overwhelming numbers counting for little on the field. Lord William knew the outcome had shaken the west's assurance, hearing many of their concerns already.

The hour was late as he left his chamber, his wet clothes cast aside for dry ones. He wore a tunic of fine crimson, adorned with golden clasps. His feet made heavy sounds on the paved floor as the torches on the walls flickered as he passed. Long had he walked those dark halls, the brightness that had once filled them now gone, leaving only shadowy stone.

Lord William's wife had died in her youth, a beautiful woman who perished far before her time. Her name was Alva, her hair rays of pure sunlight. He had loved her dearly, an affection that only grew when she brought Caitlyn into the world. He remembered the first time he saw them both together, his wife cradling their daughter's delicate head, at what was meant to be the start of their lives together as a family, though it did not last.

Shortly after bearing him one beautiful child, Lord William's wife fell pregnant with another. He loved his newborn daughter greatly but he secretly wished for a son, an heir to carry on his name. Unfortunately his wish was granted, his own wife being the price. She died giving birth to the son he had hoped for, clinging to life only long enough to name him.

Walking through the halls, as Lord William's thoughts of his lost daughter gave way only to remind him of his lost wife, he realised the son that had stolen her away was standing in front of him. Stewart wore simple clothes with a book tucked tightly under one arm. He had the look of his mother, a quality Lord William at first found comforting, knowing his wife lived on through their son. But those soft features came to haunt him, causing him to see his wife in every glance and subtle gesture.

"Father," his son said as his hands tightened around the hard leather of the book, "have you seen Lady Greyfell?"

"Drusilla?" asked Lord William with confusion, "what business do you have with her?"

"I wish to speak with her," Stewart stammered.

"She is far too busy."

"Where can I find her?"

"She's gone," he replied coldly.

"Gone where?"

Lord William began to grow angry with his son's questions, he saw his wife in Stewart's eyes and his heart reached out to her.

"I have neither the time nor the patience right now," he said sternly.

"You never do with me," said Stewart boldly, though not able to hide the fact it was laced with sadness.

"Not tonight."

Lord William continued down the hall and refused to look back, leaving his son standing there alone, seeking the comfort of a woman he did not know to be dead. He had tried to love the son his wife gave her life to bear, yet his arrival in the world only reminded him of her leaving. He wanted to remain true to her memory and love Stewart as she would have wanted and as a father should, though in time, his presence became too hurtful to bear. Despite knowing it was wrong, he found it easier to treat his son with a cold indifference, to ignore his child for his own selfish sake.

Lord Farris waited in his chamber, where he stayed as Lord William's guest along with his daughter Lady Lucille, both of which travelled back with the southern Thane across the Sea of Sails. After the battle they had made the long march to the western border, seeking refuge in Fort Morton, the home of House Gillian. The castle lay at the edge of the Rift, a coastal fortress frozen hard by the bitter winds and snows of the west. There Lord William had convinced Lord Farris to accompany him back to Black Stone, making sure he brought his daughter.

The men of the Western Realm understood the cold, for the frost never melted and the snowy wastes forever glistened white. Autumn would soon be over and winter was fast approaching, Lord William would need their support more than ever in the months to come, and he had an enticing proposal to ensure he had it.

The door to Lord Farris' chamber opened before him, the room as cold and bitter as the old man's face. He wore a cloak as white as his hair, though the fabric was stained with old blood. The fire lay bare and unlit; Lord William's breathe making wisps of heat, soon to die in the icy air.

"I can't abide this heat," said the old man as he returned to his chair.

"You left your cold winds across the sea."

"And I'll be glad to return to them," he replied with a scoff.

Lord William joined him in a chair beside the empty fireplace, the room taking on a silvery glow as the clouds made way for the moon.

"I assure you that you left your halls for good reason," he said in a calm yet forceful tone.

"One that has yet to be revealed to me."

"I see patience is not a virtue of the west."

"Neither is losing," said Lord Farris with a hard stare, "my Thane and I joined this war for the vengeance you promised us."

"And you shall have it."

"At the Lowlands they defeated us when we outnumbered them two to one, how can we win a war when faced with such odds?" replied Lord Farris with frustration, "our sons' deaths remain unanswered for and this Ewan continues to gain favour."

"Calm yourself my Lord, this is not my first war and it takes more than a single battle to win one. As for this Ewan, I don't know much about the boy but he is but one boy, he can hardly turn the tide of a Kingdom."

"So says you but there are rumours spreading that it was his plan that bested us on the field and now he's wedding King Rhain's daughter. I believe he's much more than a simple boy we need not concern ourselves with."

"Forget the boy and forget King Rhain, I have a plan that will cripple his allies and render them leaderless."

"Whatever your plans, my Thane and the west may decide to withdraw from this war entirely," said Lord Farris, dismissing any schemes.

"What if I told you that it involves your daughter finally becoming Queen of Farreach?"

The old man shifted uncomfortably in his seat, Lord William knew he greatly desired what was being offered. He longed for his daughter to one day sit beside the King in the royal halls.

"Granting Lucille such a position is far from within your power," replied Lord Farris with doubt.

"Such beauty deserves royalty my Lord, fight with me and I'll see it done."

Lord William watched as the old man considered the bright new future offered for his House, one that would lead them to the Citadel of Kings. He already knew he had him.

"If what you say is true," said Lord Farris finally, "I believe our continued support would be worth such a price."

Lord William leant forward so his eyes glowed in the pale light, piercing both shadow and flesh.

"So would I," he said with a sinister smile, "so would I."

Chapter Thirty

A New Life

Dawn's rosy fingers stole their way into the world, stretching out across the horizon. The Northern Realm lay peaceful as the rising sun silently chased down the shadows. The wooden halls of Oakenhold welcomed the morning light, the age old city basking in the warm glow.

Ewan awoke to the soft flutter of silk brushing his face, the curtains that surrounded the bed had been caught in the early autumn air, sent to gently rouse him from his dreams. The candles that surrounded the chamber had burnt out long into the night, leaving only their sweet smell. Light poured into the room from many windows, flooding Ewan's waking eyes with brightness.

Upon his chest lay his wife, the word still sounding strange even in his thoughts. Yet there she lay, more beautiful than ever. He watched her as she slept, each rise and fall of her chest filling him with a sense of completion. Ewan gently stroked her fiery hair, the long crimson curls flowing out over her soft pale skin.

Their wedding had been a thing of dreams, each moment more wonderful than the last. He had stood beneath the golden leaves of the Older Oak as Eilidh walked towards him, a river of ivory trailing behind. He had never loved her more than he had done in that moment, each step bringing her closer to him. Take, honour, hold, love, he thought to himself. He had meant every word, each one encapsulating a thousand others that were just as true.

The ceremony had ended with a kiss, a moment that was just their own, the world seemed to lessen and only their love remained. Since entering the Kingdom of Farreach, Ewan had been faced with turmoil, war, corruption and murder. Yet throughout all that, weaved the story of their love. Ewan still did not understand his arrival in that unknown land, but as his wife slept beside him, he knew it truly no longer mattered.

After Lord Michael had pronounced their marriage, a feast quickly followed. Long tables that spanned the entire length of the Carved Hall seated their many guests, Ewan recognising a mere handful of them. From all over the Eastern and Northern Realm they had come, Lords, Ladies, knights and squires. The room was full of cheer as food and wine flowed as merrily as the music. All the while he only wished for Eilidh and him to steal a moment alone.

Yet when that moment finally came, he felt entirely unprepared, the crowd of guests bid them both goodnight and they retired to their chamber. His nerves were given a brief respite as their faces were bathed in candlelight, the beauty of the room and the flickering flames overwhelming them both. Ewan had never loved another woman, Eilidh being the first to steal his heart. He trembled slightly but as his skin touched hers, it faded for nothing felt more right.

Now that morning fell upon them, the room swelled with sunlight. Carefully folded over a chair, Ewan saw his new cloak, the black fabric embroidered with the silver tree of House Anderson. Along with forming a noble name, he awoke that morning not just a husband but a Prince. He had begun his life in the Kingdom of Farreach as a mere chance rescuer, in under a year he had become a squire, a war hero and now a member of the royal family. It was strange to think that was in fact *his* heraldry he looked upon, a shining reason that he did indeed now belong in that world. Another was just starting to wake up beside him.

Eilidh's icy blue eyes slowly cracked open as she let out a small yawn, half interrupted by a smile as she noticed him staring at her.

"Good morning husband," she said as her smile grew.

"Good morning wife."

"Have you been watching me long?"

"Long enough to hear you snore," he replied teasingly, "something I feel I should have been warned about before the wedding."

"It's too late now," she said as she pulled him beneath the sheets, "you're all mine."

Eilidh kissed him as their hands intertwined, her skin pressing against his. They made love a second time, the worry and nerves of the first now gone. The light continued to stream into the room, shining through the white sheets into their hidden world.

They spent the rest of the morning in bed, not taking a single look or kiss for granted, savouring every moment together. When noon finally drew near they both dressed, passing garments between each other as naturally as words. They no longer needed to hide their affections behind a veil of propriety, making the whole process of getting ready all the longer, for each second seemed to require a kiss.

Eventually they found a way to make themselves presentable, leaving their chamber behind they walked hand in hand to the Carved Hall. One long table rested in the centre of the large room, with Eilidh's family seated alongside Lord Michael's.

"Well good morning," boomed the Thane, "or shall we say good afternoon?"

"Leave them be brother," said the Queen, "did you both sleep well?"

"We'll have no words on that matter," said Eilidh's father quickly.

"Always so serious Rhain," interjected Lord Michael.

"Shall I be less serious about your sister's wedding night?" asked the King with a smile.

To that Eilidh's bear of an uncle did not reply, he merely scoffed and gave his friend a disapproving look from behind his beard. They took their seats as food began to fill the table, Lord Michael's two youngest sons quickly beginning their first of many courses. Across from them sat Ardal, their elder brother and Lord Heir to the Northern Realm. He and Ewan had grown very close, their time together on the battlefield only serving to strengthen their friendship. His amber eyes shone amidst his dark skin as he spoke with Prince Richard.

Ewan felt the soft squeeze of his wife's hand, bringing his thoughts back to the Carved Hall, her smile letting him know the conversation included him.

"So how long will you spend in Reach?" Lord Michael was asking them.

"We don't quite know," replied Ewan, squeezing Eilidh's hand as a thank you, "we plan to stay for a few weeks."

"Beautiful countryside that far north," said the King.

"You'll both have a wonderful time," added Queen Bethan.

Eilidh's parents had arranged for them both to travel to the very edge of Forest Isle, a secluded town known as Reach, where waterfalls wove their way through hills and the stars never slept.

"Just don't miss the war," said Ardal with a smile.

"Aye," bellowed his father, "we might need another one of your plans."

"I still have a few tricks up my sleeve," answered Ewan.

"With arms as small as those I should hope so," replied Lord Michael with a laugh.

Ewan was worlds away from a family he may never see again, lost in a land and time far from his own. Yet the people that sat around him had given him a home, a sense of true belonging where there had been none. Each night he believed he would wake as if it were all a dream, and each night he hoped he would not a little more.

The branches of the Older Oak made a glistening canopy high above their heads, the undying leaves gilded and beautiful, watching over them as they ate. When finished, Lord Michael led them from the Carved Hall to a courtyard that lay beyond. Waiting there, shining brightly in the afternoon sun, was a grand carriage.

"It's a long ride to Reach," said Lord Michael, gesturing towards the carriage, "though well worth the journey."

The Northern Thane held out his bear like hand and Ewan met it with his. He had been a gracious host and an even better man.

"Take care of my niece," he said smiling as his hand tightened ever so slightly.

Eilidh left Ewan's side and ran to her parents, embracing the King and Queen as they held their daughter tightly. She had become a woman overnight but she would never stop being their child. With goodbyes said and tears shared, the newlywed couple climbed into their awaiting carriage, though before the wheels began to turn, a loud shriek was followed by hurried footsteps. A red faced and out of breath Sister Margret appeared before them.

"Forgotten about me already," she said through her panting.

"Of course not," said Ewan sincerely.

"You do make it very difficult," added his wife.

"And rightly so," the old woman smiled.

"We wouldn't have it any other way," said Eilidh.

"Look at you all grown up," Sister Margret replied with sadness in her voice, "I'm proud to see you become the woman you are."

"I had a little help."

"It was far more than just a *little* I'm afraid to say."

"You're never afraid to say anything," said Eilidh.

"True," she replied, "and I can't even blame that on old age. Promise me you'll take care of yourself and keep your husband out of trouble."

"I promise," said Eilidh as she kissed the old woman's rosy cheeks.

With Sister Margret joining the many faces that gathered to send them on their way, the carriage slowly rolled forward, bearing them out beyond the city's walls, a small host of mounted knights following behind. The wilderness surrounded them as they were engulfed by trees, carving a line through the forest.

Ewan stared out of the window as his wife rested her head upon his shoulder, her breath slightly tickling his ear. The Northern Realm rolled past them in a blur of green and gold, with light cascading through the beautiful array of colour. Despite the brilliance the land conveyed so effortlessly, it still did not compare to Eilidh.

He turned to his wife and searched the depths of her blue eyes. Although their wedding had ended, their marriage was now ahead of them, a veil of perfect uncertainty, new and wonderful and one Ewan realised he was lucky to have.

"What do you see when you look at me?" she asked him suddenly.

He thought for a moment, considering words such as love, beauty and even life, yet one stood out from all the rest.

"My future," he said softly, sealing it with a kiss.

Epilogue

The forest was alive around him, his keen senses hearing every movement as the trees swayed in unison. Beyond the leaves hung a bright blue sky, crisp and cloudless with the stars fading behind its glossy veil. Lord Michael could feel his heart beating in his chest, as calm and steady as his bow, the arrow already drawn back.

His target lay in a small clearing, a beautiful doe, quietly grazing in the soft morning light. The string tightened as the great northern bow bent in an elegant yet powerful curve. Lord Michael held the arrow still, calming its willingness to be released. He slowed his breathing and took aim, pointing the deadly shaft towards the deer, oblivious to its own fate.

Just as he was about to fire, the doe was joined by her young, three delicate fawns that came bounding into the clearing, disturbing their mother's peaceful graze. Lord Michael smiled as he lowered his readied bow; he would tell others that killing the mother would not allow her young to be hunted in days to come, though it held some truth, Lord Michael simply had too gentle a heart.

His love of the Northern Realm ran deep; it had been the home of House Dunharren since before Benathor Blackmane and the age of bears. As Thane, Lord Michael was entrusted with the protection of its lands, ensuring the safety of those that dwelt within them. He was honoured that his young niece had chosen to get married beneath the Older Oak as her mother had once done.

In the days after the wedding, with the couple on their way to Reach, the guests began to leave one by one. Soon it was time for the King and Queen to return to their white city and their marble halls. Lord Michael had loved seeing his younger sister back in her northern home, but he was proud to watch her leave with a man as noble as Rhain.

Even as boys they had been the best of friends, the distance between their two Realms never breaking their bond. As a young Prince, Rhain would spend the summer months in the north, hunting and fighting with Lord Michael for as long as the sun would allow. Bethan had always tried to gain the attention of her brother's royal friend, though back then girls were a thing to be teased and laughed at. Eventually they became young men and Lord Michael's sister a young women, the days of teasing girls turned into chasing them. Bethan had grown beautiful and fair and never failed to get the attention of any man again, not even Prince Rhain.

The wind changed and Lord Michael watched as the doe and her young sensed his presence, quickly retreating from the clearing, becoming lost in the forest that lay beyond. He had risen early that morning, dawn's clear light breaking over the walls of Oakenhold. His eyes had opened to that of his wife's, her dark hair flowing like a river of ebony. Lady Thea was the daughter of Lord Peter Rowen, Keeper of the Old Forest, a man as elderly as his lands. Whilst Rhain was chasing Bethan, Lord Michael had his own eyes on the beautiful woman that lay before him.

She kissed him as he awoke, bringing him from his dreams to a life that was even better. He held her olive skin in his powerful hands and made love to her, starting the day with a burst of passion. She had given him three wonderful sons, strong and healthy heirs to carry on his noble name. Logan and Bowen were close in their young age, it was Ardal as the eldest that would one day sit beneath the Older Oak as Thane. Lord Michael could not have been prouder seeing his son lead the bowmen on the fields of the Lowlands. He had watched Ardal grow from a boy into a brave and honourable man.

He gave his wife one final kiss before leaving her in the warmth of the bed. Their chamber rose up around them, the high ceilings supported by tall pillars, each one carved with the bears of his House. Lord Michael crossed the room, his powerful frame rivalling even the depictions of old. Upon a raised step, where light streamed down from a window above, rested an ornate carved trunk, the oak polished to a glimmering shine. Held tightly in a neat slit, with the blade buried amongst the wood, was the Thane's mighty axe, Mane.

Ardal was not built like his father; to wield such a weapon took an enormous amount of strength, one his son did not yet possess. Lord Michael had always been a powerful man, though he was skilled with a bow, he had always preferred an axe, waiting for the day Mane passed from his father's hands to his.

Leaving the axe trapped within its wooden home, he got dressed and gathered his bow. Though the axe was a force to be reckoned with on the battlefield, its place was in killing men, not deer. His three sons would be joining him on the hunt, as well as his nephew Prince Richard. He had decided to remain a guest in the Northern Realm after the wedding, in order to spend some time with his uncle's family.

Lord Michael left the chamber, giving Lady Thea one last loving stare, taking in all that she was. A smile crossed his face as he walked through the halls, his wife's beauty still lingering in his mind. He wore simple hunting clothes, the colours muted and dark like the great forests of his Realm. His great bow was slung over one shoulder, the thick wooden shaft only bending to his bear like arms.

Towards the end of the corridor, Lord Michael saw his brother by law, Edric Oakheart, speaking with a servant. The man was from humble beginnings and married to his sister Ellyn. He had not established a noble House and lived a quiet life with the Thane's sister. Ellyn was younger than Bethan and Lord Michael kept a watchful eye over her, especially now she was currently with child. Lord Michael was pleased for his sister, eager to welcome another family member into the world. He wondered whether they would have sons as he had done, strengthening the northern ranks even further.

"Edric," Lord Michael boomed, "what a beautiful morning."

"Your horses are ready and waiting," he replied.

"I see a good day of hunting ahead."

"Prince Richard was certainly eager to join you."

"Yes," he said, thinking back to the Lowlands, "Lord Peter's mailed fist certainly changed our young Prince for the better."

"Let's just hope it lasts."

As the doe soon disappeared out of sight, its young fawns close behind; Lord Michael relaxed his bow, releasing it from its taut curve. The Thane turned away from the clearing and made his way back to the company. The day went on and the dense woods of Forest Isle presented them with many more targets. Logan and Bowen each claimed a worthy prize, their young faces gleaming at their accomplishment.

At midday they decided to separate, with Ardal taking his two younger brothers and Lord Michael leading Prince Richard. He crept through the autumn leaves with his nephew, still able to hear his sons' young voices in the distance. Further and further they delved into the forest, ever searching for more pray.

Lord Michael had almost given up hope when he thought he saw something move through the trees. Raising his bow he saw Prince Richard do the same, two arrows quickly drawn and ready. They waited for some time, poised for a lethal strike, yet no target emerged. Out of the corner of his eye, Lord Michael caught a glimpse of silver ringlets beneath his nephew's sleeve, forming a steel layer of chainmail under his soft tunic.

"Richard why are you wearing armour?" he asked cautiously.

The Stag Prince slowly lowered his bow, a cruel grin spreading across his face. Lord Michael realised he could no longer hear his sons' voices, the air lay deathly quiet. In the stillness, he heard the faint sound of footsteps behind him before everything went black.

He did not dream in the darkness, a world so void of light that only pain and fear entered his mind. When finally he awoke, he tasted blood and dirt in his mouth as shapes moved as mere blurs in front of him. He soon realised that his hands were bound, the hard rope tearing at his skin.

Eventually his eyes fought through the pain, clinging to the light that was quickly fading in the eastern sky. Lord Michael saw that he was in the middle of a clearing, tied to a large post. His three sons were in a similar state but with their young mouths gagged. Armed men surrounded the Thane and his children, their shields bearing the heraldry of Lord William and the south. Amidst them stood the Stag Prince, his treacherous grin now larger than ever.

"Uncle!" he shouted, "how good of you to wake up!"

"Richard," Lord Michael managed through the pain still throbbing in his head, "what are you doing?"

"I'm ready to take my place as the rightful King."

"You fool!" he shouted, "the crown would have passed to you in time."

"Why wait for my father to die when Lord William can grant me the Kingdom now?"

"He can't just give you a Kingdom and even if he does, the cost will be too high."

"The cost of power is never too high uncle," said Richard, "Lord Farris even sold his beautiful daughter to be my Queen just to have a little bit more."

"So that's where you went after you fled the Lowlands like a coward, to plot with Lord William against your own father," he spat, "you'll have to forgive me if I don't bend a knee straight away."

"Everyone will bend a knee! Everyone!"

"Richard I pity you, for now you are truly lost."

"I don't want your pity! All I've ever wanted is the respect I deserve!"

"With treason? With murder?" Lord Michael shouted desperately.

"Uncle it's hard to find the moral high ground when we're all standing in the mud," Richard replied coldly, "you're a killer same as my father."

"And you're the same spoiled boy you've always been, you know nothing of killing."

Anger flushed the Stag Prince's face as a southern knight handed him a flaming torch.

"Let's change that shall we?" he said.

Logs and kindling were stacked beneath the four stakes, covering the ground of the deeply planted poles. Prince Richard started with Logan and Bowen, setting fire to Lord Michael's youngest sons, their gagged mouths uttering smothered cries.

"No!" their father screamed as his powerful arms fought pointlessly against his bonds.

The torch then set a fire beneath Ardal before finally being thrown at Lord Michael's feet. He watched helplessly as the flames burned ever higher around his sons.

"You're killing them!" he shouted as the fire engulfed them.

"That's the point," the Stag Prince said amidst the stifled cries.

He looked on at his three sons, seeing only fire. Lord Michael realised that he had failed not only his children, but his name, watching those that were meant to carry it on burn along with his House. After watching his youngest sons perish, Lord Michael heard only silence. Turning towards Ardal, he saw a shadow begin to grow amongst the flames.

In that moment, a thunderous roar and a loud crack of wood cut through the stillness. Lord Michael watched Ardal break free from his bonds and emerge from the flames a mighty black bear. His dark fur gleamed in the dying light as he tore through the southern ranks like the battles of old. His son had reclaimed the ancient power of their House but the enemy host was too great, even for Ardal's new and ferocious form. Lord Michael had lost two sons, their muffled calls leaving only flames and smoke. He refused to lose another.

"Go my son!" he cried, "live!"

His words echoed around the clearing, reaching the great bear. The southerners stood between him and his father, too large in number as the relentless flames kept growing. Their eyes met across the field, a wordless goodbye between father and son. The bear turned and disappeared into the trees, no man willing to follow. The fire burned ever nearer but Lord Michael stood silently, temerity not giving way to fear. Yet as the flames engulfed him, his screams were only matched by a bear's mighty yet sorrowful roar.

To be continued...

Printed in Great Britain
by Amazon